DIESELPUNK ROLEPLAYING

TOMORROW CITY

NATHAN RUSSELL

OSPREY
GAMES

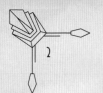

OSPREY GAMES
Bloomsbury Publishing Plc
Kemp House, Chawley Park, Cumnor Hill, Oxford OX2 9PH, UK
29 Earlsfort Terrace, Dublin 2, Ireland
1385 Broadway, 5th Floor, New York, NY 10018, USA
E-mail: info@ospreygames.co.uk
www.ospreygames.co.uk

OSPREY GAMES is a trademark of Osprey Publishing Ltd

First published in Great Britain in 2024

A catalogue record for this book is available from the British Library.

ISBN: HB 9781472849588; eBook 9781472849564; ePDF 9781472849595; XML 9781472849571

24 25 26 27 28   10 9 8 7 6 5 4 3 2 1

Printed and bound in India by Replika Press Private Ltd.

Osprey Games supports the Woodland Trust, the UK's leading woodland conservation charity.

To find out more about our authors and books visit www.ospreypublishing.com. Here you will find extracts, author interviews, details of forthcoming events and the option to sign up for our newsletter.

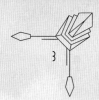

CONTENTS

INTRODUCTION 8

**THE FUTURE, BUT NOT
AS YOU KNOW IT** 8

The Revs 9

WHAT IS DIESELPUNK? 10

Themes 11

INSPIRATION 12

Books 12

Graphic Novels 12

Games 12

Film & TV 13

Music 13

ROLEPLAYING 101 14

Players 14

Game Master 15

What You Need 15

Rolling Dice 15

PLAYING SAFE 15

**THE CITY OF
TOMORROW** 16

THEN 18

NOW 19

MOTHER 20

WEIRD SCIENCE 21

THE PATTERN 22

Aberrations 22

THE COUNCIL &
THE MINISTRIES 23

CULTS & SOCIETIES 27

CRIME & LAW
ENFORCEMENT 29

CITIZENS OF INTEREST 31

CITY DISTRICTS	34	**HARM**	57
The Spindle	34	Hits	57
Inner City	36	Injuries	57
Midtown	37	Dying	58
Rimside	38	Conditions	59
The Great Factory	40	Healing	60
Underside	42	Resting & Recovery	62
Old Cali	43	Traumas	62
GETTING AROUND	44	**MOXIE**	62
		Refreshing Moxie	63
THE RULES	**46**		
		GAME TIME	64
FICTIONAL POSITIONING	46	Turns	64
PLAYING IN THE		Initiative	64
MOMENT	47	Surprise	64
TAGS	47		
CHECKS	48	**DISTANCE & MOVEMENT**	65
Making the Check	48	Movement	65
Roll Results	48	Distance & Scale	65
Modifiers	50		
Automatic and Impossible Actions	51		
One Attempt	51		
Rolling with Mastery	51		
Extended Checks	52		
PRESSURE	53		
CONSEQUENCES	53		
Soft and Hard Consequences	54		
Boons	54		
Botches	55		

CHARACTERS 66

WHAT'S A REV TO YOU?	67
TRADEMARKS	68
Backgrounds	70
Descriptors	72
Occupations	77
Pattern Weavers	83
EDGES	86
ADVANTAGES	87
FLAWS	87
DRIVES	89
TIES	90
MOXIE	91
CRED	91
GRIT	93
CUSTOMISE	93
ROUND OUT	93
CHARACTER CREATION EXAMPLE: EMILE FRANKS	94

GEAR 97

WHAT GEAR DOES	97
STARTING GEAR	98
Lifestyle	98
GEARING UP	98
Gear Cost	98
Combining Resources	99
Acquiring Gear Mid-Job	99
Encumberance	100
REPAIRING GEAR	100
GEAR TAGS	101
WEAPONS	104
PERSONAL ARMOUR	109
TOOLS	111
SERUMS	113
ROBOTS	117
VEHICLES	121

INTO DANGER 127

STORY STRUCTURE	127
The Job	128
ARGUMENTS & PERSUASION	128
CHASES & RACES	131
COMBAT	133
Organising Combats	133
Combat Turns & Actions	133
Attacking	134
Defending	134
Take-Downs	138
DOGFIGHTS	139
INTERROGATIONS & QUESTIONING	140
INVESTIGATIONS	142
PATTERN POWERS	143
RESISTING HARM	146
RESISTING HORROR	146

DOWNTIME 148

REST & RECOVERY	148
GROWING FROM EXPERIENCE	150
ADVANCES	151
School of Hard Knocks	152
CHANGES	152
RETIREMENT	153
NEW REVS	153

ON THE JOB 154

MISSIONS	154
MYSTERIES	156
Web of Clues	156
STRUCTURING JOBS	159

GAME MASTER ADVICE 160

CHARACTER CREATION	160
RUNNING THE GAME	161
GETTING THE MOST OUT OF SCENES	163
MASTERING CHECKS	164
PRESSURE	165
MASTERING MYSTERIES	167
MASTERING COMBATS	168
FLAWS & MOXIE	168
REWARDS	169

THREATS 170

ATTITUDES & REACTIONS 171

HARM 171

Mooks 171

Tough Guys 172

Villains 172

Non-Player Characters 172

THREATS & GEAR 174

MINISTRY AGENTS 174

CITIZENS 177

AUTOMATONS & ROBOTS 180

EXPERIMENTS GONE WRONG 184

TROUBLEMAKERS 187

PATTERN ABBERATIONS 192

ENVIRONMENTS 196

ORGANISATIONS 198

JOB: ESCAPE PLAN 200

APPENDIX: RANDOM GENERATORS 210

PEOPLE 210

Names 210

Distinguishing Traits & Features 211

PLACES 212

Rough Neighbourhoods 212

Classy Neighbourhoods 212

Bars, Clubs & Nightspots 213

Brands, Businesses & Factories 214

JOBS 215

Random Job Generator 215

Job Hooks 216

GLOSSARY 218

CHARACTER SHEET 220

ACKNOWLEDGMENTS 224

CREDITS 224

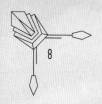

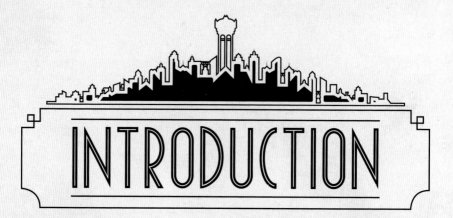

INTRODUCTION

Tomorrow City is a roleplaying game of dieselpunk adventure, dark science, and dangerous mystery. It focuses on a technologically advanced city and the people who call it home after a decades-long war that has ruined much of the world, leaving the survivors looking for new opportunities amongst the skyscrapers, alleys, and endless factories of the last great city on Earth. It is a game of pulp daring and dystopian paranoia, set against the backdrop of a dieselpunk world that takes elements of contemporary science fiction and oils them with the aesthetics of the interwar period. It is a sandbox setting and game where you can decide what aspects of the dieselpunk genre you wish to explore and how your characters will interact with the world. Perhaps they will seek adventure out in the wastelands, help citizens as they struggle to rebuild their lives in an often-dangerous city, or even work to overthrow the City Council and the potential menace of the thinking machine known as "Mother".

THE FUTURE, BUT NOT AS YOU KNOW IT

It's 1984. The Great War, known here as The Long War, has only just ended after seventy years of conflict. It's the height of the Jazz age, the art deco movement, and mad science. If you didn't know better, you would think it was sometime in the 1930s or 40s. Everyone wears fedoras, cars are big and sleek and chrome, robots roam the streets, performance enhancing drugs are popular, and gas masks are on trend…

Tomorrow City draws on many elements to create an anachronistic world that might have been – what if thinking machines had come to prominence in the early 20th century, or if World War One had dragged on for generations, or if a scientific "utopia" governed by an autocratic council had come to be? While set in the year 1984, the feel of the world in *Tomorrow City* is very much inspired by the interwar period. Imagine, if you will, that World War One just rolled into World War Two and didn't end for several more decades. While there were many scientific, military, and technological advances, art and culture have remained somewhat stagnant, stuck as they were in the 1920s, 30s and 40s of our own history. Fedoras, flapper dresses, and army surplus are common fashion, jazz and big bands play on the wireless, and pulp novels and black-and-white films entertain the masses. Now, however, the war is finally over and there is a renewed sense of prosperity as people learn to live in relative peace – many for the first time.

Still, not all is bright in this imagined future. Everyone is dealing with the trauma of a decades-long war and, while open battle has ended, a new, cold war has birthed different kinds of tension and fear. Closer to home, the citizens of *Tomorrow City* live like sardines crammed into a tin, and an unspoken class system is creating a growing friction amongst the populace. Scientists and engineers, once employed to devise new and terrible ways to win a seemingly endless war, continue their nefarious experiments. Gangsters, grifters, and petty crooks take advantage of the naïve or unwary to cement their own fortunes. The mysterious metaphysical energy known as the Pattern tears holes in the fabric of reality and spews forth horrifying aberrations. It is a city of wonder and a world fraught with danger.

The Revs

Into this mess come your characters, the Revs. The original meaning of this slang is lost in the oil-stained history of the city – maybe it was short for "revolutionary", maybe for "revolting". Today, the term "Rev" is applied to anyone who lives their life apart from the rest, takes great risks, and sometimes reaps great rewards. They are trouble-shooters, dealmakers, or even troublemakers. Some fight injustice on the poverty-stricken streets of Rimside, others hunt for old tech in the wastelands, fight sky raiders from the top of zeppelins, or make a name for themselves doing dirty jobs for the Ministries. Anything is possible on the streets and in the skies of Tomorrow City.

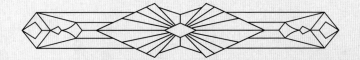

WHAT IS DIESELPUNK?

Dieselpunk is a genre of science fiction that takes place in a world that looks and feels much like our own early twentieth century. The period of 1920–50 is the predominant timeframe, but elements from earlier and later decades often find their way into the mix. It draws on media of the period, such as pulp stories and science fiction books and films, as well as more contemporary interpretations of the period and a healthy dose of postmodern storytelling. It is a broad genre where archaeologists, gangsters, soldiers, and gadgeteers could all rub shoulders with each other while taking a zeppelin trip or fighting evil robots, all to a lively big band soundtrack or under the menacing eye of a wicked overlord.

Dieselpunk media often falls into one of two broad camps. Decopunk focuses its lens on the bright hope for the future that came after the Great War; it's shiny and bright and full of wonder. Dystopian dieselpunk, however, is darker in tone and subject matter, influenced by the weariness of war, the dangers of unchecked technology, and the fear of misused power. *Tomorrow City* provides the scope for players to emphasise each of these flavours, depending on personal preference and the stories you want to tell.

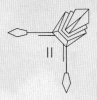

IS THIS STEAMPUNK? CYBERPUNK?

Dieselpunk is often described as being part of a continuum of genres, sitting between the hopeful optimism of steampunk and the cynicism of cyberpunk. It is dirty and gritty and incorporates elements of both these genres, as well as a multitude of others. Feel free to cherry-pick elements that you like and throw them into the mix of your *Tomorrow City* games.

Themes

Dieselpunk stories cover a broad gamut of genres and plots, and incorporate a mix of alternate history, science fiction, and even horror. They often deal with themes of survival, war and science, which *Tomorrow City* explores in the following ways:

Survival. Everyone in the city is fighting to live. Resources are scarce, the streets are dangerous, and people are constantly forced to make tough choices between doing the right thing and doing whatever they must to survive. Some take dangerous drugs to get an edge over their competitors, or make deals with nefarious organisations; others sell out their friends, steal from their employers, or abandon their principles to give their family another meal or put a roof over their heads; and a few dabble in esoteric sciences or the malignant arts of the Pattern in the hope of gaining power, prestige, or even mastery over their own fate.

War. The Long War may be over, but it is far from forgotten. Everyone has been affected by the intergenerational trauma of the world-wide conflict, and the scars are deep and fresh. The cosmopolitan City is a hotbed for old animosities and, while an uneasy peace has settled between the warring nations and city states, a new cold war has begun. The City Council and Ministry of Peace are vigilant for spies, agitators, and threats both internal and external. Beyond the city, sky raiders and bandit warbands roam the wastes, attempting to claim a slice of the new world for themselves. Everyone tries to forget what has gone before, but there is an uneasy sense that the smouldering embers of the war could reignite at any moment.

Science. In Tomorrow City, any technological advancement is a wonder to be embraced and exploited, no matter the cost. Mankind has pushed the limits of what is possible with science, creating thinking machines, alchemical serums, and devastating machines of war. Some inventions have made life much easier (for those who can afford them, at least), while others brought death to millions. Constantly searching for the next great discovery, the agents of the Ministry of Science, rogue inventors, and misguided Pattern weavers rarely stop to consider the consequences of their actions.

INSPIRATION

To get a feel for *Tomorrow City*, the kinds of stories you might tell within it, and its general look and style, you would be well served to seek out some of the following media. All of these were sources of inspiration, but the items in bold are particularly important touchstones.

Books

- **1984 (George Orwell)**
- *A Fistful of Nothing* (Dan Glasner)
- *The Big Sleep and Other Stories* (Raymond Chandler)
- *Bioshock: Rapture* (John Shirley)
- *Brave New World* (Aldous Huxley)
- *Ghosts of Manhattan* (George Mann)
- *The Grand Dark* (Richard Kadrey)
- *In Plain Sight* (Dan Willis)
- *Mortal Engines* (Philip Reeve)

Graphic Novels

- *Adventureman* (created by Matt Fraction & Terry Dodson)
- *Broken Gargoyles* (writing by Bob Salley, art by Stan Yak)
- *Ignition City* (writing by Warren Ellis, art by Gianluca Pagliarani)
- *The Manhattan Projects* (writing by Jonathan Hickman, art by Nick Pitarra)
- *The Jekyll Island Chronicles* (writing by Steve Nedvidek, Ed Crowell & Jack Lowe, art by J. Moses Nester)
- *Wild Blue Yonder* (created by Mike Raicht, Zach Howard & Austin Harrison)

Games

- **BioShock,** *BioShock 2* & *BioShock Infinite* (Ken Levine, Zak McClendon, et al.)
- *Crimson Skies* (Jordan Weisman)
- *Wolfenstein: The New Order* (Jerk Gustafsson, et al.)

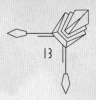

Film & TV

- *Abigail* (directed by Aleksandr Boguslavskiy)
- *Blade Runner* (directed by Ridley Scott)
- *Arcane: League of Legends* (the 2021 series)
- *Brazil* (directed by Terry Gilliam)
- *Casablanca* (directed by Michael Curtiz)
- *The City of Lost Children* (directed by Jean-Pierre Jeunet & Marc Caro)
- **Dark City** (directed by Alex Proyas)
- **Metropolis** (direct by Fritz Lang)
- *Overlord* (directed by Julius Avery)
- *The Rocketeer* (directed by Joe Johnston)
- *Sky Captain and the World of Tomorrow* (directed by Kerry Conran)
- *Shadow in the Cloud* (directed by Roseanne Liang)
- *Snowpiercer* (the 2020 series)

Music

Soundtracks for any of the films or video games mentioned above, and any electro swing

- *Abney Park*
- *Airships: Conquer the Skies* (Curtis Schweitzer, 2018)
- *Band of Brothers original motion picture soundtrack* (Various artists, 2001)
- *Batman: Mask of the Phantasm original motion picture soundtrack* (Various artists, 1993)
- *Bioshock 2: The Official Soundtrack* (Various Artists, 2010)
- *Scott Bradlee's Postmodern Jukebox*
- *Sky Captain and the World of Tomorrow Original Motion Picture Soundtrack* (Edward Shearmur and Jane Monheit, 2004)
- *This Is War (Cliff Lin, 2018)*

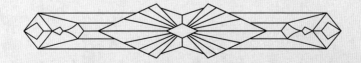

ROLEPLAYING 101

You and your friends are going to work together to tell exciting stories of danger, exploration, and intrigue against the backdrop of a futuristic city that is as much a threat to their existence as it is a refuge. Most of you will become players, who portray the protagonists of the story, while one of you will take on the role of Game Master, or "GM", who helps to guide the events of the plot and facilitate play.

The game unfolds as a conversation, with everyone working together to create a vibrant, dangerous, and exciting world to throw their characters into. The GM frames cool scenes, and the players respond by describing their character's actions. You will share ideas, listen, riff off one another, and work together to maximise everyone's fun. You all work together to create a shared world and entertaining story.

At some point, a character will try something that you aren't sure if they can succeed at; for example:

- Can you leap from the aircraft wing onto the frame of a nearby zeppelin?
- Will you disarm the crazed abomination before it hurts anyone else?
- Can you convince the Badge to let you go with just a warning?

At these moments you roll dice to see if your character succeeds and then continue by describing the outcome.

Your game will flow from conversation to game mechanics and back again. Sometimes there will be a long gap between rolling dice, while at other times you will make several rolls in a row. This is all part of the game.

Players

As a player, you take on the role of a bold, competent, determined Rev who throws themselves into danger to right wrongs, discover the lost secrets of the past, or to bring down an overbearing regime. You will describe their actions, say the things they say, and use logic and imagination to portray them. Work with the other players and GM to create a cool story about desperate characters making their way in an uncaring city.

As a player you should:

- Portray a tough, competent Rev
- Say what your character says
- Fight for what is right – for your character or for those they are helping
- Give in to your character's Flaws
- Share the spotlight with the other characters

Game Master

As the GM, it's your job to facilitate the game by bringing the city to life, portraying its inhabitants (the non-player characters or "NPCs"), and presenting challenges for the players and their characters to overcome. You help each player show off the cool things their character can do, ask and answer questions, fill in the blanks, and interpret the actions of the characters and their enemies. You are a fan of the characters, a facilitator of the action, and an arbiter of the rules.

As a GM you should:

- Make the world feel wondrous, paranoid, and dangerous
- Be a fan of the players and their characters
- Ask questions
- Do what the fiction demands

What You Need

Before you begin, you will need to gather a group of friends and:

Dice: A whole bunch of six-sided dice in two different colours.

Character sheets: Each player will need a character sheet. You can find a copy at the back of this book or as a PDF on the Osprey Games website.

Pencil and paper: For taking notes and keeping track of story details.

Rolling Dice

The rules use the following shorthand to refer to dice:

D6: A single six-sided die. You will usually roll multiples and keep the highest.

D66: Roll two D6, reading one as the "tens" and the other as the "units". For example, a roll of 5 and 3 would be read as "53".

D3: Roll a D6 and halve the result (rounding up). This gives a value between one and three. So, 1 or 2 = 1 | 3 or 4 = 2 | 5 or 6 = 3.

PLAYING SAFE

Tomorrow City explores themes of oppression, drug use, war, death, and horror. Be aware that the stories you tell could deal with challenging topics and might sometimes go in unexpected directions. You should have a conversation before play to discuss what features of the setting you wish to play down or leave out entirely. Investigate some safety tools, such as Lines and Veils, the X-Card, or Script Change and implement the one(s) that work best for your group. Remember to always aim to be respectful of others.

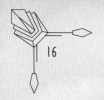

THE CITY OF TOMORROW

From the air, as one might see it when approaching by dirigible, Tomorrow City looks much like a huge spinning top, growing from a narrow base in the flooded ruins of Old Cali to a broad disc atop which sits the city proper. Here, the steel and glass skyscrapers crowd around each other, growing taller and more magnificent as they claw towards the centre of the city and the magnificent tower known as The Spindle. Sunlight glints off the art-deco adornments of polished chrome, and the buildings reflect each other in their walls of green and blue glass. As you draw ever closer to The Spindle, you can see the concentric circles that divide the city's districts and, if you linger long enough, you might even notice the slow march of these rings around their axis. The city is a bustling ant farm of industry and progress. Diesel trams speed along grand bridges before disappearing between, or even into, buildings, and huge telescreens project public notices or advertise the latest products to consumers. From directly above, the city looks like a child's puzzle, a maze of streets made of deep shadows, the pinpoints of vehicle lights marching like ghostly rats in the labyrinth.

The city's design is no accident, having been carefully planned to the last inch to maximise space and ensure the machinery beneath the streets can work to its optimal ability. At the heart of the city is The Spindle, a chrome and gold tower almost half a mile high, a monument to mankind's power to bend the world to its will. The gilded skyscraper is the headquarters of the city's Council, houses many of the most important Ministries, and forms the axis about which the metropolis' great machinery spins. It is also the abode of Mother, the all-knowing machine-mind built to guide and protect the city from now until eternity. Encircling The Spindle are the districts of the Inner City, Midtown, and Rimside, each a broad disc that turns in different directions and at different speeds according to the unknowable designs of Mother and the requirements of the machinery upon which the streets are laid.

Should you approach Tomorrow City by land, however, you will be greeted by a very different sight. While, from a great distance, you will still see the spinning-top shape and golden finger of The Spindle, the vista of the glittering city is soon lost as you and the land are cast into shadow. From beneath, the city looks unfinished, with a scaffold of steel girders hanging like vines of rusting ivy beneath it. Within this mesh sprawls the shanty town of Underside, populated by workers who cannot afford to live in the city above, refugees, and ne'er-do-wells. It is a hard place to live, with not enough to go around, and vice lurking in the corners of every tin hovel. Some unlucky urchins live their entire lives in Underside, never feeling the touch of the sun on their faces or seeing the wonder of the city that sits so close above them.

Beneath the city are the swamps and flooded canals of once-prosperous California. The months of earthquakes that destroyed much of the coastline in 1906 left the landscape scarred with deep ravines, sloshing waterways, and miles of uninhabitable marshland. This is a dank and unpleasant place, cast in permanent twilight. And yet, many still eke out an existence here, hunting wild beasts, farming pigs, fish or frogs, and trading with the city above. The ruins of the old world have also become a haunt for criminals and political dissidents, who bide their time and draw up plans for vengeance against those who live above them.

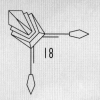

THEN

Constructed in those heady days between the fall of Old Cali and the beginnings of The Long War, Tomorrow City, then known as New Angeles, was a beacon of hope and a symbol of the prosperity of the new century. Engineers, scientists, and Pattern weavers flocked to aid in its construction – so impressive was the idea that many nations began drawing up plans for their own cities of the future. As the United States started to fracture under the strains of political dissonance and old animosities, New Angeles gained its independence, becoming an autonomous city state. Millions flocked to it, making new lives for themselves amongst the city's technological wonders and modern conveniences.

That, of course, was before The Long War, which dragged every corner of the world into the conflict. Even New Angeles, which had styled itself as a "Scientific Utopia" was caught up in it. The muddy trenches of Europe were overrun with robot soldiers and diesel-powered landships; dirigibles soared across Asia, the Pacific, and the Atlantic to deliver deadly payloads and spew forth legions of combatants. Soldiers were plied with alchemical serums to make them better instruments of war and, when injured, they were patched up with machinery and returned to the fronts.

The war raged ever on. Where one nation was bludgeoned into defeat, a new power or threat arose. Eventually, however, when the radium warheads had poisoned the air and Pattern bombs had turned the land into scars of jagged rock, the guns fell silent. An uneasy peace was brokered between the remaining nations and city states of the world, with each licking their wounds and turning to address their own internal troubles. Underground London closed its tunnels to the outside world; Leviathan submerged itself beneath the waves; Neu Prussia rumbled across the wastelands towards the Caliphates; And Tomorrow City was reborn.

1984

Tomorrow City is set in a retro-futuristic 1984. This, firstly, is a nod to George Orwell's dystopian masterpiece, *1984*. Secondly, the big gap in time between the start of The Long War and the present allows you to add or remove events, inventions, and situations to suit the needs of your story. You can decide what real-world events happened, introduce weird anachronisms, and roll in elements from your own sources of inspiration. This gives you a lot of control over how your city of the future will look and feel.

NOW

With the end of The Long War has come a new prosperity. Casting off its old name and embracing the honorific Tomorrow City, what was once New Angeles has picked up right where it left off when the war began. Jazz music is popular, people go to listen and dance to big bands, and the glamour of the moving picture once again thrills the population.

Today, the city is a place of opportunity and danger, where the wonders of science, the beauty of art, and the depravities of man coexist in equal measure. It is a city of freedom and constraint, opportunity and privation, change and contradiction.

Tomorrow City is in constant motion, turning, humming, and grinding as the concentric circles of its districts rotate about The Spindle. Sunlight streams from bright blue Cali skies and gleams off the polished towers, creating dynamic sunbursts and geometric reliefs. Steel and glass reflect the light, while chromium statues of eagles and winged gods dazzle passengers on airships and the SkyTrain. And yet, skyscrapers cast long shadows that sweep across each other like the hands of a clock and cast the lower streets in a pale grey twilight. The alleyways are dimmer still and, even in the noonday sun, they are just winding cracks between the city's monolithic structures.

At night, the contrasts between light and dark are exaggerated even further. The city is brilliant, with its cyclopean telescreens casting the streets in a blue glow and its neon billboards enticing pedestrians into nightclubs and dancehalls. Between the bright spotlights and flashing signs, however, the darkness grows so deep that it becomes a stygian wall where the desperate and horrific lurk. In the skies, spotlights sweep for aerial intruders, while dirigibles of the Ministry of Peace stab at the darkened streets in search of criminals and troublemakers.

High-rises and apartment buildings squeeze together and overflow with people. The streets bustle with crowds on their way to and from work, or out for an evening's entertainment. Someone is always starting or finishing a shift somewhere, hustling for a few dollars more, or scraping by doing anything that pays. Tens of millions call the city home, and all the variety of life can be found in this cosmopolitan melting pot. Space is at a premium and used for multiple purposes wherever possible. Broad walking paths, sky bridges or roofs serve double duty as parks, sporting fields, open-air plazas, or aircraft runways; balconies are also meeting places or storefronts; and the tram tunnels house the uncounted destitute. The haves and have-nots rub shoulders with each other across the city, though it is certain that you will see more of the wealthy in the Inner City and an increasing number of the working class the further from The Spindle you go.

Beneath the streets are the shadowed machine halls where workers toil in the smog-filled factories, pump stations, and engine houses. It is a world of oil-stained gloom, where the unwashed masses work in the glow of warning lights and furnaces. Hundreds of feet below, the flooded ruins of old California exist in the permanent shadow of the turning metropolis. Here, stunted trees and sprays of sickly reeds struggle to grow between the tumbling ruins of once-great buildings. It is a wilderness of decay and a maze of canals, where the foetid soil and dying brush hide a multitude of dangers.

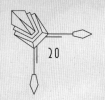

MOTHER

A great thinking machine known as "Mother" guides the city on its journey into the future. Little is known of Her origins, who built Her, or when; She has simply always been there, at the heart of Tomorrow City, conducting its population through the turmoil of The Long War and ensuring the continuance of the great metropolis. Her calculating devices and analytical engines are infinitely complex and woven into the very structure of the city itself.

While Mother's chrome visage is regularly broadcast on telescreens throughout the city, no one outside the City Council and Ministry Directors has ever spoken with Her. Her vast intellect, wisdom, and benevolence are manifest simply through the continuing prosperity of the city and the propaganda created by the Ministry of Truth. Most citizens accept this unquestioningly, with many even revering Mother as a deity – the personification of the future, brought to life with electricity and veiled in chrome. There are some, however, who question whether a machine should hold such a position of power within the city, or refuse to recognise Her authority at all. The Anti-Robot League, for example, distributes anti-automaton pamphlets and argues for the dismantling of Mother, while certain cells of The Revolutionists also decry the reliance on a machine to govern the future of humanity.

AUTOMATONS & ROBOTS

Mother is the most sophisticated thinking machine ever constructed, but She is not the only artificial life in the city. Automatons, each with a tiny spark of Mother's intellect, watch over the city, report on the citizens, and intervene whenever and wherever Mother sees fit. Less advanced but just as incredible are the tens of thousands of robots built and programmed to complete simple tasks to make life easier. Across the city you will see robots pouring drinks, delivering parcels, working construction sites, and doing any number of other everyday tasks.

WEIRD SCIENCE

This is a world of ambitious invention and science pushed to the very edges of what is possible. The Long War saw the greatest minds of the age turn their talents to creating new and devastating ways to kill and destroy – weapons and fighting vehicles were refined and mechanical soldiers were built in their legions. Now that an uneasy peace has settled, scientific minds look to other things. Much of the city is automated, and moving sidewalks, escalators and dirigibles get people about with relative ease. Robots, artificial limbs, and complicated instruments help with everyday activities, making work, pleasure, and life in general that much easier for the population.

Perhaps the advancement that has changed society the most, however, is the alchemical serum. First devised to improve a soldier's stamina and aggression, or to deaden them to the horrors of war, a multitude of uses have since been found for them. Serums can increase a user's strength, perception, or speed; cure them of a variety of ailments; or allow them to perform seemingly super-human feats. When soldiers returned home, they continued to use their "special medicines", which then soon found their way into the hands of the general populace. Today, serum use is commonplace and, in some industries or social circles, expected.

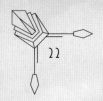

THE PATTERN

The Pattern is a corrupting energy that seeps into the world through tears in the fabric of reality. Wherever it appears, buildings, objects and even people become warped and distorted. Individuals attuned to the Pattern can manipulate it, bending it to their will and shaping the world to their own design. During The Long War, metaphysicists such as Oppenheimer and Einstein used their knowledge to develop devastating Pattern Bombs that ripped apart reality and turned huge areas into surreal hellscapes of jagged glass and swirling energy.

Whether by accident or design, the complex geometry of Tomorrow City concentrates the Pattern. Its tapestry of buildings, roads, raised tramways, and open spaces stretch the fabric of reality so thin in places that it splits and spills forth hideous aberrations or deadly energies. Many buildings now adorn themselves with complex designs of strange geometry in the hope of diffusing or distributing the chaotic force.

Aberrations

Strange lifeforms of geometric shapes, swirling patterns, and abstract thought brought to life, aberrations are creatures infused with Pattern energy. Most are spewed forth from reality tears and, unable to understand our world, go on devastating rampages that destroy or warp large swathes of the city. Others were once normal people, but exposure to tears, weapons, or other strong Pattern energy has turned them into hideous mockeries of their former selves.

IS THIS MAGIC?

What was it Arthur C. Clarke said? "Any sufficiently advanced technology is indistinguishable from magic." The Pattern is like that. It works under its own laws, but can be studied, investigated, and exploited like any science. Many already have, as seen with the invention of Pattern Bombs and Fractal weapons.

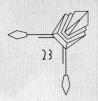

THE COUNCIL & THE MINISTRIES

The everyday administration of the city falls to the Council, an ineffective bureaucracy of politicians and power-hungry public servants, its authority long ago subverted by the Ministries. Council members busy themselves with creating or repealing meaningless laws, kissing babies, undermining their opponents, and preparing for the next debate in an endless season of elections.

The Ministries are the powerful administrative arms of the city, in charge of everything from agriculture to transportation, manufacturing to sanitation. Each Ministry is attended to by legions of clerks, bureaucrats, and agents, and overseen by cunning and dangerous Directors. Ministries cooperate with each other when their roles and agendas align, but each fiercely protects its domain, often secretly working against each other.

While every Ministry plays an important part in running the city's infrastructure, the most powerful are the so-called "Big Three" – the Ministry of Peace, the Ministry of Truth, and the Ministry of Science.

The Ministry of Peace (MoP)

Peace Through Force
Crime, justice, and public safety are the purview of the Ministry of Peace. Once the War Department in charge of military operations, its new role is to minimise public disturbances and address any threats to the peace, both internal and external. The police department, known as "Badges", are the public face of the MoP, but there are many other branches. Most notorious are the black-clad Peace Officers who are said to arrive unannounced to remove persons deemed threats to the peace. Many who are taken away are never seen again.

Important Departments:

- **Badges**: The city's police force.
- **Department of Defence**: While reduced in size, the city continues to maintain a strong military garrison to protect it from external threats.
- **Department of Public Safety**: This organisation oversees internal security, monitoring the public and dealing with subversives. The Peace Officers are their enforcement arm.
- **Justice Department**: The courts and judicial system is administered by this department.

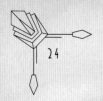

The Ministry of Truth (MoT)

In Truth We Trust

The Ministry of Truth is responsible for the distribution of news and information. It is their solemn duty to ensure the citizens of Tomorrow City are informed of current events and kept from anything that might cause panic or public unrest. Sometimes, this means bending the truth or falsifying documents. The MoT influences, if not outright owns, most of the radio stations and film studios, and controls the majority of the telescreens throughout the city. Through these great cathode ray displays, found on almost every major intersection, the Ministry can monitor the city, as they operate as both cameras and projectors.

Important Departments:

- **Public Affairs Division**: This department runs radio stations, newspapers, and the city's telescreens.
- **Department of Art & Culture**: In charge of art galleries, museums, and censorship.
- **Department of Democracy**: The clerical arm of the City Council, also responsible for running elections.
- **Advocacy Division**: This department runs charitable organisations and education facilities.

The Ministry of Science (MoS)

Knowledge Is Power

Once in charge of developing deadly weapons and machines of war, today the Ministry of Science focuses on creating new ways to make life more comfortable or efficient for the city's citizens. At least, that's what their mission statement says. In reality, many of the philomaths in their employ continue the morally questionable investigations that began during The Long War. While based at the University of Science & Technology, the MoS has many sites spread throughout the city, each specialising in one esoteric topic or another. Some are obviously Ministry buildings, while just as many are hidden workshops or laboratories positioned to watch the citizens they are secretly experimenting on.

Important Departments:

- **Department of Contemporary Archaeology**: This department funds expeditions into the wastelands in search of lost technology and valuable objects.
- **Metaphysical Affairs**: In charge of researching the Pattern and associated phenomena.
- **Medical Science Division**: This department focuses on serums, medicines, and the biological sciences.
- **University of Science & Technology**: The city's most prestigious institution of higher learning.

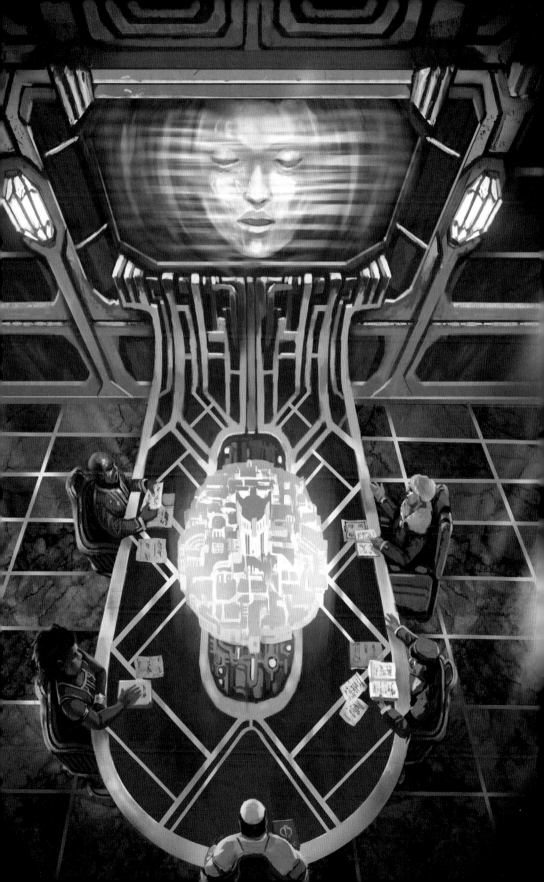

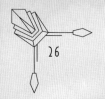

Other Ministries

Some other significant Ministries that play important roles in the governance of the city include:

The Ministry of Agriculture

Responsible for the factory farms of Rimside, the wasteland ranches, food safety, and all associated administration, the MoA holds an apparent monopoly on produce and food. However, their reliance on the Ministry of Transport to get the goods to customers and a competitive black market have meant they rarely hold as much power as the other Ministries. They are often derisively referred to as Porkers, a reference both to their extensive piggeries, and the reputation of high ranking bureaucrats being exceedingly greedy.

The Ministry of Public Works

This Ministry oversees the maintenance of public property, sanitation, government construction programmes, building approvals, and property law. They are responsible for awarding contracts to pipe runner crews, who can be seen across the city conducting maintenance and ensuring the rotation of the districts goes smoothly. The MoPW also technically oversees The Great Factory, but due to a complex net of laws, contracts and back-room deals they all-but ceded their control long ago.

The Ministry of Revenue

The government's accounting arm, the MoR is responsible for monitoring the taxes created and collected by the other Ministries. They are also in charge of Ministry payrolls. Auditors of the MoR are often accompanied by robotic assistants who carry overly large briefcases that unfold to reveal complex counting machines. Auditors divide their time between assisting other Ministries in the collection of their taxes and resources, and assessing those same organisations to ensure compliance. For this reason, they are equally despised by the general population and the bureaucracies of government.

The Ministry of Transport

Roads, tramlines, subways, and the SkyTrain are the purview of this Ministry. They maintain the infrastructure that keeps things moving in the city, and work with the MoPW to ensure tunnels, stations and lines are kept in good working order. In recent years the MoT has had to deal with increasing unionisation among its workforce, which it has unsuccessfully tried to break through force, coercion and bribery. An attempt to replace drivers with robots was met with violent opposition, said to be inflamed by members of the Anti-Robot League.

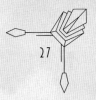

CULTS & SOCIETIES

Organised religion is not as popular as it was before The Long War, with people instead flocking to groups that make them feel like they belong or give their life purpose. Secret societies, private clubs, revolutionary groups, and quasi-religious cults are common.

The Anti-Robot League

A disorganised coalition of like-minded individuals, the Anti-Robot League seeks an end to the use of robot labour. Primarily consisting of the working class and poor, many of the ARL's members have lost their jobs to robot replacements. Viewed as loud but mostly harmless, the ARL devotes its energy to printing pamphlets and organising marches with plenty of banner waving and drum beating but not much else. Occasionally, however, a drunk, foolish, or particularly angry group will attack a robot, break into a factory, or attempt to sabotage a business that relies on robot labour.

The Followers of Moloch

A growing number of drones from the Great Factory have turned to the worship of Moloch, the hungry Machine God. Said to be a personification of The Great Factory itself, the followers believe that Moloch must be constantly appeased with their literal blood and sweat. They shave their heads and bodies and wear cloth belts or headbands to catch their own sweat as they work, which they later offer to their deity in simple rituals. Some cut themselves or indulge in self-flagellation as acts of worship, and it is said that a few of the more blood-thirsty sects kidnap victims to sacrifice. Many citizens see the Followers of Moloch as deluded fanatics, but their growing numbers are beginning to worry many within the Ministries.

The Court of Pigeons

Governed by the mysterious Feathered King, the fanciers of the Court of Pigeons are a web of spies, informants, and information brokers. They maintain large pigeon lofts that tumble across many rooftops in Midtown and operate a messenger pigeon service for those who would rather avoid using the telephone. Dressed in dirty docker caps and grey dust coats, they are a frequent site on rooftops across the city, where they keep tabs on the comings and goings of the city's movers and shakers. Many astute business owners pay the Feathered King large sums to keep their secrets private, or to gain an advantage over their competitors.

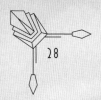

The Revolutionists

Demanding a change to the current political regime, members of this group work to undermine the authority of the City Council and the Ministries. They paper the city with anti-government posters and graffiti and launch attacks on important infrastructure. Their symbol, a spiralling circle with an arrow at one end, is often seen painted over signs or scratched into handrails or walls. Branded as radicals and subversives, the Ministry of Peace deals harshly with anyone suspected of working with the Revolutionists.

Archeocults

Popular amongst younger citizens, the many different archeocults worship the strange, dangerous, or lost technologies of the past. Most begin with the discovery of an abandoned piece of machinery deep beneath the city, or the arrival of an odd artefact in one of the markets. The young, inquisitive, or gullible are then often drawn in to believing the item has astounding properties and soon develop all manner of rituals or habits to interact with it. Most archeocults only last a short time, but a few have persisted for years and have grown in influence in parts of the city.

Other Organisations

There are a multitude of clubs, societies, and organisations pursuing their own agendas in the city. Some others include:

- **The Huntington Lodge**: An exclusive club for the city's elite. Rumours abound that its members engage in bizarre rituals and dabble in dangerous Pattern weaving activities.
- **The Prussian Band**: The Ministry of Truth regularly warns citizens to be alert for members of this subversive group who act as agents of foreign powers. They are said to identify each other by wearing dark blue ribbons, sashes, or scarves. Whether the band actually exists is a matter for debate in many social clubs.
- **The Society of Philomaths**: Recognisable by their clear rubber coats and belts of sinister instruments, these scientists and academics have earned a reputation as dangerous eccentrics who take their pursuit of knowledge too far.
- **The Temperance League**: They want one thing – the return of prohibition and the criminalisation of alcohol and serum use. They are quite militant about it.

SECTS & FACTIONS

Every cult and secret society of the city is split by internal strife and divided by ideological differences. This gives you room to make each as ineffective, troublesome, or dangerous as you need for your story.

CRIME & LAW ENFORCEMENT

Crime is rife in the city. Petty crooks looking to make a quick buck, crimes of passion and opportunity, organised criminal enterprises and racketeering, and even conspiracies to bring down the Council, Mother, or the entire city are frequent. In a place where only the cunning or strong survive, people all too frequently turn to illicit means to make ends meet or to find an edge over their competition.

To make things worse, the criminal justice system is overburdened and ineffective. Most police precincts are left to determine whether criminal activity should be escalated to the courts, or if minor punishments can be meted out ad-hoc. Dangerous criminals and malcontents found guilty by the courts are either banished or sent to New Alcatraz.

The Badges

The first line of defence against crime are the Badges – the metropolitan police department. They have precinct houses scattered throughout the city, but are understaffed, poorly equipped, and as corrupt as any other city institution. All too often, they turn a blind eye to the activities of criminals, either out of apathy, laziness, or in return for kickbacks. When they do investigate crimes and get involved in public disturbances, the Badges are often heavy-handed and indiscriminate. They jump to conclusions quickly, arrest everyone in sight, or deal swift justice with their batons and boots.

Vigilantes & Private Eyes

With such an ineffectual police department, some citizens have taken it upon themselves to right wrongs and address perceived injustices. Private eyes, mercenaries, and vigilantes are common, many making up the ranks of the Revs. While licensed P.I.s are tolerated, vigilantes are viewed as criminals by the Ministries, as they often interfere in official business or disrupt the smooth operation of the city. The citizens of Tomorrow City have varying opinions of vigilantes, and Revs in general, depending on whether or not they believe what the Ministry of Truth says about them.

The Belafonte Crime Family

Notorious Midtown gangsters, the Belafonte family run various criminal enterprises across the city, including illegal gambling operations, extortion rackets, and prostitution rings. Despite everyone knowing exactly what the family does, "Papa" Belafonte and his children are well respected in the district as they give generously to the community and keep gang trouble to a minimum.

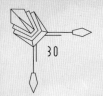
The Collector

Running an extensive smuggling operation that brings in artefacts from as far away as Europe and Japan, the Collector is a mysterious figure in the city's underworld. Said to be a wealthy skyriser, nobody can confirm their identity, due to the fact that they do all their business through a strange and highly advanced robot known as Karada. Standing seven feet tall and fashioned to look like a samurai warrior, Karada is the menacing face of the organisation who sometimes appears in seedy parts of town to hire Revs for risky, but profitable, jobs.

Hood Scum

Gangs of youths, unemployed thugs, and petty criminals often congregate on street corners, in dingy bars, under bridges, or in dark clubhouses. They play pool, dance, steal cars, break and enter, menace locals, and brawl with other gangs for the rights to a particular patch of turf. Belonging to a gang is a mark of respect for many younger citizens, while for others it's a means of survival.

The Pillbox Mafia

Popularised by a series of newspaper articles about female bank robbers, it is unclear whether the so-called "Pillbox Mafia" even exists. Named for the distinctive style of hat they're said to wear, this band of dangerous femme fatales are believed to be responsible for a swathe of crimes across the city, including heists, extortions, and murders. If they do exist, they must be highly organised and extremely smart, as no arrests have ever been made. They have, however, made the pillbox hat very popular amongst women of certain social circles.

CITIZENS OF INTEREST

There are many important and influential people in the city. Some make headlines every week, while others work quietly in the shadows to fulfil some hidden agenda. Some of the most noteworthy characters include:

Aunt Maude

Grey-haired and craggy-faced, Maude is a fixture on the steps of the Concourse of Prosperity. She whiles away her days throwing breadcrumbs to the pigeons and watching the comings and goings of Councillors and Ministry officials. She is happy to talk with anyone who stops and vigorously denies being a member of the Court of Pigeons.

Carmine Grant, Director of Public Safety

Head of the Ministry of Peace, Carmine Grant revels in the power and authority of his position. A decorated soldier, much of his body was rebuilt with automaton parts after being injured on the front lines of The Long War. Some say this has left him incapable of empathising with the public he has been entrusted to protect.

Eleanor Braithwaite

When the industrial tycoon Douglas Braithwaite and his sons were killed in the Factory Riots, Eleanor was left with the reigns of the family company and fortune. Since then, she has used her wealth to build medical centres and shelters in Rimside, in hopes of avoiding another tragic uprising. Her peers see it as an unsightly waste of money, while many in Rimside are suspicious of her real motivations.

Foreman Enoch

Broad chested, bald headed, and with a great red beard, Enoch is a popular leader of the cult of Moloch. Passionate and charismatic, he proselytises throughout The Great Factory and Rimside, seeking to bring more worshippers to the furnace of his God.

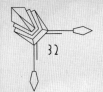

Fran Tutti

If you need gossip on the city's movers and shakers, then Fran is the person to see. A flamboyant performer and owner of the Tropicana Cabaret Club, Fran always dresses to shock in sequinned outfits and bold headpieces. They love to give impromptu performances, and Fran's private parties are always the talk of the town.

The Green Gargoyle

Public enemy number one, the so-called Green Gargoyle is a vigilante who delivers justice with a pair of automatic pistols. Recognisable by his black cloak and green felt fedora, he has had several violent run-ins with the Badges. He is a folk hero in some neighbourhoods of Midtown and Rimside.

Harold Manning, Director of the Ministry of Truth

Manning has a great deal of influence on how information is disseminated and controlled in the city. Newspapers and radio stations all defer to his word, and he personally approves all new propaganda campaigns. He gained a reputation in his early career for crafting devastating smear campaigns based on rumour and gossip, earning him the sobriquet "Hearsay Harry" – a nickname he is said to hate.

Jasper Trock

Short and rotund, with a bushy black moustache and cheerful smile, Jasper oversees Rimside's huge freight elevators, which provide the only easy vehicle access to the surface. Don't let his friendly demeanour fool you, he is a shrewd operator who makes good money smuggling items and people in and out of the city.

Marcus Craig, Councillor

A representative of the Inner City, the paunchy, balding Craig is the most well-known of the Council Members. He owns several companies in a variety of industries and has a distinct interest in maintaining the status quo. He bullies and cajoles to get his own way, and many believe he has extensive blackmail files on many of the other Councillors.

Roderick York III

Fighter pilot ace, movie star, and heir to the York fortune, Roderick is the darling of the society pages. He spends his days sleeping and his nights revelling in the most fashionable nightspots in town. Nobody believes the rumours that his war records are manufactured.

Siegfried Lutz

The stoop-shouldered Chief Engineer of Energy Distribution and Logistics, Lutz is an oddity amongst the many high-ranking Ministry officials as he seemingly eschews power and politics. He prefers to spend his time attending to the capacitors beneath The Spindle and directing his engineers about their daily business.

Vivian Lafayette

Known as "The Fixer", Lafayette holds no particular position in any Ministry, yet works for all of them. She is a shrewd and dangerous woman, who hires Revs on behalf of Ministries, Councillors, and wealthy business magnates who would rather keep their identities secret.

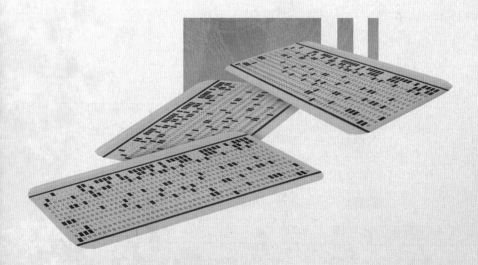

CITY DISTRICTS

Tomorrow City is divided into five distinct districts. The Inner City, Midtown, and Rimside each lie on one of the huge discs that turn about The Spindle on the city's surface. Beneath the streets, deep into the funnel-shaped structure of the city, is The Great Factory. Hanging from underneath the city like a lattice of rusting ironwork is the shanty town of Underside. The districts are further divided into a multitude of neighbourhoods, each with a distinct identity and fluctuating borders.

IMAGINING THE CITY

To help you imagine what Tomorrow City looks and feels like, picture any great American city of the inter-war period and add another layer of grime and industry. Anything you might have found in one of those great metropolises is here, just bigger, more crowded, covered in pipes and cables, or decorated with exaggerated art deco ornamentation. When describing city locations, visualise a similar historical place, but make it darker, brighter, or more dangerous. Use a real city map if you like but turn it upside down and move the prestigious suburbs or boroughs to the Inner City or Midtown, the factory districts to Rimside, and the worker's shanties to Underside.

The Spindle

Quiet Efficiency, Watchful Guards, Snobby Bureaucrats, Polished Marble, Pneumatic Tubes, Shining Chrome, Red Tape & Paperwork, Whispering, Large Clocks, Ornate Fixtures, Aunty Maude on the Concourse Steps, Imposing Entrances, Everything in Its Place, Banks of Elevators, Air Charged with Electricity, A Terse Reprimand, Icons of Mother

At one hundred stories tall, the magnificent art deco structure known as The Spindle is the tallest and most impressive building in the city. Visible from almost any point, and from many miles beyond the city, it glistens in chrome and gold and glass. Sometimes it even shimmers with the raw energy that courses through its structure.

The Spindle is seat of the City Council and the home of Mother. Public offices and reception areas fill great indoor plazas on the lower levels of the tower, serviced by officious Ministry agents and dead-eyed robots. The higher levels of the tower are reserved for Councillors and important Ministry personnel. Here they watch over the city from their thick, glazed windows and debate the fate of the metropolis in grand meeting rooms.

- **The Spire Dock**: At the very top of The Spindle is a private airship dock for Council Members and VIP guests.
- **Barracks**: The Spindle Guard have extensive barracks and training facilities on the sub-street levels of The Spindle, allowing them to quickly respond to threats.
- **The Capacitors**: The Spindle is not only an impressive piece of architecture but also an essential part of the city's machinery. It is the axis about which the great discs of the city revolve and the point at which the engines of The Great Factory direct their vast stores of energy. In the very bowels of the tower, far beneath the streets, are great capacitors and batteries that store and distribute power to the city, according to the needs and purposes determined by Mother and the Council.
- **The Concourse of Prosperity**: Crossing the granite paving of the concourse will take you to one of the six great entrances to The Spindle. Each is a broad art deco arch almost two stories in height and flanked by a pair of Spindle Guard in their ceremonial ironside armour. On any given day you will find knots of reporters or gawking citizens gathered to hear the latest pronouncement from the City Council, or catch a glimpse of a high-ranking Ministry official.
- **The Core Pin**: Once a year, the viewing rooms are opened, allowing citizens to peer through thick glass at this steel rod, said to be the precise centre of the city. Its purpose is unknown, but it runs the length of The Spindle, from its spire to its unfathomable depths.
- **The Great Calvaria**: The hall where Mother's ornate face resides. It is here that the Council confers with Her. It is always guarded by four Angels.
- **The Lobby**: Polished marble floors, bold art deco ornamentation and an enormous visage of Mother greet visitors when they enter the cavernous lobby. The great oak counter is almost five feet high, requiring you to crane your neck to speak to the clerks.
- **The Old Shafts**: It is rumoured that a series of secret elevator shafts, used during The Spindle's construction, lie buried deep within the skyscraper.
- **The Terrace**: On the twentieth floor is a manicured greenhouse and public park that wraps around the tower. Paths of crushed granite wind between garden beds, with kiosks selling newspapers, tobacco, toys, postcards, and freshly cut posies at their many intersections.

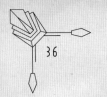

Inner City

Tall Skyscrapers, Spotlessly Clean, Watchful Doormen, Well-dressed Residents, Gilt Statues, Classy Nightspots, Moving Sidewalks, Robotic Servants, Polished Wood, Regular Patrols, Grand Open Plazas, Music from a Jazz Club, Expensive Brands, Obsequious Staff, Celebrities Stalked by Paparazzi

The domain of the rich and powerful, the dazzling skyscrapers of the Inner City reach almost as high as The Spindle itself. Immaculate apartment buildings with broad balconies, luxurious penthouses, rooftop terrace gardens, and glass-walled skybridges are features commonly associated with this part of the city. Here, sleek automobiles glide along spotless streets, well-heeled residents shop at prestigious boutiques, and uniformed security guards watch through glass-fronted buildings, alert to any disturbance of the peace. While it is the smallest of the city's districts, its proximity to The Spindle makes it a sought-after place to live and an ideal location for powerful organisations or prestigious businesses.

The Inner City is home to major banks and several important Ministries, such as the Ministry of Peace and the Ministry of Science. It is the economic centre of the city. Here, the wealthiest citizens look across the city from their sprawling apartment complexes and immaculately furnished boardrooms, surveying the city that revolves around them.

- **The Beecroft**: The city's most exclusive hotel, it is the residence of choice for rich celebrities and visiting dignitaries. Paparazzi often lurk here in the hopes of capturing a candid picture.
- **Enterprise Plaza**: Perhaps the most famous intersection in the city, Enterprise Plaza is a dazzling spectacle of telescreens and neon-lit billboards. Many Midtown and Rimside visitors make a pilgrimage here just to see the lights.
- **First Capital Bank**: Said to be the most secure privately owned building in the city, the headquarters of the First Capital Bank is an imposing black granite skyscraper. As well as secure vaults and lockboxes that any bank can offer, First Capital also employs dozens of Metaphysical Geometrists to create and maintain private extradimensional spaces for clients' valuables.
- **Justice Precinct**: The heart of the Ministry of Peace's power. The MoP's headquarters are here, as are the courts and several other associated buildings.
- **The Magic Castle**: Salvaged from the ruins of Los Angeles, this elaborate mansion now sits atop a twenty-story skyscraper. While it primarily operates as a nightclub, it is rumoured to be home to a secret society of Pattern users.
- **New City Station**: Looking like an art deco cathedral, this grand transport hub spreads several city blocks and is sixty stories high. Cables, tracks, and roads pass through it from all directions, and it is said that all SkyTrains originate and terminate here.
- **Nightclubs & Nightlife**: If you're looking for a good time, you cannot do better than the glittering clubs and dance halls of the Inner City. Anyone who's anyone wants to be seen at the entrance of glamorous nightspots such as The Tropicana or The Teslatron, or rubbing shoulders with the rich and famous in front of a big band at Clash. Even citizens of Midtown and Rimside can have a fun night out at any one of the neon-lit jazz clubs that come to life across the Inner City after dark.

- **The Steps**: With few natural hills in the city, the architects had to get creative. The Steps is a prestigious neighbourhood of brownstone terraces accessed by broad banks of electric escalators.
- **Silver Lane**: This eight-story galleria spans an entire city block and is covered by a curved glass roof made of geometric panes. If you are after expensive jewellery, finely tailored clothes, or antiques of questionable provenance, then this is the place to visit. The boutiques here commission the city's finest craftsmen and designers to create bespoke fashion objects, and many employ finders to obtain interesting objects for them to intrigue and amaze the bored citizens of the Inner City.
- **Sky Walks**: Beautiful arched bridges, strung between high-rise buildings and filled with planter boxes of mature trees, the sky walks provide park-like facilities high above the bustle of the street.

Midtown

Busy Streets, Crowded Markets, Rattling of Trams, Flashing Neon Signs, Dark Subway Entrances, A Honking Car Horn, Children Playing in the Street, Busy Delis, A Nosy Neighbour, An Automat, A Dead Pigeon, Tree-lined Street, A Paper Boy, The Smell of Exotic Cooking, Old Men Playing Chess, A Trash Can Piled With Garbage, Pipe Runners Working on a Rooftop

High-rise apartments, picture theatres, replica brownstones, department stores and mom-and-pop shops squeeze against the pavement in Midtown, all overrun by pipes, ducting, and cables like industrial-proportioned ivy. The nicer neighbourhoods have lush, tree-lined avenues; every street corner has a hydrant, post box, or drinking fountain; and many apartment buildings have rooftop gardens, pigeon lofts, or airship docks. The SkyTrain and tram are the preferred transportation options for getting around, and people regularly travel to eat out at their favourite restaurants or buy their groceries from corner stores. Apartments are small and the streets are crowded, but life is not all that bad in this district.

The streets of Midtown are busy with predominantly middle-class citizens, from a melting pot of cultures and backgrounds. The residents here include clerks, minor bureaucrats, teachers, scientists, and businesspeople. Some, like the residents of Little Novgorod, are refugees of The Long War, while others have lived in Midtown for generations. For the most part, the people of Midtown go about their business in relative ignorance of the hardships of Rimside and Underside, but always in the shadow of the Inner City and its immense wealth.

- **Delis & Markets**: An essential part of life in Midtown are the delis and grocery stores found on many street corners. These small businesses meet the needs of their neighbourhoods, providing everyday items, fresh produce, meals, and a place to meet and chat for the locals.
- **Little Novgorod**: When the Russian Union collapsed, a great exodus of people made their way to Tomorrow City and began their lives anew in this neighbourhood. Here, you can find fur-clad babushkas talking in huddles, young toughs smoking in street cafes, and the best pirozhki in the city.

- **Midtown River**: A broad canal that separates Midtown from Rimside, the River runs the entire circumference of the district like a modern-day moat and is a consistent five hundred feet wide, with bridges at regular intervals. Originally intended as both a reservoir and place of recreation, it has become a thriving hub of commerce and transportation.
- **New Venice**: This river-front neighbourhood got its name after several of its sub-street tunnels collapsed and flooded. The lack of car access, the stench of stagnant water, and the threat of disease-carrying mosquitoes has made it one of the least desirable places to live in Midtown.
- **Old Town**: One of the earliest inhabited neighbourhoods, positioned close to the border with the Inner City. Once the domain of the workers who built the city, it has since been gentrified, its tall, narrow apartment buildings updated with modern lifts and large windows that afford impressive views of The Spindle.
- **Rooftop Gardens**: Many high-rise apartments have rooftop gardens where fruits and vegetables are grown by residents or tended to by members of the Provedore Union. These tend to be lush oases of neatly ordered planter boxes and net-covered fruit trees.
- **The Roosts**: The high-rise sanctuaries of the Pigeon Court, these ramshackle forts of scrap wood and wire are attended to by a network of pigeon fanciers and spies who dress in dirty docker caps and grey dust coats.
- **Ruth Field**: Home of the Skyrockets and playground of the masses, Ruth Field is the largest sports stadium in the city. You can catch a game of baseball, football, or even more esoteric sports on almost any night of the week here, and it is always a sell out on the weekends when the inter-district competitions run.
- **The Tunnels**: A warren of access corridors, broad sewers, and disused trolley tunnels that form a honeycomb under the streets of Midtown. Some can be entered from basement trapdoors or subway tunnels, while others can only be accessed through drains or filthy sewer vents.

Rimside

Filth and Grime, Delivery Dirigibles, Smog, Crowded Tenements, Dirty Children, Cables and Chains, Narrow Alleys, Cargo Containers, Battered Labour Bots, Factory Whistles, Rusting Cranes, Shifty Smugglers, A Maze of Crates, Rumbling Trucks, An Alarm, Soot Stains, Washing Lines Hung Between Buildings, Grumbling Labourers, Old Women Gossiping from Windows

The largest of the surface districts, Rimside is a sprawling landscape of warehouses, factories, and tenements. Here, commercial industries are king, with assembly lines, smokestacks, and workshops all sharing space with diesel refineries, loading docks, and manufacturing plants. Workers scurry about in short sleeves and caps, sweating under the hot Cali sun. They congregate for a joke and a smoke before the boss commands them back to work with a glare. Delivery trucks and transport dirigibles arrive and depart every hour of the day and goods are loaded onto tram cars to be delivered to storehouses and shops further into the city.

Rimside is also home to the enormous greenhouses, rooftop stockyards, hatcheries, and vertical farms that supply much of the city's food. They stink of livestock and fertiliser, and the cries and mews of animals carry across the district. These sprawling properties are supported by slaughterhouses, canneries, mills, food processing plants, and breweries. Despite all this food production infrastructure, there is still not enough to go around, with the majority of produce sent to the Inner City and wealthier neighbourhoods of Midtown.

- **The Airfield**: Airship docks rise like lattice towers, and long airstrips are marked off along the top of industrial buildings across the district. The so-called airfield is a particularly dense collection of towers and runways, serviced by elevators, cranes, mechanics, and longshoremen.
- **The Bodyworks**: Officially the General Robotics Factory, the Bodyworks gets its name from the rows of lifeless robots that stand on its dock ready for shipment across the city. Most of the city's commercial robots are built and repaired here.
- **The Crematorium**: While there are many funeral homes and morgues, the black chimneyed Municipal Crematorium is the final resting place for most of the city's deceased. It is said the orderlies here steal gold teeth, artificial limbs, and even clothing from the dead, to sell on the black market.
- **The Elevators**: Huge freight elevators, large enough for several trucks or even a small landship, descend some fifty stories from Rimside to the surface of Old Cali. They are used by those heading out to or returning from the wastelands, and to collect the produce farmed in the soggy swamps beneath the city.
- **Piggeries**: A complex of multi-story farms, slaughterhouses and butcheries, this disturbing place reeks of blood and death. The Belafonte crime family holds a controlling interest in this place – it is said that, if you upset Papa, the last thing you may ever hear is the squealing of the pigs.
- **Reclamation Yards**: The city's waste is brought here for sorting before being bulldozed into great chutes and dumped in the swamps below the city.
- **The Tenement Towers**: Tall, narrow tenement buildings house the workers and their families. Life is hard here. The buildings are dirty and poorly maintained, and there is not enough to go around, including power. The elevators never work, the lights are dim, and blackouts are common.
- **The Wall**: At the very edge of the district, where the city finally meets the sky, is a ten-story high wall. Covered in gantries, thick pipes, scaffolds, and hanging worker's huts, it marks the extreme border of the city. Many younger citizens see it as a rite of passage to stand atop the wall, between the two worlds of the city and the wastes beyond.

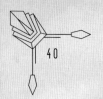

The Great Factory

Noisy Machinery, Thick Smog, Soot Stains, Narrow Corridors, Giant Pistons, Deep
Shadows, Noxious Fumes, Oil and Grease Stains, Clanging Pipes, Stifling Heat, Chant-
ing of Moloch's Followers, Deep Pits, Rattling Catwalks, Shouts and Calls, An Angry
Foreman, Hissing Steam, Large Pressure Gauges, Stench of Sweat

The subterranean city of The Great Factory is a world of shadow and noise, choking
smog and scorching steam. Machinery and engines of unfathomable purpose churn
away every minute of every day in vast halls the size of entire city blocks. Some
chambers are entirely filled with great pistons, crankshafts, and rocker arms, while
others have bundles of pipes with enormous gauges and valves. Gyroscopes and
flywheels connect with motors and dynamos via chains or belts as thick as a trolley car,
constantly lubricated by teams of filthy workers. It is a hive of industry that literally
keeps the city turning.

Each part of The Great Factory is attended to by an army of drones and specialised
engineers who have been trained to know every intimate detail of their specific piece
of machinery. Over generations, the knowledge of how the differing parts operate and
interact with each other, however, has become compartmentalised. Today, there is no
person living who understands how The Great Factory works in its entirety.

- **Deep Well**: At the centre of The Great Factory is the deep shaft of the funnel,
  extending hundreds of yards down into the bedrock of Old Cali. It is used
  to draw up ground water to cool the factory's engines and supply the city.
  Working a shift in the heat and damp at the bottom of Deep Well is often used
  as punishment for insubordinate drones.
- **Dormitories & Washrooms**: While most Factory families live in the crowded
  tenements of Rimside, or in the squalor of Underside, younger workers reside
  in the dormitories that are crammed between the machine halls and engine
  rooms. These stinking rooms, little more than corridors, are packed with triple-
  bunk beds that are shared by different shifts, the only personal space consisting
  of metal lockers just large enough for a change of clothes and a brush or photo
  frame.
- **The Great Maze**: The Factory is sometimes called the Great Maze, as its
  winding tunnels and narrow corridors are almost impossible to navigate.
  Drones use coloured pipes, distinctive gauges, damaged bulkheads, and other
  landmarks to find their way between their dormitories and places of work.
- **The Hall of Workers**: Rows of benches and tables fill this cavernous cafeteria
  and meeting place. Here, exhausted drones congregate after long shifts to eat,
  talk, and relax before returning to their dormitories.
- **The Mouth of Moloch**: A cathedral to the Machine God; at the centre of this
  darkened hall is a screaming maw of blackened steel, the flames of a furnace
  spewing tongues of fire. Followers of Moloch gather here to worship and
  sacrifice.
- **The Shift Clock**: Not a single clock, but an object found throughout the
  factory-city. These large brass time pieces measure the length of shifts and

drones sometimes half-joke that they change depending on the needs of the factory and its overseers.

- **The Old Vents**: Long ago blocked off by construction on the surface, and since abandoned by the factory workers, a thick miasma of poison gas swirls about these old airshafts. Criminals sometimes make their way down here to hide out or plan their next enterprise.

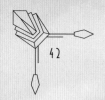

Underside

Rusting Steel Girders, Howling Wind, Tin Shacks, A Crying Child, Permanent Gloom,
Thugs Huddled Together, Narrow Steel Beams, A Maze of Alleys, A Fifty-Story Drop, Canvas
Flapping in the Wind, Eyes Watching from Darkened Hovels, The Tinkle of Rusting Wind
Chimes, Rope Ladders and Nets, Lanterns Hung from Chains, The Scrape of Metal on
Metal, A Broken Ladder

Underside is a shanty town of patched-together hovels hanging precariously beneath the
city on rusting steel girders and catwalks. It is always dark in the umbra of the city, the
sun only brushing the outer edges of the slum as it falls below the horizon each evening.
The tin shacks, patched with scrap wood and tattered canvas, lean together like a house of
cards, rattling in the chill wind and ready to collapse without warning. The narrow alleys
formed by thin walls, stacked crates and flapping curtains are a confusing warren and many
walkways are little more than scraps of tin or rotting wooden planks ready to give way to
an unlucky footstep.

Families of destitute workers and refugees, gangs of hood scum, and wanted criminals
huddle in tiny shacks and crowd the benighted lanes and gantries. They trade in scraps of
clothes, stolen goods, or access to water and gas pipes tapped from the city above. With
so little to go around, crime and violence are everyday occurrences here. It is a treacherous
place to live, but most of these people have no other place to go.

- **Breezeway**: The longest, widest walkway in Underside, everyone passes through here
  eventually. Lit by strings of lightbulbs wired to the city above, many seedy gin joints
  and doss houses are found along this street.
- **Crow's Nest**: Many smugglers, refugees, and criminals make use of this illegal airship
  dock, slung beneath Breezeway.
- **The Drip**: One of Underside's primary water sources, this rivulet from a broken drain
  somewhere high in the city is a meeting place for locals. They share stories and gossip
  here as they fill water containers or wash themselves with slivers of blackened soap.
- **Dump Station Two**: A gaping hole in one of the refuse chutes used by the Rimside
  reclamation yards. Workers here scoop out useful items or rotting food as it tumbles
  its way to the surface below. It can be dangerous work, however, and many have been
  dragged down the chute by an unexpected rush of garbage.
- **The Flush**: Raw sewage pours from pipes here at the edge of the city, covering
  everything nearby with filth. When the wind blows the wrong way large portions of
  Underside get caught in the sewage spray.
- **The Hammocks**: The poorest citizens of Underside cannot even afford the comfort of a
  tin hovel. Instead, they make their beds in swaying nets and hammocks, slung between
  girders, above shacks, or even suspended in the open air. Many who make a spot in the
  hammocks find it hard to leave and survive by begging handouts from those who pass
  them by.
- **Laddertown**: While there are many ways to get to Underside, this neighbourhood is a
  central hub where several paths, tunnels, and old access stairs converge. Pan handlers,
  urchins, and hood scum often congregate here, ready to pounce on any traveller that
  looks like they might have some coins to spare or belongings to steal.
- **Narrow's End**: It is said the wretches who live in this pitch-black alley indulge in
  cannibalism and use hidden trapdoors to capture unwary wanderers.

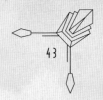

Old Cali

Endless Desert, Rusting War Machines, Foetid Swampland, Buzzards Circling, Weathered Nomads, A Cloud of Poison Gas, Clumps of Spikey Vegetation, An Abandoned Minefield, The Distant Rumble of a Vehicle, A Coming Storm, A Crumbling Building, A Pattern-warped Animal, Twisted Trees, A Passing Airship, A Ghost Town

Beyond the city lie the endless wastelands of ruined America, from the radium-poisoned deserts and seas to the broken mountain ranges and twisted forests. Scattered settlements dot the wilderness, eking out a meagre existence in the mud. Most of the great cities of North America were destroyed when the United States broke apart and the rest were decimated during The Long War. There are no creature comforts out in the wilderness beyond the city, only hardship and danger. Bands of tainted raiders, merciless sky pirates and the last vestiges of the old state militias harass the few remaining communities for their resources.

Still, there are treasures to be found here. Lost weapons of strange and devastating designs, secret laboratories, buried cities, and autonomous factories are scattered across the wilderness. Persistent and lucky scavengers can make a fortune for themselves, should they survive the journey into and back out of the wastelands.

- **The Fragments**: Pattern bombs left vast areas as disfigured hellscapes of jagged colour bursts and pulsing reality tears. Journeying through a fragment is like trying to navigate a kaleidoscope, the motley prism tumbling and shifting as you move. Aberrations infest these territories and occasionally stumble into passing caravans or nearby settlements.
- **The Grave Lands**: Rusting, bone-strewn battlefields, pitted with shell craters, collapsed trenches, and the corroded hulks of gun batteries and tanks. Crashed dirigibles and the monstrous remains of landships tower above the crimson-stained earth like skeletal carcasses. Acres of barbed wire and long-forgotten minefields lie in wait for anyone foolish enough to pass through these lands.
- **Herd Farms**: Small communities of freeholders and ranchers have returned to the wastelands, raising malnourished cattle and other livestock to sell to Tomorrow City. These are a tough people, ones who don't trust strangers and take no risks with their livelihoods.
- **New Alcatraz**: Floating high above the ruined coastline is the flying prison of New Alcatraz. The most dangerous criminals and subversive elements of the city are sentenced to imprisonment here, where they rot in tiny cells with little hope of escape.
- **The Swamplands**: Immediately below the city, extending hundreds of miles north and south, are the flooded canals, saltmarshes, and muddy swamps of Old Cali. Pocked with the jagged fingers of ruined cities and towns, this foetid expanse is difficult to traverse. Still, settlements persist, with hunters, toad farmers, exiles, and tainted mutants lurking in half-sunken hovels or gathering in temporary barge communities.

GETTING AROUND

The streets of the city wind, bend and seem to fold back on themselves in impossible tangles that make no sense to the casual observer. This is only compounded by the fact that the city is in constant motion – the streets literally move – and parts of the city rise and fall in correlation with the machinery beneath. Pipes, tracks, bundles of thick cable, and broad ducting weave between, across, and over the buildings of all districts, and teams of pipe runners constantly scurry across the city to service them, pull them up, or lay new connections as the city moves. The result is to make it almost impossible to map the city, as dead ends appear where there were none last week, and new rail networks are constantly being laid by city engineers.

Cars and trucks are common, but the congested streets, masses of pedestrians, and constantly changing routes make them slow. Still, the wealthy persist in using their private vehicles and chauffeured limousines, while trucks and vans make deliveries across the city to locations where the freight trams cannot go. For everyone and everything else, there is public transport.

Though constantly being rerouted and modified, the overhead SkyTrain and winding tram lines offer the most direct routes between districts. Beneath the streets are the dark tunnels of the subways that connect the neighbourhoods of a district. Due to the constant rotation of the districts about The Spindle, the subway lines never cross district borders and changing lines or moving between transport hubs is common.

It is difficult to get anywhere quickly in the city, and it can sometimes take hours to move a relatively short distance. Use the following times as a guide for travel around the city. These are for ground movement, perhaps on foot, or by using the subway, trams, and SkyTrain. Air travel is considerably quicker, particularly when travelling longer distances.

- Moving between nearby neighbourhoods in the same district: 2–12 minutes (2D6 minutes).
- Moving between distant neighbourhoods in the same district, or nearby neighbourhoods in different districts: 5–30 minutes (1D6x5 minutes).
- Moving between distant neighbourhoods in adjacent districts (e.g. from Midtown to Rimside): 10–60 minutes (1D6x10 minutes).
- Moving between non-adjacent districts: 30 minutes to 3 hours (1D6x30 minutes).
- Finding an entrance to The Great Factory: 5–30 minutes (1D6x5 minutes). It might be a tight squeeze, dirty, or unpleasant.
- Getting to Underside from anywhere in the city: 10–60 minutes (1D6x10 minutes). There is no telling exactly where in the slums you might arrive.

MAPPING THE CITY

There is no definitive map of Tomorrow City, firstly because it is always on the move, and secondly so that you can place things where they need to be! Make choices about distances and the locations of different neighbourhoods based on what makes sense for your story and what is most interesting. Over time, you will develop your own impression of how all these pieces fit together.

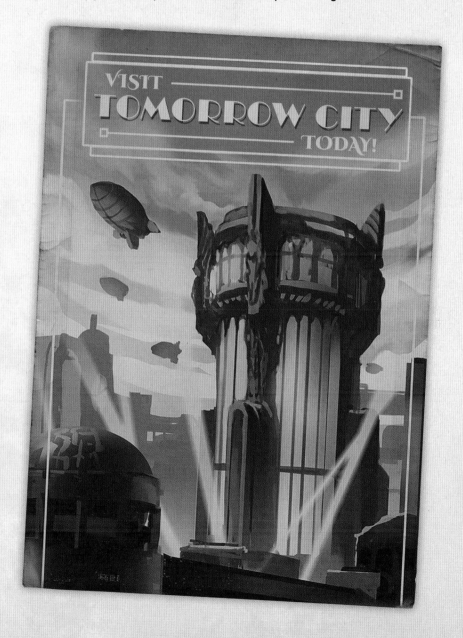

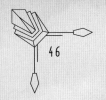

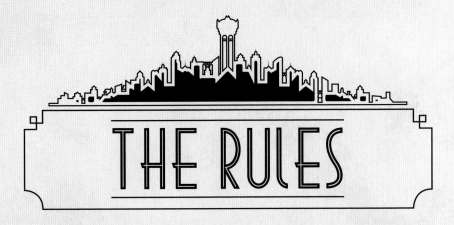

THE RULES

When you play *Tomorrow City*, everyone should be working together to tell an exciting story. Use your common sense, do what is most interesting or logical in any given moment, and drive play towards the features of the plot that seem most in keeping with the genre and tone of your story. Keep the following in mind as you play.

FICTIONAL POSITIONING

"Fictional positioning" is a term for all the facts and details that you have established in your story and being aware of how they might impact the actions of all the characters involved in a scene. It's basically a fancy term for "common sense" as it applies to your story and the characters involved, including where they are and what they are doing. Have you tripped the Tainted Bloater and now stand over them with your pattern blaster? That's fictional positioning. Is your character filled with rage and wants the East Side Dock Master dead, no matter the cost? That's also fictional positioning.

PLAYING IN THE MOMENT

During play, both the players and the GM are discovering the story together, so don't plan too far ahead. The GM sets the scene, the players decide what their characters do, and you let the situation unfold as it needs to. Act and react to things as they arise and play in the moment. Players might ask about what they see, hear, or smell, if they know some guy, or can do some action. GMs might ask how the characters are feeling, what they are thinking, or what is worrying them right now. Use the answers to fill in the blanks and drive the story towards the next interesting moment. When things get tricky, or you don't know what happens next, roll the dice and find out how your story changes.

TAGS

Tags are words or short descriptive phrases that convey significant details about your story's characters, locations, and events. A character might be *Quick* or *Covered in Mud*, a floor safe is *Heavy*, and a room might be *On Fire*. Sometimes tags will be written down on a character sheet, a map, or a sticky note where everyone can see it. At other times, they will simply be details described during play.

Tags can do any or all of the following:

- Describe the world, its inhabitants, and the features that might be interacted with. Tags help to breathe life into your world.
- Grant permission to do something. To attack a foe at a distance you will need an appropriate weapon, like your *Chromium-plated Pistol*. To enter the Ministry of Truth's secure facility you will need a *Coded Punch Card*.
- Make actions more or less likely to succeed. Helpful Tags will add Action Dice to checks, while other Tags might impede an action by adding Danger Dice.
- Inspire action and suggest ways to approach or overcome challenges. The gun is *Loud*, the security guard is *Angry*, and the bag full of explosives is *Precariously Balanced*.

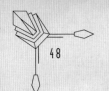

CHECKS

When you need to know if a character successfully breaks into a secure Ministry building, survives a fall from a skyrise balcony, re-wires the brain of a broken automaton, or does some other cool thing, make a Check. A character might have to make a Check when they:

- Try to overcome a tough problem
- Attack something
- Defend themselves or someone else
- Interact with an unfriendly or uncooperative NPC
- Use their skills or knowledge when under pressure
- Try something beyond the scope of their Trademarks

Making the Check

You will need a pool of Action Dice and Danger Dice, which are normal D6 in two different colours.

Tell everyone what your character is doing. Describe their action, what you want to achieve, and how your character is going about it.

1. Create a dice pool. Start with one Action Die. Add further Action Dice and Danger Dice based on the situation and action. Anyone can make suggestions, but the GM has the final say.
2. Roll all the dice. Each Danger Die cancels out a matching Action Die – discard both. Find your highest remaining Action Die, and this is your result.
3. Describe the outcome of your Check, using the result to guide the fiction and move the story along.

Only players make Checks. This leaves the GM free to focus on creating cool scenes and encounters.

Roll Results

Your highest remaining Action Die determines how successful the action is.

6: Success – You do the thing without too much difficulty. If you have additional 6's left over, each extra is a Boon. Boons let you add more detail to the action or gain some other advantage.

4 or 5: Partial Success – You achieve your goal, but at a price. Perhaps you don't achieve everything you wanted, maybe the action cost you something, or the situation changes in an unexpected way.

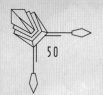

3 or less: Failure – You don't succeed, things have gone wrong, and you might now be in an even worse position.

Botch: If all the remaining Action Dice show 1's, or all the Action Dice have been cancelled out, you have critically failed. Things have gone very, *very* wrong, and the consequences will be terrible.

Modifiers

The following circumstances might add Action or Danger Dice to a pool. It is common practice to talk through the action description, Tags and other details and pick up dice as you go. This helps everyone better imagine the scene and understand what is going on. You don't need to incorporate every tag or scene detail into a dice pool, just pick out the most obvious advantages and disadvantages and use them as a guide.

ADD AN ACTION DIE FOR...	ADD A DANGER DIE FOR...
Trademark: A single relevant Trademark. Players may make an argument for why it is useful.	**Danger Rating:** Add Danger Dice equal to the Danger Rating of the enemy or problem being acted against.
Edges: Each relevant Edge attached to the Trademark being used.	**Harm:** Each different hindering Condition or Injury the character currently has.
Tags: Each Tag on a Threat or Scene that can be exploited for advantage.	**Tags:** Each Tag on a Threat or Scene that makes an action harder.
Position: You have a better position, are acting on a careful plan, or have plenty of time to prepare.	**Position:** The enemy has a better position; or the character is surprised, rushed or unprepared.
Gear: An item of equipment that has a useful Tag or provides a clear advantage in the situation. Just having an item does not grant an Action Die.	**Gear:** Not having a required item or having to improvise it. Some actions may be impossible without the right equipment.
Help: When you have assistance from one or more allies.	**Scale:** Facing an obstacle that is bigger, more numerous, tougher, more skilled, or very powerful.

Emile Franks is running from a group of robotic hounds that have been set upon him. The GM calls for a Check.

Player: *I start with one Action Die and have the Quick Trademark with the Duck & Weave Edge. That's three Action Dice. I also have a bit of a head start, does that give me an extra Action Die for position?*

GM: *Sure. The hounds have a Danger Rating of 1, so add a Danger Die for that, and another because there's a lot of these things chasing you.*

Emile's pool is four Action Dice and two Danger Dice. The player rolls all the dice, scoring 2, 3, 5 and 5 on the Action Dice and a 5 and 6 on the Danger Dice. The Danger Die scoring 5 cancels one of the matching Action Dice and they are both removed. Emile's best remaining Action Die is a 5, which is a partial success.

Automatic and Impossible Actions

Depending on the description and intent, an action might automatically succeed or be impossible to complete. In these cases, simply describe the outcome and continue without a Check.

One Attempt

In most situations, characters are limited to a single attempt to complete an action. They make the roll and must deal with the consequences. If you really want to make another attempt, you will need to find a new approach to the problem.

Rolling with Mastery

Some characters have special Advantages that allow them to "roll with Mastery". When making a Check with Mastery, you may re-roll a single Action Die before comparing and cancelling dice. Simply pick it up and roll it again. You must keep the new result, even if it is worse. Multiple instances of Mastery do not stack – you can only ever re-roll one Action Die for a given Check.

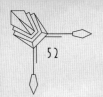

Extended Checks

Usually, when you make a Check, the action succeeds or fails, and you move on with the scene. However, sometimes an action requires more time or effort to complete and has a greater chance for things to go wrong along the way. In these situations, the GM will call for an Extended Check, indicating that three successes are required before the situation or action is resolved.

Make a Check as normal. For Extended Checks, both partial and complete successes count towards the required successes. You can also count Boons as successes. When you have accrued three successes the Extended Check succeeds.

Each failure you roll when making an Extended Check is a strike against the character. A Botch might apply two strikes against the character, or end the action completely, depending on the situation. If you accrue three strikes before achieving three successes, the Extended Check ends in failure.

When making Extended Checks, describe how the situation changes after each roll. The character might be making sound progress towards a goal, or they may have suffered a minor or serious setback. The player can describe how the character adjusts their approach before continuing with the next Check if they wish. It is very likely that the dice pool will change after each roll as the situation unfolds. If things have gone well, an Action Die might be added, while one or more additional Danger Dice could represent a complication from a partial success, failure, or Botch.

Alexi wants to climb onto the roof of a Ministry of Science facility and enter through a skylight. The GM decides this requires an Extended Check. Alexi's first roll is a 6 – that's one success. The player describes Alexi scaling a sturdy drainpipe.

A 4 on his next Check means he accrues another success but, as it's a partial success, something has gone wrong; the GM describes a wrench tumbling out of his tool belt, making a noisy clang. The guards have become suspicious, and a Danger Die is added to Alexi's dice pool.

He only rolls a 2 on the next Check, indicating a failure; Alexi has reached the roof, but he can now see several guards standing directly below the skylight. The player marks a strike and, because the situation has become much harder, another Danger Die is added to the pool.

He rolls again, getting a 5 on his next Check, giving him enough successes to complete the task, with another consequence. It is agreed that Alexi has managed to drop down into the warehouse but is now surrounded by several alert security guards.

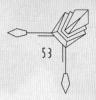

PRESSURE

Pressure is an abstract measure of the growing danger that the characters find themselves in. It represents the accumulation of little mistakes, wasted time and just plain bad luck.

Pressure begins at 0. After making a Check, each uncancelled Danger Dice that shows a 6 will increase the Pressure by +1. The GM should track the rising tension somewhere everyone can see, such as on a piece of note paper or with a large die. When the Pressure reaches a total of 6, something bad happens – more enemies arrive, the villain enacts the next step in their plan, an alarm sounds, an opponent reveals a new ability or weapon, or perhaps an ally is put in danger. The exact details of what happens will depend on your story and the moment in which the Pressure tips.

> *After making a Check and cancelling dice, the player is left with 1, 4, and 5 on your Action Dice and 3, 6, and 6 on the Danger Dice. Their result is a partial success (the 5 on the Action Die). However, because two Danger Dice that show 6's remain, the Pressure is also increased by +2.*

Once the Pressure reaches 6, it remains there until the GM decides to reset it to 0. This usually happens after they reveal the new trouble, but does not have to be (sometimes, the trouble happens "off-screen").

CONSEQUENCES

When the dice hit the table, things change. Characters do cool stuff, suffer setbacks, or overcome an obstacle. They are now in a better, worse, or simply different situation. Change the scene in some interesting way and use the Check result, the fiction, and your best judgment to guide the description of consequences.

Consequences often fall into one of the following types.

- **Cost**: The action costs something. Perhaps time is wasted, an item is lost or broken, a resource is used up, or a favour is now owed.
- **Complication**: Something happens to make the situation tougher or more difficult. It might be an unexpected problem or finding out that something they did not want to be true, in fact, is.
- **Tags**: The scene changes in some way. Add or remove a Tag from a character, a Threat, or the Scene itself.
- **Threats**: Add a new Threat to the Scene or increase the power or scale of an existing one.
- **Harm**: Someone suffers Damage or a Condition, representing some physical, mental, social, or emotional harm. It might be the acting character, an opponent, or an innocent bystander. Most attacks and other forms of Harm cause 2 Damage.

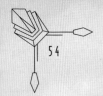

Soft and Hard Consequences

In broad terms, the intensity of a consequence can be described as "soft" or "hard". A soft consequence applies stress but gives a character a chance to react or stop whatever is about to come. A soft consequence might be used when the stakes are low, the characters are in a good position, or the GM wants to escalate a situation and see how the characters respond. Soft consequences set characters up for action, with time to prepare for the danger, attempt an escape, or change the situation to their advantage. Partial successes often result in soft consequences; the danger is imminent, but the really bad stuff hasn't happened yet. A soft consequence is often followed by the question: "What do you do?"

When characters really mess up, fail to respond to the clear warnings of imminent danger, or do something really dumb, they get hit with a hard consequence. This might be actual harm, but it doesn't have to be. The problem is right here, right now, and there is no stopping it or getting away before it happens. Failed Checks often result in hard consequences, especially if the character was attempting something obviously dangerous or difficult. Hard consequences should not come as a surprise and they should be a logical follow-up to the narrative and action. Botches should always result in hard consequences.

Boons

When you make a Check and roll multiple 6s, things have gone particularly well. The first 6 rolled indicates that the action succeeded, while each additional remaining six is a Boon. The player and GM are free to decide how this "critical success" is conveyed, with either person making suggestions. The GM, however, always has the final say on the consequences of the action.

Think of Boons as "and" statements; "I succeeded and I also...". Each Boon you roll can add some extra detail or improve the overall effect of an action. Common uses for Boons include the following:

- **Increased Effect**: Spend a Boon to make your success even better. Describe how your outcome is greater in scale, influence, or effect.

You leap from one rooftop to the next and have caught up with the target you were pursuing.

- **Set Up an Ally**: Spend your Boon by describing how your action helps another character. They then get a bonus on their next action if they take advantage of this Boon.

You trip your opponent and your ally's next attack is particularly effective, adding an extra Action Die to their roll.

- **Add a Tag**: Add a useful Tag to the Scene or to a Threat. It must be relevant to the action that generated the Boon.

You throw a Molotov cocktail at a tessellated aberration, burning it. You use your Boon to declare that the thing is now "Melting". The GM thinks this is cool and describes how its actions are now slowed.

- **Extra Successes**: If making an Extended Check, a Boon can be spent as an additional success, helping to achieve the goal quicker.

Botches

In contrast to Boons, Botches indicate that things have gone very badly. If all your Action Dice have been cancelled by Danger Dice, or if the only remaining Action Dice show 1's, the action has failed in the worst possible way. The GM is encouraged to really bring the pain in whatever fashion seems appropriate to the situation. Some example Botch effects include the following:

- **Increased Danger**: Reveal a detail that makes things much worse for the character.

The enemy is more numerous or powerful than expected; a grenade sails through a window; you lose control of the car and spin out of control; a man enters with a gun.

- **Add a Tag**: Add a hindering Tag to the Scene, the acting character, or an ally, or give a Threat a new Tag that helps them. It should relate to the failed action and make the situation worse.

You shoot at some escaping thugs but roll a Botch. Not only do your bullets miss, but they punch a hole in a pipe that lets out a gush of poisonous fumes. The room now has the "Filled with Poison Gas" tag.

- **Inflict Serious Harm**: The acting character, or an ally, suffers 4 Damage instead of the usual 2. Alternatively, they might suffer two levels of a Condition, or a combination of damage and Conditions.

You attempt to avoid the swing of a Hood Scum's club, but Botch the Check. The GM could inflict 4 Damage on you, but decides you suffer the normal 2 Damage and must take the Dazed condition.

- **Extra Strikes**: If making an Extended Check, the player character suffers an additional strike against them.

HARM

Harm is the physical, emotional, or social trouble that a character might find themselves in, perhaps because of a Check, or the result of an action by another character or enemy. In *Tomorrow City*, Harm comes in three forms: Hits, Injuries, and Conditions.

Hits

Characters can soak up a certain amount of Harm before they really start to feel the effects: this is represented by their Hits. The maximum number of Hits a Rev can have is equal to their Grit value. When a character suffers physical Harm, you remove a number of Hits equal to the Damage. Most situations and attacks inflict 2 Damage on a target, so your Hits will quickly be depleted if you rush into dangerous situations without a plan or the right equipment.

Injuries

An Injury is a Tag that represents some serious ongoing physical, mental, or emotional Harm.

If a character suffers Damage but has reduced their Hits to zero, the damage rolls over to Injuries instead. When this happens, distribute the excess damage among one or more new or existing Injuries. When you add a new Injury, make it painful and troublesome, such as a deep wound, broken bone, bullet wound, or serious psychological condition. Some example Injuries might include the following, though the GM always has the final say over the exact nature of the Harm a character suffers:

- **Broken/Crushed:** Arm, Leg, Fingers, Toes, Ribs, Jaw, Heart, Spirit
- **Wounded/Punctured:** Gut, Chest, Eye, Face, Arm, Leg, Hand, Pride
- **Lost:** Fingers, Hearing, Toes, Eye, Ear, Self-control
- **Bruised:** Hand, Arm, Ribs, Spine, Throat, Chest, Kidneys, Ego
- **Damaged/Ruined:** Hearing, Nervous system, Depth perception, Reputation, Self-esteem
- **Frail:** Heart, Knees, Lungs, Immune system, Resolve, Spirit

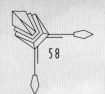
Emile is attacked by a malfunctioning robot and suffers 2 Damage. Unfortunately, he only has one Hit left. After marking off the last Hit he still has one Damage remaining, so must write a new Injury, or increase the severity of an existing Injury. He writes a new Injury, recording "Bruised Hand" and marking a single point of Damage against it.

Later in the combat, Emile suffers another 2 Damage. He could add both points to the existing Bruised Hand, create a new Injury with two points of Damage marked, or even write two new Injuries with one point of Damage each. He decides to add a new Injury for both points, writing "Broken Nose".

Each Injury can have up to three damage marked against it and a character can have a number of different Injuries equal to their Grit value at any one time.

Emile has a Grit of 3, so can have up to three different Injuries recorded.

When you add more Damage to an existing Injury, you can change the description to convey the increased severity. For example, a "Bruised hand" injury with one point of Damage might become a "Broken hand" if it has three points of damage marked. This helps to add to the drama of the story but is entirely optional.

Dying

If a character must write an Injury, but has already suffered their maximum, they instead begin Dying. A Dying character can do nothing beyond moan or crawl a few feet and will die in D3+Grit turns if they are not Stabilised.

Anyone can attempt to Stabilise a Dying character by making a Check, with a Danger Rating equal to the number of Injuries the target currently has.

If a Dying character suffers any further Damage, it is an Automatic Death and they die immediately.

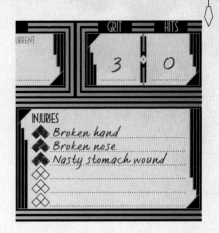

After a series of unfortunate encounters, Emile has accrued three Injuries, each with 3 Damage marked. When he falls down a flight of stairs, he takes another 2 Damage. As he can have no more than 3 injuries at a time, and has no more space to add Damage to his Injuries, he starts Dying. He rolls a D3, getting 2, and adds his Grit value of 3 – he will die in 5 turns if he isn't Stabilised.

Conditions

Conditions are temporary physical, emotional, or social consequences that are applied when dramatically appropriate, because of a Check, or as the result of an action by a character or enemy. Each Condition is a Tag that can influence the story and affect dice pools. These Tags can be suffered multiple times, indicating the growing severity of the Condition. Suffering the same Condition three or more times can have serious consequences for a character.

The character sheet includes the following Conditions that characters might commonly suffer, but you are encouraged to make up your own as necessary.

- **Angry**: You are filled with rage, which clouds your judgment and may cause you to act without thinking things through. This is problematic in moments that require careful consideration but could be useful in some conflicts. If you suffer three Angry Conditions, you become so enraged that you are incapable of any rational thought and will turn your anger on the nearest, easiest target. Clear this Condition when you have time to calm down and think things through rationally.
- **Dazed**: You are distracted, concussed, or confused, slowing your reactions and making it difficult to concentrate or focus. You will act after enemies in combat. If you suffer three Dazed Conditions, you are completely stunned or knocked unconscious and can do nothing until at least one level is removed. Clear this Condition when you have a chance to clear your head, rest, or come to your senses.
- **Shaken**: You are intimidated, scared, or overwhelmed by someone, something, or the environment in general. Acting against the cause of the fear is particularly difficult. If you suffer the Shaken Condition three times, you become a terrified, gibbering mess incapable of rational thought or action. You might freeze in place or flee in terror – whichever is most inconvenient. Clear this Condition when you have spent some time away from the source of anxiety.

- **Tired**: You are weary or exhausted and struggle to maintain activity, concentration, and resolve. Acts of sheer willpower are particularly challenging. If you suffer three Tired Conditions, you collapse exhausted or fall asleep. Clear this Condition when you have time to sleep or rest for an extended period or take time to eat a meal.
- **Poisoned**: You are suffering from the effects of a dangerous toxin, such as a deadly gas, noxious fumes, or a poisoned weapon. You have a fever, look ill, and are wracked with pain, which makes it particularly difficult to interact with others or concentrate on details. If you suffer the Poisoned Condition three times, you are rendered unconscious and might even begin Dying, at the GM's discretion. Some poisons may have other, specific effects. Clear this Condition when you are administered an antidote, receive effective medical assistance, or have time for the toxins to clear from your system.
- **Weakened**: You are stripped of energy and strength, perhaps from overexertion, lack of nourishment, or the effects of some serum or weapon. Carrying heavy equipment, performing feats of athleticism, or carrying out physically demanding tasks is very difficult. If you suffer the Weakened Condition three times, you collapse unconscious. Clear this Condition when you have an opportunity to rest and eat a meal.

When a character "clears" a Condition, they remove it completely, regardless of how many times they might have suffered it.

INJURIES, CONDITIONS & CHECKS

Marking an Injury or Condition multiple times makes it harder to shake off and increases the chance of a more serious consequence in the future. No matter how many times each Condition or Injury is marked, it will only apply a single Danger Die to a relevant check.

Healing

Characters can make a Check to heal themselves or someone else. Add Danger Dice equal to the number of different Injuries the target has. A successful Check heals 1 Damage, +1 per Boon. You may remove damage from Hits or Injuries, as the player chooses. Partial successes and failures might waste time or resources, give the target or healer a Condition, draw unwanted attention, or cause characters to miss other opportunities. A Botch, however, could result in damage being inflicted or some other serious consequence!

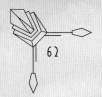

Resting & Recovery

When a character rests in relative safety for an extended period – several hours at least – they can heal and recuperate from the Harm they have suffered. The character must do very little to gain this benefit – sleep, eat a meal, talk with their friends, or watch a film, for example. What constitutes relative safety will depend on the action of your story.

After resting, a character heals all their lost Hits and removes one point of damage from each Injury. You can re-write an Injury to reflect that it has improved if you wish. Resting is often enough time for characters to also clear any Conditions they are suffering, at the GM's discretion.

Emile has removed all three of his Hits and has two Injuries, with 1 Damage on his bruised hand and 2 Damage on his broken nose. After a rest, he restores his hits to the max of 3 and gets to reduce the Damage on each Injury by one. His bruised hand is completely healed, and the broken nose goes down to 1 Damage.

Traumas

If a character suffers a particularly grievous Injury, the GM may decide it is a Trauma. Traumas should only be inflicted when dramatically appropriate, perhaps as the consequence of a Botch or as a result of narrowly avoiding death. Traumas count as 3-Damage Injuries that cannot be healed during the timeframe of a Job. They may even require expert medical attention or months of recovery time. A Trauma can be downgraded to a standard Injury during some future Downtime.

MOXIE

Sometimes pure skill and chutzpah aren't enough to overcome a tough situation. When things really hit the fan, you need nerve, determination, and a little serendipity. That's what Moxie is for. It represents a character's focus, willpower, and luck, which you will spend and regain throughout a case.

You can spend a point of Moxie to do one of the following:

- **Demonstrate Expertise**: Use a second Trademark in a Check. Declare which two Trademarks you are using and add Action Dice for each, along with additional dice for each relevant Edge in both Trademarks. The GM might ask clarifying questions and can veto Trademarks or Edges that are not appropriate. You can never use more than two Trademarks for a single Check.

- **A Little Luck**: Change a single rolled die up or down by one result; for example, you could turn a 5 into a 6, or a 4 into a 3. This can be done for Action or Danger Dice, an Initiative roll, a serum duration, or for any other dice roll you make for your character. You can spend multiple Moxie points to alter a die by several pips, to adjust several dice, or a combination of both. No die result may be increased above 6 or below 1. When adjusting a Check result, do so before cancelling Action Dice and Danger Dice.

- **Take a Breath**: Use an action to reduce the severity of a Condition by one step, heal one point of Damage from an Injury, or heal D3 Hits. Your Character must be able to pause a moment, take stock of your current situation, and regroup. Taking a breath during combat or another conflict is possible but may give an opponent some advantage or an opportunity to act.

- **Useful Detail**: Add an interesting or helpful detail to the Scene. This might reveal some helpful information or introduce a useful item or contact. Such details might become Tags, complicate or improve a situation, or add an Action Die to a Check. A useful detail cannot contradict established facts and the GM has the final say over whether the declaration is appropriate.

Refreshing Moxie

Moxie represents a combination of good fortune and sheer willpower and will eventually run out. A character's Moxie is refreshed when one of their Flaws causes significant difficulties for them and/or an ally. This might result in one or more Danger Dice being added to a Check, suffering a Condition or Damage, or simply incur story repercussions. After the ramifications of the Flaw are resolved, refresh all used Moxie points.

Carol's research leads them to an exclusive nightclub in the Inner City. Seeing an opportunity to refresh their Moxie pool, Carol's player points out they have the Flaw "Always Filthy", which might cause a problem in this situation. The GM likes the idea and roleplays the bouncer refusing to let them enter the club. The Revs must find another way in, and Carol's Moxie is refreshed back to its starting value.

GAME TIME

Most of your story will play out in Scenes. This is the conversation that goes back and forth between players and GM to establish the details of a situation and how the characters respond. The GM frames the Scene by describing the sights, sounds, and details the characters know or notice. The really important features of a Scene might be Tags that will affect character actions and Checks.

The players portray their Revs while the GM takes on the role of everyone else. Sometimes you might talk like your character and say what they say, and other times you will just describe their actions. Most of the time, a Scene's action will unfold in whatever order makes sense; sometimes this will involve discussion or negotiation between players and GM, but most of the time it is a smooth conversation of action and counteraction.

Turns

If it's important to know the specific actions of each character and the order in which they occur, a Scene can be divided into Turns. During a Turn, each character can perform one Free Action and one Action.

- **Free Actions**: Any almost automatic action is a Free Action, including things like moving a few steps, drawing a weapon, or shouting a few words.
- **Actions**: A character can both move Near and perform a Quick Action, such as making an attack, providing first aid, using a serum, saying something witty, or throwing an object to an ally. Alternatively, they can perform a single Focused Action, like moving Far, carefully aiming and shooting, examining something closely, or diffusing a bomb.
- **Bonus Actions**: Some characters have special Abilities that grant them a "bonus" Free Action or Quick Action. These are in addition to the standard number of Actions a character can take.

Initiative

When you first begin acting in Turns, each player determines their Initiative by rolling a single D6. If the result is 4 or higher, their character will act before any enemies or NPCs in the Scene. If the result is 3 or less, they will act after the GM-controlled characters.

Surprise

If one side in a conflict or Scene has surprised the other, they get a free Turn. This may count as having a better position, with Action or Danger Dice applied to Checks as appropriate. After the surprise Turn(s) has been completed, players should roll for Initiative as normal.

DISTANCE & MOVEMENT

All distances in Tomorrow City are kept abstract, describing position relative to the other characters or features in the Scene.

- **Close**: Face-to-face, at arm's length, or even physically entangled. This is the distance at which most close combats occur. Up to about 10 feet.
- **Near**: A short distance, more than an arm's length but still only a few strides away. You're probably in the same room as a target and you can easily fire a pistol at this range. Up to about 50 feet away.
- **Far**: Yelling distance, or a short run away. You can still see a target clearly, though perhaps not all the details. Up to about 250 feet or a city block.
- **Distant**: Probably within sight, but well out of reach of most weapons. This range is too far away to hold conversations or make out clear details.

Movement

Movement changes the relative position of characters and objects. If a character was Far from a rooftop fire escape and used their whole Turn to approach it, they would now be Close. Likewise, if a character started Near an enemy and used their Quick action to move away from them, they might now be Far from them. Use common sense and clear descriptions to keep things organised.

Distance & Scale

All distances are relative and change based on the scale of the Scene. When characters are interacting in a room or building, Close may mean only a few yards away. When flying aircraft and engaged in a dogfight, however, Close might instead represent dozens, or even hundreds, of yards.

CHARACTERS

You're a Rev, a dangerous, passionate, and skilled mercenary prepared to do whatever it takes to get a job done. Revs come from all walks of life; they might be millionaires just looking to have fun, tired drones working to bring down the current regime, or dangerous criminals only interested in serving themselves. In Tomorrow City, it takes all kinds to get a job done, and necessity often makes for strange bedfellows.

You create your character by doing the following:

1. **Visualise your character** – Who are they? What do they do?, What trouble makes their life more complicated? (p.67)

2. **Choose or create three Trademarks.** These are broad Tags that describe the most important, interesting, or useful things about your character. (p.68)

3. **Choose three Edges.** An Edge is a particular focus, specialisation, or advantage that your character can make use of. (p.86)

4. **Choose three Advantages.** An Advantage is a special ability, piece of gear, or other unique bonus. You may select one from each of your Trademarks. (p.87)

5. **Choose or create two Flaws.** Flaws are troubles, problems, passions, or disadvantages that your character must deal with. (p.87)

6. **Write one Drive.** A Drive is a motivating desire that pushes your character to act. (p.89)

7. **Describe two Ties.** Ties are important relationships that your character has. (p.90)

8. **Set your Moxie, Cred, and Grit to 3.** You may switch points between these values if you wish. (p.91)

9. **Gear up.** Note down the mundane items your character has. You will spend Cred points at the start of each Job to acquire more specialised gear. (p.68)

10. **Round out your character.** Give them a name and description. Tell the other players about your Rev and how they deal with the problems they encounter. (p.93)

WHY REVS?

All cool groups of troublemakers and problem solvers should have an iconic name that conjures up what they do and where they come from. In Tomorrow City, it's Rev. Like the revving of a diesel engine, the revolving city streets, the rumbling of a coming revolution, the shocking revelations of scientific progress, or the revolting masses of the underclasses, Revs are loud, dangerous, and cannot be ignored for long.

WHAT'S A REV TO YOU?

Before diving into character generation, discuss as a group the kinds of story everyone wants to play and what role your characters will take. Some Revs operate legitimate businesses, others launch criminal enterprises and are little more than gangsters or common hoodlums, and yet others do the dirty work of the Ministries – either on or off the books. Will you be a formal organisation, a loose affiliation of like-minded individuals, or lackeys for someone more powerful? Will you be seeking to improve the city, to line your own pockets, to stir up a revolution, or a little bit of everything? Framing your campaign in broad terms right at the beginning will make it much easier for everyone to create interesting characters that have a reason to work together.

Some ideas to get you started include:

- Troubleshooters for one of the Ministries or the City Council
- Vigilantes or guardians seeking to protect the citizens of their local neighbourhood from the many dangers of the city
- Secret agents of Mother herself, doing things her automaton servants cannot
- Agitators working for one of the city's many subversive factions, such as the Anti-Robot League, Revolutionists, or Followers of Moloch
- Mercenaries, out to earn their next big pay-day in whatever way they can
- Scavengers, traders, or explorers seeking artefacts and technology lost during The Long War

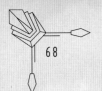

TRADEMARKS

A Trademark is a conceptual idea that helps to define who your character is, what they can do, and their place in the world. They are broad Tags that convey an important or interesting detail about a character's past, occupation, or unique talents. Each Trademark is an important descriptor that is used to determine what a character is good at and what they can do when they take on a Job.

Define your character by choosing three Trademarks. They are divided into four lists, and you may select from any list, using common sense to pick ones that fit your character concept. For example, you might choose one Background, one Descriptor and one Occupation; two Occupations and one Pattern Weaver; a Background and two Descriptors; or any other combination.

Each Trademark includes the following details:

- **Name**: A descriptive name that sums up what the Trademark represents. You can change or adjust the name to better reflect your concept if you wish. A Trademark's name is a Tag.
- **Description**: A broad description of what the Trademark is all about. Use it as a springboard for your own ideas and to tailor the Trademark to your character.
- **Traits (⊕)**: These represent the skills, physical attributes, and knowledge that are an intrinsic part of a character with the Trademark. Use them as inspiration to determine when a Trademark is useful. Some of these Traits will be turned into Edges a little later in the character creation process.
- **Flaws (⊖)**: Each Trademark provides example Flaws to inspire you later in the character generation process.
- **Gear (◓)**: Suggestions for basic starting equipment a character might have.
- **Advantages (⊛)**: These are special abilities, talents, or unique gear that a character with the Trademark might have. Each Trademark will give you three Advantages from which you will choose one.

EXAMPLE TRADEMARK

A description of what the Trademark is all about.
   ⊕ A list of example skills or abilities common to this Trademark. Use these as inspiration for Edges.
   ⊖ A list of example Flaws that your character might have.
   ◓ A list of the equipment that a character with this Trademark begins with.

   ⊛ **Advantage 1**. Description/effect of the Advantage.
   ⊛ **Advantage 2**. Description/effect of the Advantage.
   ⊛ **Advantage 3**. Description/effect of the Advantage.

HEY, WHERE'S MY SKILL LIST?

Tomorrow City does not have a definitive list of Traits or detailed explanation of what each does. They are prompts to inspire action and you should interpret them through the lens of your character.

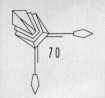

Backgrounds

Backgrounds describe some aspect of a character's past, such as their social class, upbringing, or a traumatic event that defined who they became in later life. You may choose a maximum of one Trademark from this list, and only during character creation.

DRONE

You were born to serve as a factory drone, toiling in the underground engine rooms that keep the city running. You are immensely strong and capable of working for many hours without rest.

- ⊕ Strong, Endurance, Repair, Awareness, The Great Factory, Scavenger, Brawl
- ⊖ Dim-witted, Clumsy, Always Filthy, Illiterate
- ⊛ Dirty Overalls and Cap

- ⊛ **I Must Work Harder.** You may spend a Moxie point to completely clear a Dazed, Tired, or Weakened Condition as a bonus Free Action.
- ⊛ **Face in the Crowd.** You look and dress like every other factory worker in the city. You can disappear into groups of drones, factory workers, or the poor with ease. You are difficult to detect until you take an action that draws attention to yourself.
- ⊛ **Low-light Vision.** You can see in dim, low-light situations as clearly as if the area was well-lit.

RIFFRAFF

You grew up in the gutters of the metropolis or the shanties of Underside. Your life has been hard and has honed your survival instincts.

- ⊕ Awareness, Sneak, Pickpockets, Run, Streetwise, Underside, Brawl
- ⊖ Shifty Eyes, Always Filthy, Steals Food, Nervous Disposition
- ⊛ Filthy Clothes, Knife, Someone's Tooth

- ⊛ **Scrounge.** When you Rest, instead of healing, you can declare that you are looking for a specific piece of gear. Roll a D3 – if the result is higher than the item's Cost, you find it.
- ⊛ **Filthy Urchins.** You have a network of contacts who see all sorts of things from the gutter. When you try to get information or gossip from the streets of Rimside or Underside, roll with Mastery.
- ⊛ **In This Together.** When you are desperate for somewhere to hide out, roll a die. On a 4 or higher, someone in Rimside or Underside will hide, shelter, or feed you. There is always a price.

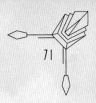

SKYRISER

You are a member of the city's elite, born into privilege and able to take advantage of all that entails. You were born to rule and raised to believe that the poor need to toil for their own benefit.

- ⊕ High Society, Impeccable Style, Well-educated, Bureaucracy, Inner City, Healthy, Eye for Detail, I Make Commands Not Requests
- ⊖ Arrogant, Black Sheep, Soft-looking, Imposter
- ⊙ Expensive Clothes, Cheque Book, Gold Watch

- ⊛ **High Society.** When you enter a social situation involving the wealthy and powerful, you can immediately identify who has the highest social status or most authority. Gain +1 Action Die on your first social interaction with this person.
- ⊛ **Born to Rule.** When you make Checks to bully or push around minor city officials and bureaucrats, roll with Mastery.
- ⊛ **Lackey.** You have a bodyguard or personal assistant that is treated as an NPC with Grit 3 and two Tags of your choice. You may purchase gear for them with your Cred. Your Lackey is loyal but will not recklessly endanger themselves. If injured, killed, or lost in some way, you may hire a new lackey during Downtime.

  Example lackeys:
  - **Assistant.** Grit 3, Bureaucracy, Quiet
  - **Bodyguard.** Grit 3, Brawl, Intimidate
  - **Chauffer.** Grit 3, Drive, Etiquette

WASTELANDER

You're not from around here. You have lived a difficult life in the harsh wastelands, the sodden swamps beneath the city, or some distant land. You are obviously out of place, but sometimes that is an advantage.

- ⊕ Awareness, Survival, Endurance, Hunting, Shoot, Wastelands, Dodge
- ⊖ Rough Around the Edges, Naive, Wide-eyed Stare, Uncouth, Illiterate
- ⊙ Strange Clothes, Pocket of Odd Knickknacks

- ⊛ **Obvious Outsider.** When you behave poorly in polite company or are caught somewhere you shouldn't be or doing something you shouldn't do, city folk are quick to believe it is because of your wild background and ignorance. Gain +1 Action Dice on Checks to convince them so.
- ⊛ **Stalk.** You are an expert hunter. When you track a target, roll with Mastery.
- ⊛ **Animal Companion.** You have a small, loyal pet such as a rat, raven, ferret, or cat. It may or may not be mutated. The animal companion is treated as an NPC with Grit 2, the Small Tag and two other Tags of your choice. If it is killed, you suffer the Shaken Condition. You may find and train a new pet during Downtime.

  Example animal companions:
  - **Rat.** Grit 2, Small, Quiet, Bite
  - **Crow.** Grit 2, Small, Fly, Alert
  - **Cat.** Grit 2, Small, Climb, Silent

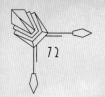

WINDBORN

You spent most of your life in a sky colony, perhaps as part of a nomadic airship caravan that traverse the wastes, with sky pirates, or on a floating citadel.

- ➕ Steady Feet, Pilot, Quick and Wiry, Geography, Endurance, Scrounge, Climb
- ➖ Naive, Rough Around the Edges, Arrogant, Risk-taker
- 🔘 Warm Jacket, Goggles, Rope

- ✪ **Head for Heights.** When making Checks related to moving and working at great heights, roll with Mastery.
- ✪ **Ship Gunner.** When you make an attack using a vehicle-mounted weapon, roll with Mastery.
- ✪ **Diplomatic Immunity.** You hold an important position in a community outside of Tomorrow City. You can exploit this position to get out of minor misdemeanours and can roll +1 Action Die when leveraging your political credentials.

Descriptors

Descriptor Trademarks indicate strong personality traits or attitudes, or an important physical, emotional, or intellectual aspect of a character. You may choose a maximum of two Trademarks from this list when creating your character.

BOLD

You are confident and courageous, with nerves of steel and a can-do attitude. The way you assess a situation, make a plan, and take action often inspires others.

- ➕ Awareness, Brave, Inspiring, Tenacious, Command, Quick Thinking, Fast Reflexes
- ➖ Death Wish, Arrogant, Life is Cheap, Need to be Loved
- 🔘 Rugged Jacket, Satchel

- ✪ **Inspiring.** Once per Scene, after successfully making a Check, you may spend any Boons generated to give other characters Moxie points (one for one). This cannot increase a character's Moxie point total beyond their starting maximum. You cannot inspire yourself.
- ✪ **Steely.** When you resist something frightening or intimidating, roll with Mastery.
- ✪ **Into the Breach.** If an ally fails or Botches an attack, you can use your next action to attack the same target with +1 Action Die.

BROKEN

You were injured and disfigured, perhaps during The Long War, or maybe in a factory accident. Technicians and surgeons put you back together as best they could, but you are a jigsaw of machine and flesh now.

- ⊕ Metal Plates and Screws, Endurance, Awareness, Frightening Appearance, Unnatural Strength, Hide, Iron Will
- ⊖ Battle Scars, A Broken Gait, Nightmares and Weariness, Thousand-yard Stare, Vulnerable to Electro Damage
- ⚫ Hooded Jacket or Cloak

- ⊛ **Mostly Machine.** You can last twice as long without food, water, or oxygen as a normal human can, and are immune to the Poisoned Condition. You recover Damage during rests as normal but cannot benefit from healing. A repair Check can be made to heal Hits or remove Damage from Injuries, in the same way that someone else might receive first aid.
- ⊛ **Part-Automaton.** You can sense the signals from automatons and can make a Check to gain an impression of their surface-level "thoughts" (usually their current attitude, mood, or intent).
- ⊛ **Auxiliary Limb.** You have either an extra mechanical limb or a detachable hand (choose when you select this Advantage). The extra limb is an arm or tail that ends in a claw that can grip and hold things but cannot attack or perform precise actions. The detachable hand works like a Tiny, Simple robot (p.117). You may select this Advantage a second time, taking the alternate option.

CARING

You are incredibly empathetic and seek to ease the suffering of others. You often give freely of whatever resources you have and look out for those who cannot help themselves.

- ⊕ Empathy, Eye for Detail, First Aid, Animal Empathy, Naturally Calm, Friendly Smile, Amateur Psychologist
- ⊖ Soft-hearted, Gullible, I Will Not Harm a Helpless Person
- ⚫ A Portion of Coffee, A Handful of Sweets

- ✪ **Rally.** Once per Scene, you can use a Quick Action to clear a psychological Condition, such as Angry, Shaken, or Dazed, from another character who can see or hear you. You can spend Moxie to rally additional characters (one-for-one) or to clear additional Conditions at the same time. You cannot rally yourself.
- ✪ **A Little Kindness.** When you tend to an ally during a Rest, they can remove one additional point of Damage from a single Injury.
- ✪ **Calm Under Pressure.** Spend a point of Moxie after you make a Check to negate any Pressure generated by the roll.

CHARMING

You have an easy charm that draws others in and makes them feel at ease. You have a knack for making suggestions that others find reasonable and tend to get your own way.

- ⊕ Winning Smile, Persuasive, Seduction, Interrogate, Disguise, Convincing Liar, Empathy
- ⊖ Caught Up in Your Own Charm, Lothario, Weak-willed, Compulsive Liar
- ◉ Mirror, Nice Clothes

- ✪ **Dreamy.** If you take time to listen to, study, or investigate a target you can adjust your demeanour and appearance to make yourself very appealing to them. Gain +1 Action Die when interacting with the target in social situations until they see through your subterfuge or you cause them harm (physically or emotionally).
- ✪ **Winning Smile.** When you attempt to persuade someone with your charm and magnetism, roll with Mastery.
- ✪ **Orator.** You can easily draw a crowd and hold their attention for a short period. While you are speaking to them, they will remain focused on you, unless something loud, dangerous, or disruptive occurs.

GENIUS

You are incredibly intelligent, well educated, or wise from life experiences. You have an uncanny ability to retain information and solve problems that others cannot.

- ⊕ Smarts, Science, History, Research, Exceptional Memory, Perceptive, Obscure Facts
- ⊖ Arrogant, Soft-looking, Curious
- ◉ Notepad, Glasses, Nice Jacket

- ✪ **Academic Rigour.** When you research information or call on academic knowledge, roll with Mastery.
- ✪ **Mastermind.** If you carefully make a plan, spend time preparing, and explain it in detail, any ally who follows through gains Mastery on a single non-combat Check related to the execution of the plan.

⊛ **Tactician.** If you spend a Quick Action assessing a situation and telling an ally exactly where to shoot or how to hit a target, they gain +1 Action Die on their next attack Check.

HUGE

You are big, muscular, and very strong. You can easily lift great weights and regularly engage in physically demanding tasks. While you are tough and strong, you are sometimes not the most graceful of individuals.

- ⊕ Strong, Dead lift, Smash Things, Tough as Nails, Fists like Iron, Intimidate, Endurance
- ⊖ Clumsy, Graceless, Don't Fit into Regular Clothes, Two Left Feet
- ⊛ Poorly Fitting Clothes, Club

- ⊛ **Heavy Lifter.** You may ignore the Cumbersome Tag on one item of gear you carry.
- ⊛ **Iron Sinews.** When performing feats of strength, such as lifting or breaking items, roll with Mastery.
- ⊛ **Diehard.** Your size and natural constitution make you hard to bring down. You may suffer one additional Injury than your Grit would normally allow.

PERCEPTIVE

You notice things that others miss and often have uncanny insights into situations or people. You focus on details, put the pieces together, and always seem to spot vital clues.

- ⊕ Awareness, Keen Eyes, Human Lie Detector, Eye for Detail, Investigate, Search, Asks all the Right Questions
- ⊖ Distracted by the Little Things, A Little Too Blunt, Obsessed with the Details
- ⊛ Magnifying Glass, Notepad and Pen

- ⊛ **Simple Deduction.** When you spend some time observing and analysing a target, you can accurately determine which part of the city they have recently been in and gain a helpful insight about their past, habits, or recent activity.
- ⊛ **Detail-Oriented.** When you make Checks to spot, notice, or search, roll with Mastery.
- ⊛ **Danger Sense.** You are never surprised at the start of combat and may instead roll for Initiative as normal.

QUICK

You are quick on your feet, fit, and nimble. You act with speed and agility and have excellent hand-eye coordination.

- ⊕ Fleet-footed, Duck and Weave, Athletic, Sleight of Hand, Alert, Gymnastics
- ⊖ Hot-headed, Careless, Butterfingers, Run at the Mouth
- ⊛ Loose-fitting Clothes, Good Shoes

- ⊛ **Parkour.** When you make Checks to run, leap, or climb, roll with Mastery.

(A) **Counterstrike.** When you successfully avoid Harm from a close combat attack, you can spend any Boons generated to inflict 1 Damage on your attacker. You can also spend Moxie to inflict additional Damage, one for one.

(A) **Quick Hands.** You can make two Free Actions each Turn.

SNEAKY

You are sly and devious by nature, getting by in life with half-truths, stealth, and deception. You have a talent for going unnoticed, tricking others, or getting into places you otherwise shouldn't be able to.

(+) Awareness, Stealth, Sleight of Hand, Lie to Your Face, Pickpocket, Cunning, Break & Enter

(–) Shifty-looking, Greedy, Cynical, Powerful Enemy

(•) Dark Clothing

(A) **One With Shadows.** Whether by natural talent or an affinity with the Pattern, you become virtually undetectable when you remain perfectly still in the shadows, even to mechanical aids such as night-vision goggles and infrared cameras.

(A) **Natural Born Liar.** When you lie to or deceive someone, roll with Mastery.

(A) **Sneak Attack.** When you attempt a Take-Down on an unaware target, roll with Mastery.

TAINTED

Exposure to radium, serums, or other chemicals has left you permanently changed. This might be subtle, or could manifest as horrible boils, glowing eyes, or dark pulsing veins.

(+) Tough, Serum Expert, Intimidate, Identify Toxins, Stealthy, Notice

(–) Frightful Appearance, Poor Eyesight, Cynical, Hates Scientists, Glows in the Dark

(•) Concealing Clothes, Syringe and Glass Vial

(A) **Toxin Resistance.** You can spend a Moxie point to clear the Poisoned Condition as a Free Action. In addition, serum side effects with a random duration last half as long as usual (rounding down).

(A) **Toxic Blood.** Your blood is either acidic or poisonous (choose when you take this Advantage). You can suffer 1 Damage to draw a vial of blood to use as a tool. Anything that bites you suffers 1 Damage.

(A) **Mutation.** You have one of the following obvious physical mutations that grants you a bonus Action Die when appropriate:

Cat's Eyes. You have excellent night vision

Gills. You can breathe under water

Huge Ears. You have excellent hearing

Scorched skin. You have the *Resistance (Fire)* Tag

Occupations

A character's job, position, calling, or all-consuming interest is defined by the Occupation Trademarks. They are what a character does. You may select up to two Trademarks from this list when creating your character.

APOTHECARY

Part doctor, part alchemist, you are an expert at making serums, tinctures, and salves that enhance a user's skills or abilities. You work the streets or from hidden laboratories, dispensing aid to whoever needs it.

- ⊕ Serum Expert, Medicine, Science, Poison Expert, Research, First Aid, Forensics, Calm Under Pressure
- ⊖ Soft-hearted, Blunt, Squeamish, Serious Debt
- ⊙ Surgical Mask, Syringe, Doctor's Bag

- ⊛ **Fully Stocked.** You begin a Job with a number of free Serum Spikers equal to your starting Cred. Each is fully stocked with serums.
- ⊛ **Brewmeister.** During a Rest, or when you have time to work, you can attempt to brew up a specific serum, poison, acid, or similar product. The Danger Rating is equal to the Cost of the chosen serum or tool, and can be further modified by circumstances as normal. A successful Check creates D3 doses. Boons can increase the total doses by +1, or may have other effects.
- ⊛ **Combat Medic.** When you heal yourself or someone else, roll with Mastery.

AVIATOR

You're a pilot, airman, or dirigible sailor. As a veteran of air combat and a bold aviator, you are at home soaring through the skies in anything that can get you there.

- ⊕ Skilled Pilot, Dogfighting, Stunt Flying, Repair, Dirigibles, Gunnery, Quick Reflexes, Brave
- ⊖ Reckless, Arrogant, Major Debts, Dangerous Rival
- ⊙ Aviator's Jacket and Goggles

- ⊛ **Aircraft.** You own (or have access to) a Cost 3 dirigible or aircraft, such as a Sky Cab or Stormwind Fighter (p.124). If this is damaged or destroyed, you can repair or replace it during Downtime. You may select this Advantage a second time, increasing the value of your personal craft to Cost 5.
- ⊛ **Dogfighter.** When you make a Manoeuvre Check during dogfights, roll with Mastery.
- ⊛ **Brace! Brace! Brace!.** You always have time to bail out from a damaged or destroyed vehicle. In addition, when you do, you can spend a Moxie point to survive completely unscathed – tell everyone how you managed this!

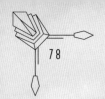

CROOK

You are a grifter, thief, or petty criminal, skilled at breaking the law to achieve your goals. You deal in the illicit and have probably been locked up at least once.

- ⊕ Spot Trouble, Stealthy, Break & Enter, Climb, Criminal Underworld, Safecracking, Sleight of Hand
- ⊖ Wanted by the Ministry of Peace, Huge Debts, Shifty-looking, Brand (or other mark of a criminal)
- ⊙ Rumpled Clothes, Knife

- ⊛ **Expert Entry.** When you make a Check to pick locks, override security, or break and enter, roll with Mastery.
- ⊛ **Easy Mark.** If you have time to observe a target, their habits, and their routines, you can learn a secret or weakness. Gain +1 Action Die when exploiting this weakness.
- ⊛ **Rogue's Gallery.** You have met, worked with, and maybe informed on a lot of bad guys. When you encounter a new villain or criminal, you may declare that you have history with them. The GM decides what that history is and how they feel about you.

ENGINEER

You are a mechanic, grease monkey, demolitions expert, or roughneck responsible for maintaining and repairing city infrastructure, airship engines, or other large machinery.

- ⊕ Repair, Jury-rig, Engineering, Demolitions, Vehicle Maintenance, Endurance, Disable Device
- ⊖ Always Filthy, Blunt, Butterfingers, Secretly Worships Moloch
- ⊙ Dirty Overalls, Hard Hat, Headlamp, Tool Belt

- ⊛ **Grease Monkey.** When you attempt to repair or disable vehicles and machines, roll with Mastery.
- ⊛ **Wreck it.** When you use a Focused Action to attack a vehicle, robot, or automaton, a successful Check deals +1 Damage.
- ⊛ **Demolitionist.** When using an explosive, you can spend a Moxie point to add one of the following Tags to it: *Anti-Material, Electro, Fire, Huge Blast, Radio Detonator, Stun,* or *Timer.*

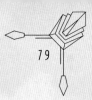

GADGETEER

Part scientist, part engineer, you are a natural at building, repairing, and inventing things. There isn't a machine you can't fix or a problem you cannot solve with a little time and a custom-built gadget.

⊕ Smart, Notice, Robots, Science, Repair, Problem-solving, Disable Devices, Gunsmith

⊖ A Little Too Curious, Jittery, Absent-minded, Better With Machines Than People

⊙ Utility Belt, Half-finished Blueprints

⊛ **Inventor.** When you have the time and space to work, and materials to work with, you can build weapons, tools, or even vehicles. This requires a Check with a base Danger Rating equal to the gear's Cost. Boons can add more Tags or reduce the build time. A partial success might mean the build takes longer or has a negative Tag, such as Unreliable, One Use, or Dangerous. The base construction time is one hour per point of Cost (so a Cost 2 item will require at least two hours to build).

⊛ **Gadgets.** As a Free Action, you can spend a Moxie point to declare you have a small, useful item of gear with up to one Tag. The item rarely lasts for long.

⊛ **Bot Builder.** You begin with a single free robot with a Cost equal to your Cred +1. Robots you purchase cost 1 Cred less (to a minimum of 1).

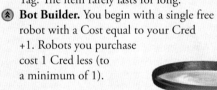

GARGOYLE

You are a vigilante and defender of the weak, haunting the night on the prowl for trouble. You mete out justice where there might otherwise be none.

⊕ Stealthy, Brawl, Climb, Awareness, Investigate, Shoot, Dodge, Intimidate

⊖ Cynical, Cold-hearted, Soft-hearted, Old Injury

⊙ Baton, Dark Clothes

⊛ **Mask.** You wear a frightening Gargoyle Mask. If lost or broken, you can spend a Moxie point during a Rest to repair or replace it.

   - **Gargoyle Mask.** *Night Vision, Intimidating, Immunity (Gas)*

⊛ **Whirlwind Attack.** You never suffer a penalty for being outnumbered in close combat. In addition, when fighting Mooks in close combat, gain +1 Action Die.

⊛ **Fear Itself.** When you make a Check to intimidate or frighten someone, roll with Mastery.

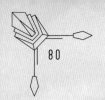

GUMSHOE

You dig the dirt, find the clues, and seek answers to things that some people would prefer you left alone. You are a private investigator and troubleshooter.

- ⊕ Investigate, Notice, Interrogate, Law, Follow Leads, Human Lie Detector, Brawl, Shoot
- ⊖ Personal Code, Hard Drinker, Blunt, Old Injury
- ⊙ Trench Coat, Private Investigator's License

- ✸ **Just One More Thing.** When you seek information by questioning or interrogating someone, roll with Mastery.
- ✸ **Tarnished Badge.** You have close ties to or a helpful contact in the Badges. You can leverage this relationship to learn a piece of inside information, look at reports, get into crime scenes, or even speak to prisoners. There may be a price to pay.
- ✸ **Hardboiled.** You're tough as old boots. You can spend a Moxie point to ignore the effects of a single Injury for the remainder of a Scene.

MUCKRAKER

You're a reporter, agitator, or neighbourhood gossip. You sway opinion, reveal unwanted truths, and inform on current events by digging-up evidence.

- ⊕ Interrogate, Spin a Tale, Detect Lies, Keeps an Eye on the Telescreens, Investigate, Persuade, Notice, Gossip, Knows the Ministry of Truth's Tricks
- ⊖ A Little Too Curious, Reputation for Lying, Stubborn, Wanted by the Ministry of Truth
- ⊙ Notepad and Pen, Press Pass

- ✸ **Cam-bot.** You have a small spider-legged robot with a camera that can record or project up to 60 seconds of footage (no sound) or send a live signal back to a connected telescreen. If lost or broken, it can be replaced or repaired during Downtime.
  - *Cam-bot.* Small Typical robot (p.117), *Record, Project, Climb.*
- ✸ **Rumour Mill.** When you have time to Rest, you can spread rumours, gossip, and lies instead of healing. On a successful Check, people in a nominated neighbourhood believe this information. Boons can increase the number of neighbourhoods influenced.
- ✸ **People Reader.** When you attempt to determine if a target is lying or their attitude or motivations, roll with Mastery.

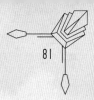

SCRAPPER

You're a professional fighter, making your living with your fists. You take work where you can get it, competing in the underground fight circuits, bodyguarding the rich and powerful, or doing dirty jobs for dangerous people.

- ⊕ Brawl, Disarm, Grapple, Threaten with Violence, Dodge a Blow, Spot a Weakness, Fight Dirty, First Aid
- ⊖ Soft-hearted, Blunt, Squeamish, Serious Debt, Criminal Record, Old Injury
- ⬤ Boxing Gloves, Gym Bag

- ⊛ **Thumpers.** You are equipped with diesel-powered fighting fists known as Thumpers. If the Thumpers are lost or destroyed, you can repair or replace them during Downtime.
    - **Thumpers.** *Powerful, Parry, Demolish Stuff.* Choose one of the following Tags for free: *Deadly, Electro, Fractal (*and *Rare), Rapid Fire,* or *Stun* (and *Non-Lethal).*
- ⊛ **Assess An Enemy.** If you spend a Focused Action watching a living opponent, you can identify a weak spot. You roll with Mastery on close combat attacks made against them for the remainder of the Scene or until you assess a new target.
- ⊛ **Brawler.** When engaged in close combat, you can spend a Moxie Point to make one bonus attack Action in a Turn.

SHARPSHOOTER

You are a gunslinger, sniper, or trick shooter. You are familiar with all manner of firearms and can hit a target at a hundred paces while blindfolded.

- ⊕ Shoot, Gunnery, Trick Shot, Take Cover, Hide, Awareness, Pistols, Long Shots
- ⊖ Show-off, Bloodthirsty, Nightmares, Shaky Hand
- ⬤ Trench Coat, Bandolier of Bullets

- ⊛ **Special Ammo.** You may spend a Moxie point to load a ranged weapon with special ammo. This lets you add one of the following Tags to the weapon: *Accurate, Deadly, Stun, Electro,* or *Fire.* The special ammo lasts until the Scene ends, you decide to load a different special ammo, or you Botch a roll with the weapon.
- ⊛ **Ricochet.** When making a shooting attack, you may bounce a projectile off hard surfaces. Add +1 Danger Die for each surface you bounce off.
- ⊛ **Guns Akimbo.** When you shoot with two pistols at the same time, roll with +1 Action Die and deal +1 Damage on a successful attack.

SKY RANGER

You are or were a member of the Sky Ranger Corps; elite warriors who literally flew into the action. You utilise shock and awe to overcome enemies and diffuse situations before they can escalate further.

- ⊕ Duck & Dive, Swoop, Shoot, Brawl, Pilot, Breach, Restrain, Shock & Awe
- ⊖ Overconfident, Old Injury, Show-off
- ⚅ Flight Suit, Sky Ranger Helmet, Trench Dagger (counts as a Knife)

- ⚇ **Rocket Pack.** You are equipped with a sophisticated rocket pack. If it is lost or damaged, you can repair or replace it during Downtime.
  - **Rocket Pack.** *Fly, Fast, Agile, Noisy*
- ⚇ **Dynamic Entry.** When you enter a room, vehicle, or aircraft with force, any enemies present count as surprised for the first Turn of combat.
- ⚇ **The High Ground.** When you attack a target from above, roll with Mastery.

VETERAN

You saw action during The Long War, probably posted to the front, and bore witness to unspeakable horrors. You are a seasoned soldier and weary veteran.

- ⊕ Shoot, Fight, Warfare, Endurance, Command, Drive, Take Cover, Run
- ⊖ Thousand-yard Stare, The Shakes, Nightmares, Bloodthirsty, Detached
- ⚅ Tattered Uniform, Worthless Medals

- ⚇ **Trench Life.** Used to catching some shut eye wherever you can, you gain the benefits of a Rest in just three hours.
- ⚇ **Serum Soldier.** Soldiers were encouraged to take whatever they had to keep them in fighting condition. Increase the duration of serum effects by +1. Side effect duration is not altered. In addition, you begin each Job with one free Serum Spiker filled with serums.
- ⚇ **Armour Optimisation.** At the start of a Mission, after you gear up, you may add one of the following Tags to a piece of armour you are equipped with: *Resistant (Fire), Resistant (Electro), Immune (Gas), +1 Armour*. You may select this Advantage up to three times.

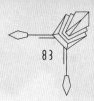

Pattern Weavers

The Pattern is a mysterious energy created by and connected to the strange geometry of the city. Characters with Pattern Trademarks can manipulate this energy to do remarkable, sometimes horrifying, things. You may choose a maximum of two Trademarks from this list when creating your character.

Many of the Pattern Weaver Trademarks have Advantages that allow them to create amazing effects and manipulate reality. Refer to "Pattern Powers" in the Into Danger chapter (p.143) for more information on how these work and what a Pattern Weaver can do

ABERRATION TRACER

Part bounty hunter, part killer, you are committed to hunting down and destroying manifestations of the Pattern. You have honed your skills to track and destroy, particularly aberrations and dangerous Pattern users.

- ➕ Detect the Pattern, Manifest the Pattern, Fight Aberrations, Track Aberrations, Resist the Pattern, Brawl, Shoot, Aberration Weaknesses
- ➖ Beacon to Aberrations, Cynical, Bloodthirsty, Self-righteous
- 💧 Knife, Rugged Clothes

- 🔼 **Fractal Blade.** You can manifest a blade of Pattern energy with a thought, as a Free Action. Taking this Advantage a second time allows you to spend a Moxie point to give a weapon you can see the Fractal Tag for the remainder of the scene.
  - **Fractal Blade.** *Parry, Fractal, Powerful, Concealed*
- 🔼 **Barren.** You can make a Check to create a field where Pattern energy is suppressed. A success creates a field out to Close range around you, and Boons can increase its size or have other effects. Aberrations in the barren field reduce their Danger Rating by one. The field requires a Free Action to maintain each Turn.
- 🔼 **Pattern Tracing.** When you make a Check to detect the Pattern, follow the trail of Aberrations, or navigate areas warped by the Pattern, roll with Mastery.

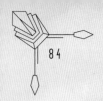

METAPHYSICAL GEOMETRIST

You have explored the city and uncovered the secret paths of the Pattern as it flows through the mortar of buildings, or the spaces between lamp posts. You have learned to move and interact with the world in seemingly impossible ways.

➕ Detect the Pattern, Manifest the Pattern, Analyse a Room, City History, Secret Paths, Architecture, Direction Sense, Find a Shortcut, Manipulate the Pattern

➖ Fastidious, Nervous, Sly, Weird Vibes, Easily Distracted

💧 City Map, Flashlight

⊛ **Destination Anywhere.** Before you open a door, you can declare it leads to a room, hallway, or other space familiar to you. The destination must have a door you can enter through. On a successful Check, you are correct and, while the door remains open, you (and others) can step between the locations, no matter the distance between them. Less familiar destinations and places far away are harder to connect to.

⊛ **Tesseract.** With a thought, you can open a trans-dimensional space about the size of a small safe or lockbox. You can store and retrieve small items from the tesseract as necessary. Whenever you retrieve an item, roll a D6; on a 1, something else also exits the box. Anything stored in the tesseract exists out of time and space and does not decay or grow old. You may select this Advantage a second time, increasing the size of the tesseract to that of a small closet.

⊛ **Four-dimensional Vision.** Spend a Moxie point to see through the walls of buildings as if you had X-Ray vision. Lasts for up to 1 minute.

SYMBOLIST

You have learned to manipulate the Pattern through symbols, images, and writing, forcing it to your will. You use these skills to fashion glyphs and marks that benefit or harm others, to change the way objects work, and to interpret symbols and writing.

➕ Detect the Pattern, Manifest the Pattern, Resist the Pattern, Lock & Unlock Things, Cyphers, Read Foreign Languages

➖ Fastidious, Obsessive, Cautious

💧 Chalk, Fountain Pen, Book of Glyphs

⊛ **Glyph.** You draw a complex symbol on an item of gear or other object, imbuing it with a little Pattern energy. On a successful Check, the item gains one Tag of your choice which will last for up to one Scene. Boons can add more Tags, increase the duration, or have other effects. Tags can be any descriptive effect (such as *Locked, Strong, Weakened, Glowing*, etc) or an actual gear Tag.

⊛ **Symbol of Protection.** You can use a Free Action to draw a shield of Pattern energy, granting you one of the following Tags until the beginning of your next Turn; *Deflect, Parry, Resistant (Fire), Resistant (Electro)*. You may spend Moxie to apply additional Tags, one-for-one.

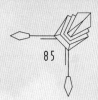

Fabricated Image. You can make a Check to draw an image of an inanimate object on a wall, floor, or other surface. On a success, the drawing takes on a realistic appearance, good enough to pass a cursory glance. Boons can be used to improve the detail or realism, while partial successes indicate the drawing took a long time or has some obvious flaw. The illusion lasts until interacted with or inspected closely.

WEIRD

You have a strange affinity with the Pattern and the way it flows around and between people. This gives you uncanny insight into the actions of others but often makes you seem different from the world around you.

Detect the Pattern, Manifest the Pattern, Summon Aberrations, Awareness, Empathy, Direction Sense, Resist the Pattern, Unsettling Stare, Alert to Danger

Uncomfortable Stare, Daydreamer, Creepy Vibes, Unsettling Aura

Notebook and pencil

Jinx. If you have no Moxie points, you may gain one when another player's Check creates Pressure.

Pattern Reading. As a Focused Action, you can make a Check to see and read the Pattern as it flows around a living target. On a success, you gain insight into their current mood, motivations, attitude, or intentions. This knowledge comes to you as impressions of colour, shapes, and feelings and better rolls reveal clearer information.

Phase Imp. You have bonded to an impulsive and chaotic aberration, no larger than your hand. The imp has animal intelligence, Grit 2 and one Tag from the following list: *Distracting, Fast, Fly, Impossibly Thin, Sharp Edges, Tough.* If you concentrate, you can see through the imp's eyes, but it doesn't like it. If the imp dies you suffer the Weakened Condition. You may summon and bond with a new imp during Downtime.

SPECIALISING

Characters with three very different Trademarks will be better prepared for a variety of situations, while a character with two similar Trademarks can excel at a specific activity under the right circumstances. However players choose to create their characters, it is strongly advised to have a broad range of abilities and backgrounds across the group of Revs.

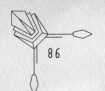
EDGES

Edges are specific advantages, skills, or benefits associated with or derived from a Trademark. They often represent a focus, interest, specialisation, or talent related to the broader concept.

Your character has the Scrapper Trademark, making them adept at things like brawling, dodging blows, and even how to patch themselves up after a fight. If you take the Edge "Fight Dirty", you are telling everyone that your character is well versed in underhanded tactics, low blows, and probably how to avoid them.

Your character begins with three Edges. Each Edge must be associated with a Trademark, which you will write it under on your character sheet. You can choose how many Edges to assign to each Trademark – you might write one Edge for each of your Trademarks, put all three into a single Trademark, or any other combination.

Players are free to choose their Edges, but each one should be a specific aspect or specialisation of the Trademark. If unsure, the list of Traits is a good starting point; either use them as written or as inspiration for your own.

TRADEMARKS, TRAITS, EDGES, & TAGS

A Trademark is a concept for a group of thematically related knowledge, skills, and abilities. It is often a broad archetype that everyone at the table can instantly recognise and understand. A Trademark is a Tag that will provide advantages at different times during play.

Your character is good at all the things listed as Traits (and probably a bunch of other things, too). Traits are not Tags but help to define the scope of a Trademark. Think of them as giving permission to know or do stuff; "*Because I am a [Trademark], I am good at [Trait]*". The Trait list is neither exhaustive nor set in stone – add to it or change it to suit your needs. If you are ever unsure whether a Trademark is relevant in a specific situation, refer to your Traits. Use them throughout play to guide your actions or justify why a Trademark is useful in a specific situation.

An Edge is a Tag that represents your character specialising in an aspect or feature of a Trademark. It indicates that the character has a distinct advantage or is very good at that thing; "*Because I am a [Trademark], I am good at [Traits], but I am exceptionally skilled at [Edge]*". Two characters with the same Trademarks could still have different skill sets based on their Edges.

In game terms, when you do something related to a Trademark, you add an Action Die to your Check. If you have any useful or relevant Edges listed under that Trademark you might get to add another Action Die for each.

ADVANTAGES

An Advantage is a unique special ability or piece of equipment that allows your character to do something cool and further defines their place in the world. Some let you use amazing powers, others grant you companions, and many break the rules of the game or change the way in which your character interacts with the world. You may choose one Advantage from each of your Trademarks. If you are unsure which to pick, just go with which seems most fun, roll a die, or select the first option, which is an iconic Advantage for the Trademark.

Advantages represent potential pathways to develop your character. As your Rev grows and changes, you might choose to gain new Advantages, but you do not have to. Select Advantages that help to define your concept of who your character is and forget the rest.

You have the Muckraker Trademark and imagine your character as a sneaky paparazzi who makes their money selling photos to the tabloids. Taking the Cambot Advantage is a perfect choice for your character. The People Reader Advantage, however, doesn't fit your ideas for the character, so you will ignore that option as the character develops and grows.

FLAWS

Revs are passionate, dangerous, and flawed individuals with bad habits, physical drawbacks, vices, desires, social problems, and dark secrets that regularly make their lives more difficult. In *Tomorrow City*, these negative impulses and personal troubles are represented by Flaws.

Flaws provide opportunities to draw a character's background into play, introduce new challenges, and help to make them feel like they have a life beyond the Job they are currently working. They are primarily roleplaying tools, but, when a Flaw complicates a Scene, you get to refresh your character's Moxie pool.

Each Trademark has a list of Flaws that reinforce or contradict its features and you are free to choose from these or make up your own. Troublesome personality traits and physical weaknesses make particularly good Flaws, as they can cause your character problems at virtually any time or in any place.

Write two interesting Flaws and weave them into your character's background. Consider how each relates to their past or their present situation, career, or skills. Did your Veteran's laziness make them a pariah amongst the rest of the company? Or does your Skyriser's arrogance always get them the wrong kind of attention?

> *Don't just write the Flaw "Wanted" but clarify who is after you. Are you "Wanted for a murder you didn't commit", "Hunted by the Spindle Guard", or "Hounded by a hungry aberration"? Maybe your Genius is "Arrogant", or perhaps they "Think they are more talented than everyone else".*

You will want Flaws to come into play, so make them something you find interesting or would like to see happen. Flaws should not be so debilitating that they affect everything a character does, but, when they do kick in, they need to present a serious obstacle or problem.

Use your imagination, the Trademark examples, and the following suggestions for inspiration.

- **Attitude.** You have a strong belief, worldview, or personality trait that often gets you into trouble. What is it? What always makes you say or do something? When would you never voice your opinion?

  Might Makes Right, Selfish, Anarchist, Timid, Arrogant, Too Compassionate, Show-off, Bully, Stickler For the Rules, Loudmouth

- **Hunted.** A powerful individual or group is after you, and they turn up at the most inconvenient times. Who is after you? Why? What are they going to do if they catch you?

  Wanted by the Ministry of Peace, Chosen to Feed Moloch, The Ministry of Science Wants to Experiment on You, Denton Pryce Wants Your Head – Literally!

- **Hygiene.** Due to work, illness, personal circumstances, disease, or upbringing, you have poor personal hygiene or bad habits. It makes some social situations much more difficult and can have other effects on your ability to complete a Job. Why is your hygiene so poor? When does it get worse? How do people usually react to you?

  Body Odour, Soiled Clothes, Long and Dirty Fingernails, Spits, Bad Breath, Rotting Teeth, Filthy Hands, Unwashed and Matted Hair, Boils or Sores

- **Old injury.** You have an injury that never healed properly or that makes some actions challenging, time-consuming, or unpleasant. When is this injury most inconvenient? What do you do to minimise its impact? What do people do, say, or ask about it that really upsets or angers you?

  Pronounced Limp, Missing Fingers, PTSD, Broken or Disfigured Limb, Trust Issues, Constantly Weeping Wound, Terrible Scars

- **Sickly.** You have an illness or ailment that causes inconveniences and makes doing some things much more difficult. What makes life much harder for you? When does it get worse? What helps to relieve the symptoms?

Persistent Cough, Bad Allergy, Stomach Issues, Weak Heart, Malnourished, Always Short of Breath, Nasty Rash, Ulcers

- **Self-control.** You have poor self-control, lack restraint, or easily lose your composure under certain circumstances. What is it you can't help doing? When are you at your weakest? What might others do to help you?

  Greedy, Anger Issues, Phobia, Serum Addict, Hedonist, Bloodthirsty, Womaniser, Alcoholic, Impulsive, Gambling Addiction, Thrill-seeker, Hates the Sight of Blood

FINDING FLAWS IN PLAY

You can choose to leave one or both Flaws for now and see how the character evolves during your first session or two. As you throw your character into difficult situations, their Flaws might reveal themselves. Alternatively, if you write a Flaw now but find a more interesting drawback as play unfolds, discuss changing it with the GM.

DRIVES

Revs are driven by strong desires, important relationships, and all-consuming goals. They throw themselves in harm's way to protect their loved ones or right wrongs; they take risks for a little cash or a chance to stick it to an authority figure; and they sign on to dangerous Jobs if it means getting a little closer to a personal objective.

Write a single Drive for your character. It can be anything you think will be fun to play, or that rounds out your character. Your drive might suggest the kinds of Jobs you want to get involved in (*Make the people of Slender Row feel safe*), be related to a Flaw (*Give up on gambling once and for all*) or tie in with a Trademark or backstory (*Get back at the Ministry of Truth for ruining my family's name*). Your character's Drive should give some insight into them, provoke ideas for interesting stories, and provide reasons for them to throw themselves into tough situations. Try answering one or more of the following questions to inspire your own Drive:

- Who has wronged me? How? What am I going to do about it?

  Vinnie Black killed my brother. I'm going to kill him.

- What's wrong with the city? How will I change it?

  The Ministry of Truth tells too many lies. I will prove this to the citizens of Rimside.

- What is my biggest weakness? How will I fix it?

  My ruined leg causes me so much pain. I will find someone to heal it.

- Where do I want to be in a year's time? What's stopping me?
  I'm gonna own me a fancy Inner City apartment. All I need is the cash.

- What mystery has always fascinated me? Where do I find answers?
  What lies at the centre of the Nevada Fragment fields? I need to get out there.

- Who most needs my help? Why? What can I do?
  Pops Hurley is going blind. I'll find a way to pay for his surgery.

- What secret do I need to keep? How will I protect it?
  I killed the leader of the West Street Hoods. I need to frame one of their own.

TIES

Ties are the pre-existing connections and relationships between the player characters that help to ground them in the world. They are like Traits in that they define aspects of your character but are not Tags.

Work with the other players to give each character Ties with at least two other Revs. Use the examples below as inspiration, but flesh them out further to expand your backstory and the details of the relationship.

Ties with People and Places

- _____ and I both hate the Ministry of Science. (Why?)
- I met _____ while investigating the South Side Slaughter. (What was that?)
- The gangster Papa Belafonte wants _____ and me dead. (What did you do?)
- _____ and I lived with the homeless in Underside for a while. (How did you get out?)
- I used to stir up trouble with _____ on the Rimside loading elevator. (What enemy did you make?)

Positive Ties

- I am secretly in love with _____. (Why haven't either of you acted on this?)
- _____ is just a kid and I need to look out for them. (Do they want your help?)
- I once saved _____ from a scrape with a serum brute. (Are they thankful? Or maybe resentful?)
- _____ and I are family. (Siblings, Parent/Child, from another Mother?)
- _____ and I are old war buddies. (What terrible thing did you do to survive?)

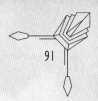

Problematic Ties

- I don't trust ____. (Why?)
- ____ betrayed my confidence. (How did this happen? Have you confronted them?)
- ____ has a bad habit I cannot tolerate. (What is it? Do they know?)
- ____ and I used to be rivals. (What changed?)
- ____ has spurned my advances. (How do you feel about them now?)

ROLEPLAYING HOOKS

A character's Drive and Ties are primarily roleplaying tools used to ground your character in the world you are creating and help to flesh them out. Playing to these hooks will also earn Experience Points, which are used to change and improve your character.

MOXIE

Moxie represents a character's luck and willpower. You spend your Moxie points over the course of a Job to do cool stuff and improve your character's chance of success at various actions. When all your Moxie has been spent, it will not refresh until you have suffered considerable trouble from one or more of your Flaws. You begin with a Moxie point pool of 3.

CRED

Cred is an abstract measure of a character's resources, wealth, and reputation. You spend Cred to acquire gear at the start of a Job and it might be temporarily increased or reduced as a consequence of an action. It does not translate to a specific social class, position, or level of wealth, but rather is your ability to get the items you need at any given time. You begin with 3 points of Cred, which refreshes at the start of each new Job.

GRIT

Grit is a character's toughness and ability to resist Harm. Your character can suffer damage equal to their Grit value without any long-lasting effects. It also determines the total number of Injuries a character can have without falling unconscious or dying. Your character begins with a Grit value of 3.

CUSTOMISE

Your character's Moxie, Cred, and Grit each begin with a value of 3. You may swap points amongst these as you wish, so long as no value is lower than 1 or greater than 6. You may also choose to remove points from these values to "buy" additional Edges. Increasing and decreasing any of these values will change the way your character feels in play, giving them an advantage in some situations, but making things more difficult in others.

You decrease your character's Moxie and Cred by one point each, giving you two points to play with. You decide to increase your Grit to 4 and take one new Edge. The character will be below average in luck and won't have as much cool gear as other characters but is going to be quite resilient and have the bonus Edge to get them through tough situations.

ROUND OUT

Your character is now almost complete; all that is left to do is give them an evocative description, a cool name, and share them with the other players. You should already have an idea of what your Revs are going to do in the setting, and Ties with a couple of the other player characters, so now is the time to flesh out your relationships and bring things to life.

Names in Tomorrow City vary depending on background, social class, and personal preference. The most common names are those that were popular during the interwar period, so looking at the credits of movies from the 30s and 40s is a good start. Many Revs go by nicknames or have epithets that indicate a trait or hint at a reputation. The Appendix (p.210) has a table of random names that you can use for inspiration.

CHARACTER CREATION EXAMPLE: EMILE FRANKS

Charli is creating a character for a new game and begins by browsing the Trademarks to see if anything sparks some ideas. The **Windborn** and **Veteran** Trademarks jump out at them as interesting, and an idea of a well-travelled character who was reluctantly dragged into service during The Long War begins to form. Charli notes down those two Trademarks on their character sheet and decides on **Quick** for their third one. This gives the character quite a broad range of skills and abilities to draw on in play.

Next, they need to choose three Edges for the character. These are things they will be especially good at. Looking over the Traits for each Trademark, Charli sees several things that would be cool to turn into Edges and, after some thought, writes one for each Trademark; **Pilot** under *Windborn*, **Shoot** under *Veteran*, and **Duck & Weave** under *Quick*.

Advantages are cool abilities, equipment, or amazing talents that characters have, and Charli gets to pick one for each Trademark. Considering both the character's background and what would be cool during stories, they decide on **Head for Heights**, **Armour Optimisation**, and **Parkour**. These three Advantages will give the character a little boost in specific situations during play.

Flaws are the next thing that Charli needs to consider. There are lots of interesting examples listed under each Trademark and they particularly like the idea of **Nightmares**. Charli thinks the character might be suffering trauma from their experiences in the Long War, and the nightmares might make getting a good rest difficult. This could have serious repercussions for the character during Jobs, and everyone at the table agrees this is a cool idea. Charli isn't sure about a second Flaw, so decides to leave it for now – they will discover what it is during play.

Next up are the character's Drive and Ties. Charli is going to keep this pretty simple – the character wants to get back to the skies, but needs to raise enough funds to buy an airship. They write *"**Acquire an airship and escape the city.**"* After describing their character to the other players and discussing potential relationships and backstories, Charli writes the following two Ties: "*I have Carol Grime's back because we're both outsiders in the city*" and "*I don't trust Alexi because he only seems to look out for himself.*"

Charli notes down the character's starting Moxie, Cred, and Grit as 3 each. Then they adjust the Cred value down to 2, reasoning that they are an outsider and are struggling to raise money for their airship. Charli uses this spare point to buy another Edge, noting *Fight* under the Veteran Trademark.

All that is left to do now is give the character a name and description. Charli decides on the name **Emile Franks** and writes the following description:

"Once a member of La Republique airship colony, and later a frontline soldier, Emile is a wiry and gaunt individual with hollow cheeks and close-cropped hair. Hearing of the destruction of his home, he now drifts through life, hoping to make enough to one day buy an airship and rebuild his beloved sky fleet."

TOMORROW CITY

NAME
Emile Franks

DESCRIPTION
A gaunt veteran who seeks an escape from the city

TRADEMARKS

Windborn
◇ Steady feet
◆ Pilot
◇ Quick & wiry
◇ Geography

◇ Endurane
◇ Scrounge
◇ Climb
◇ ....
◇ ....

Veteran
◆ Shoot
◆ Fight
◇ Warfare
◇ Endurance

Command
◇ Drive
◇ Take cover
◇ Run
◇ ....

Quick
◇ Fleet-footed
◆ Duck & weave
◇ Athletic
◇ Sleight of hand

Alert
◇ Gymnastics
◇ Parkour
◇ ....

◇ ....
◇ ....
◇ ....
◇ ....

◇ ....
◇ ....
◇ ....

ADVANTAGES
Head for heights
Armour optimisation
Parkour

FLAWS
Nightmares

DRIVES
Acquire an airship and escape the city

TIES
I have Carol's back because we're both outsiders here
I don't trust Alexei

MOXIE

MAX | CURRENT

3

CRED

MAX | CURRENT

2

GRIT | HITS

3

CONDITIONS

◇
◇
◇
◇
◇
◇

INJURIES

◇
◇
◇
◇
◇
◇

WEAPONS	RANGE	CATEGORY	TAGS/NOTES

ARMOUR	HITS	TAGS/NOTES
Airship Gunner's vest	3	Parachute, Cumbersome

GEAR

Warm jacket, Goggles, tattered uniform, Worthless medals, Good shoes

NOTES

Wiry, pale, hollow cheeks, close-cropped grey hair, permanent grimace.

Once a member of La Republique airship colony, and later a frontline soldier, his home was destroyed and he now drifts through life, hoping to make enough to one day buy an airship and rebuild his beloved sky fleet.

XP

◇◇◇
◇◇◇
◇◇◇
◇◇◇
◇◇◇
◇◇◇
◇◇◇
◇◇◇

GEAR

Gear is all the stuff a character might use during a Job to overcome obstacles and get things done. It covers everything from the clothes on a character's back to their tools, weapons, armour, and vehicles. Gear can be either basic or specialised. Basic gear is described with just its name, like *rope, pocketknife*, or *binoculars*. It has no Tags or special rules associated with it and is primarily for storytelling purposes. Specialised gear tends to be more difficult to acquire and has one or more Tags listed after it, like *shotgun (spray)*. While almost anything can be basic gear, things such as ranged weapons and armour are always special.

WHAT GEAR DOES

Gear gives you permission to do something; you can't shoot someone without a gun, you can't drive somewhere without a car, and you can't pick a lock without lockpicks, a hairpin, or a paperclip! Sometimes having a useful piece of gear will make a task easier to complete; scaling the outside of a skyscraper, for example, will be much easier with climbing gear or a grappling gun than without.

Whether or not a piece of equipment affects a Check will depend on the fiction. As a rule, basic gear does not automatically grant any bonuses beyond letting a character try something. Specialised gear has one or more Tags or special rules that might improve the chance of success at an action or grant some other bonus.

STARTING GEAR

Characters begin with the clothes on their back and any basic equipment that makes sense to their Trademarks and current situation. Revs typically travel light, as it can look strange running across the city with a pack full of odds-and-ends.

Lifestyle

You get to decide where and how your character lives. Where in the city do they make their home? How do they afford their lifestyle and typical expenses? You might use your Trademarks to guide you, but don't have to. Perhaps your Skyriser has fallen on hard times and now hides out in Underside; maybe your Wastelander has powerful political backers and lives it up in a prestigious part of Midtown. These choices can all influence the way stories unfold and how your character approaches given situations.

GEARING UP

At the start of a Job characters get to "gear up", grabbing equipment from their stash, purchasing items, or fashioning custom gear that they think will be useful. Some characters will always choose the same items, while others will make selections based on the needs of a given mission brief.

After characters have been given the Job's hook and know what they need to do, they can spend their Cred and declare what gear they have.

Gear Cost

All gear has a cost. You can have any Cost 0 items that make sense – this is your basic gear. You can purchase any other items that have a Cost equal to or lower than your current Cred value. However, each time you acquire an item with at least a Cost of 1, you must reduce your current Cred value by one. Purchasing gear in this way means your character can have a total number of specialised items equal to their Cred value.

> *You have a Cred value of 3. This means you can have up to three special items. You buy a Cost 3 **Sniper Rifle** (Accurate, Deadly, Silent) and reduce your Cred total by one. It is now 2, so you can buy anything up to the value of 2. You decide to buy a Cost 2 **Bulletproof Vest** (Armour 1, Concealed). Your Cred value now drops down to 1. You can buy a single Cost 1 item, and you decide to buy a spiker of serum. With this final purchase, your Cred drops to 0 and will remain there until the end of the Job or you have a chance to refresh it.*

A character's Cred rating is usually refreshed at the end of a Job, during Downtime. Sometimes, however, they may gain money or influence that allows them to regain one or more points of Cred during a Job.

SPENDING CRED

Select your special gear one piece at a time, starting with the most expensive item. Write it down, reduce your Cred value by one, and then select your next item. Continue doing this until your Cred is reduced to zero or you have acquired everything you are after.

Combining Resources

During the gearing up phase of a Job, two or more characters can combine their resources to acquire an expensive piece of gear. The players declare they are working together, and the GM might ask how each character contributes to procuring the item. If the explanation is satisfactory, and the characters' combined Cred equals or exceeds the Cost of the item, it can be obtained. All characters involved in the acquisition must then reduce their current Cred value by the number of characters who combined their resources.

The players decide that a 2 ½ ton truck (Cost 5) would be the perfect transport out into the wastelands. Two characters, each with a Cred value of 3, decide to work together to procure the truck, each explaining how their money, influence, or contacts help to get it. The GM agrees, and the vehicle is leased from a shifty army quartermaster. Both characters then reduce their current Cred value by two.

Combining resources in this way means virtually any item of gear is within the players' reach, but it will come at a heavy cost. Oftentimes, it may be better to set up a small Job to procure an important item that is required for a future mission.

Acquiring Gear Mid-Job

Characters that don't use up all their Cred at the start of a Job (or who are thrown straight into the action without a chance to gear up), can acquire gear during the events of the story. They will need to find a store, vendor, or other source for the item, and pay for the gear in just the same way as described above.

If characters find or are given specialised gear, they can use it for the remainder of a Job. If the found object is particularly complex or unusual, the GM might also require a Check, careful study, or practice to unlock its inner workings or use it properly.

Encumbrance

While there are no hard rules on how much gear a character can carry, you should use your common sense. Also, bear in mind a Rev who is carrying a lot of stuff will soon draw unwanted attention from the authorities, opportunists, or suspicious citizens. While it is not uncommon to see people in military surplus, a gasmask, the odd bit of armour, or carrying a weapon, someone bristling with blades and guns, or other strange equipment is bound to get noticed.

REPAIRING GEAR

Weapons, machines, and other equipment can malfunction, break down, or get wrecked. Sometimes it is destroyed and becomes utterly useless, while, other times, it can be fixed with a little time, effort, and a few spare parts.

Repairing Damage

Armour and equipment with a Grit value, such as vehicles and robots, can be repaired in the same way a character might be healed. Add Action Dice for relevant Trademarks and Edges, and Danger Dice if you don't have the appropriate tools, workspace, or knowledge of whatever is being repaired. A successful Check will repair D3 damage, +1 per Boon. Repair times can be long – up to an hour per point of damage removed though partial successes might increase this – and Boons could also be spent to reduce the total time required.

Repairing Other Gear

Other items of equipment, such as tools and weapons, can be repaired at the GM's discretion. This also requires time and a Check, with Danger Dice added for the level of damage and other relevant factors. An item's Cost is a good baseline for how many Danger Dice might be added to the pool. A successful Check will get most items functioning again, though a partial success might mean that it took a long time, some resource was used up, or the item now has a negative Tag. Repair time will vary depending on the size of the item and the extent of the damage.

GEAR TAGS

While specialised gear can have virtually any word or descriptor as a Tag, in *Tomorrow City*, some Tags have specific game effects. Below are the most common ones you might find in the equipment lists. Use them as inspiration for your own equipment Tags.

Positive Gear Tags

Each of the following Tags provides a specific benefit when using an item. Positive Tags typically increase the Cost of an item by +1 or +2.

- **Accurate.** This weapon is well crafted, and its attacks are more precise. Roll attacks using this weapon with +1 Action Die.
- **Agile.** This vehicle is particularly responsive and is very good at tight turns and high-speed manoeuvres.
- **Anti-materiel.** On a successful attack, this weapon deals double Damage to vehicles, machines, and huge robots/automatons. Double the Damage before factoring in Boons and other bonuses.
- **Armour X.** This item can soak up to X Damage from attacks or other sources of Harm.
- **Blast.** This weapon affects everyone/thing within Close range of the target.
- **Blast (Huge).** This weapon affects everyone/thing up to Near range of the target.
- **Cargo (Light).** This vehicle can carry up to about 1 ton of cargo.
- **Cargo (Medium).** This vehicle can carry up to about 3 tons of cargo.
- **Cargo (Heavy).** This vehicle can carry up to about 10 tons of cargo.
- **Cargo (Massive).** This vehicle can carry 50–100 tons of cargo.
- **Concealed.** This item is hidden and/or difficult to spot.
- **Deadly.** On a successful attack, this weapon deals +1 Damage to living targets.
- **Deflect.** Gain +1 Action Die when defending against ranged attacks.
- **Detonator.** This explosive has a wire running to a detonator, up to a Far distance. Someone must manually detonate the explosive. Sometimes the wire breaks. Radio detonators are large, expensive, and have a range of Far, but the signals are easily affected by electrical devices and other interference.
- **Electro.** On a successful attack this weapon deals +1 Damage to automatons, robots, and electrical devices.
- **Fast.** This vehicle is much faster than others of its type.
- **Fire.** This item can set things on fire. Objects set on fire suffer 1 Damage per turn until extinguished. Fire deals +1 Damage to flammable targets.
- **Flashy.** This vehicle draws attention wherever it goes.
- **Fractal.** This weapon is imbued with Pattern energy and is particularly effective at harming aberrations.

- **Fuse.** This explosive will detonate D3 Turns after lighting the fuse. It is a free action to light a fuse. If you cut a short fuse, the explosive will explode the same turn you light it, but it gains the Dangerous tag.
- **Immune (X).** You do not suffer Harm from X.
- **Off-road.** This vehicle is designed to travel across rough terrain.
- **Parry.** Gain +1 Action Die when using this item to defend against close combat attacks.
- **Powerful.** On a successful attack, Boons can be spent to deal this weapon's Damage instead of the usual +1.
- **Rapid Fire.** You can choose to roll 1, 2 or 3 additional Action Dice when using this weapon. Add an equal number of Danger Dice to the pool.
- **Resistant (X).** You take 1 less Damage from X.
- **Silent.** This item is very quiet.
- **Spray.** This weapon affects everything in a cone-shaped area directly in front of it, out to Close range. The target-end of the spray has a radius of about ten feet.
- **Spread.** When you make a successful attack with this weapon, each Boon can be used to inflict the weapon's damage on another target within Close range of the first.
- **Stun.** This weapon inflicts the Dazed Condition, in addition to any Damage. Boons can be spent to apply additional levels of Dazed.
- **Thick Armour.** This vehicle halves all Damage suffered from weapons that do not have the Anti-materiel Tag. Round fractional Damage down.
- **Timer.** This explosive can be set to detonate at any time in the next twelve hours. The timing is rarely exact.
- **Tripped.** This explosive is set off by a target stepping on it or pulling a tripwire. It requires a Check to accurately set it in place, or effectively conceal it.

Negative Gear Tags

These Tags indicate poor design, inefficiencies, or problems that a character might encounter while using a piece of gear. Negative Tags typically reduce the Cost of specialised gear by half a point, rounding up. They can never reduce the cost to below 1.

- **Cumbersome.** The item is large, heavy, or difficult to carry. You suffer +1 Danger Die to actions requiring dexterity or stealth while equipped with this item. This penalty is cumulative for each piece of *Cumbersome* gear you have.
- **Dangerous.** When making a Check with this item, failures count as Botches.
- **Explodes.** If this vehicle, robot, or piece of armour loses all its Grit, it is very likely to explode, inflicting 4 Damage to anyone or anything within Near range.
- **Flammable.** This vehicle is particularly vulnerable to fire-based attacks.
- **Inaccurate.** Suffer +1 Danger Die when attacking with this weapon.
- **Light.** Vehicles with this Tag become very difficult to manoeuvre in bad weather and/or high winds.

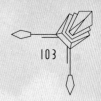
- **Mounted.** This weapon is too heavy for a single individual to carry or fire. It can only be used when fixed on a vehicle or building.
- **Non-lethal.** This weapon causes no damage to a target. It often has other effects.
- **Obvious.** This item is hard to conceal and/or draws unwanted attention.
- **One Use.** This item can only be used once before it is used up, useless, or destroyed. This might be for a single action, or a single scene, depending on the item. It cannot be repaired.
- **Rare.** This item is hard to find, expensive, or difficult to build. Increase this item's Cost by +1. When attempting to repair this item, add +1 Danger Die to the Check.
- **Reload.** This weapon needs to be reloaded after each use. Reloading is a Quick Action.
- **Slow.** This vehicle is much slower than others of its type.
- **Sluggish.** This vehicle does not handle very well and can be difficult to control through tight manoeuvres.
- **Unreliable.** If you generate Pressure when using this item, it stops working for a number of Turns (or minutes if not in combat) equal to the Pressure generated. This is in addition to any other consequence. One Use items cannot be Unreliable.

Custom Gear

Players and GMs are encouraged to create their own strange dieselpunk weapons, tools, and vehicles to fit the needs of their stories. The best approach is to use the examples provided in this chapter as a baseline and cost new items appropriately. Gear with positive Tags should never have a Cost lower than 1.

Gear construction is quite flexible, and you should feel free to create new Tags or special rules as needed. Discuss ideas as items are built. Be aware that while this system gives you a lot of control over your gear, it won't hold up to min-maxing; remember to play to the spirit of the game and genre.

THE STATE OF TECHNOLOGY

The world of *Tomorrow City* is at a technological level like our own world's early 1940s. Common items might be mass produced but still have the look and feel of handcrafted objects. The transistor has not been invented and there are no advanced electronics, computers, or portable phones. Nuclear weapons and energy are things of science fiction, with massive diesel engines providing power and Pattern bombs destroying the landscape in their place. Medicine is much the same as in the 40s, though the ability to replace damaged body parts with machinery has prolonged the lives of many, if not made them better. Alchemical serums have become popular, and their use is accepted across all classes of society, though some older citizens may look down their noses at them.

WEAPONS

Weapons fall into four broad categories: close combat, ranged, heavy, and explosives.

Close Combat Weapons

These weapons are for up-close and personal attacks. Common close combat weapons include knives, baseball bats, machetes, and knuckle dusters. However, you might occasionally see swords, pneumatic boxing gloves, or even chainsaws!

Close combat weapons are always used at Close range and deal 2 Damage on a successful attack. Unarmed attacks also count as close combat weapons and deal 2 Damage.

CLOSE COMBAT WEAPONS	COST	TAGS/RULES
Knife, Club, Knuckledusters	0	
Aberrant Fang	2	*Fractal*
Arc-rod	2	*Electro, Spread*
Boot Knife	1	*Concealed*
Chainsaw	1	*Deadly, Powerful, Cumbersome, Obvious*
Electro-rod	1	*Electro*
Great Weapon	1	*Deadly, Cumbersome*
Pneumatic Gloves	1	*Stun*
Shock Baton	1	*Stun, Non-lethal*
Spring Blade	2	*Parry, Concealed*
Sword	1	*Parry*
Thunder Fist	3	*Electro, Anti-materiel, Rare, Cumbersome*

Close Combat Weapon Upgrades: *Concealed, Deadly, Electro, Fire, Intimidating, Parry, Spray, Spread,* and *Stun* are +1 Cost each. *Fractal* and *Anti-materiel* increase Cost by +2 each. Anti-materiel close combat weapons also gain the *Cumbersome* tag. Each negative tag reduces the cost of a close combat weapon by ½ a Cred point (round fractions down).

Ranged Weapons

Ranged weapons are anything that can attack a target from a distance. Pistols are common in the city, and rifles will occasionally be seen slung over a shoulder or carried by government or private security. Larger weapons tend to draw more attention.

Ranged weapons are listed with a range value that indicates the optimal distance at which to attack with them. You can use them at other distances, but the action might become more difficult.

Ranged weapons deal 2 Damage on a successful attack.

	RANGED WEAPONS	COST	RANGE	TAGS/RULES
ONE-HANDED	Chem Pistol	2	Close	Spread, Silent, Non-Lethal. Inflicts the Poisoned, Tired, or Dazed Condition on targets (choose when attacking). Boons can apply additional levels of the chosen Condition
	Dart Pistol	2	Near	Silent, Deadly, No effect on non-living targets
	Fractal Ray Pistol	3	Near	Fractal, Rare
	Hand Cannon	3	Near	Deadly, Inaccurate, Intimidating
	Pistol	1	Near	
	Stun Gun	1	Close	Stun, Non-lethal
	Zapp! Gun	2	Near	Electro
TWO-HANDED	Arc Gun	3	Near	Electro, Spread
	Crossbow	1	Far	Silent, Reload
	Heavy Rifle	3	Far	Deadly, Powerful
	Light Machine Gun	3	Far	Rapid Fire, Deadly, Cumbersome
	Pattern Blaster	4	Near	Fractal, Spray, Rare
	Rifle	1	Far	
	Sawn-off Shotgun	1	Close	Concealed, Inaccurate, Reload
	Shotgun	2	Close	Spray, Reload
	Sniper Rifle	3	Distant	Accurate, Deadly
	Submachine Gun	2	Near	Rapid Fire

Ranged Weapon Upgrades: *Anti-material* ranged weapons increase their Cost by +2. *Accurate, Concealed, Deadly, Electro, Intimidating, Powerful, Rapid Fire, Spray, Spread* and *Stun*, are +1 Cost each. *Fractal* increases Cost by +1 and must also take the *Rare* Tag for an additional +1 Cost. Each negative Tag reduces the cost of a ranged weapon by ½ a Cred point (round fractions down).

Heavy Weapons

Heavy weapons are intended to bring down large, heavily armoured, or powerful targets. They include things like machine guns, anti-tank rifles, cannons, and teleforce weapons.

Heavy weapons deal 4 Damage on a successful hit. In addition, they always have the *Cumbersome* Tag. Like the ranged weapons above, the range value indicates the optimal distance to attack with heavy weapons. Attacking at less or greater than this range could incur a penalty.

HEAVY WEAPONS	COST	RANGE	TAGS/RULES
Anti-Air Rocket Launcher	3	Far	Anti-materiel, Inaccurate, Cumbersome. May only attack flying targets
Anti-Tank Rifle	4	Far	Anti-materiel, Cumbersome
Cannon	7	Far	Blast (Huge), Powerful, Mounted
Flamethrower	5	Close	Spray, Rapid Fire, Fire, Cumbersome, Dangerous
Heavy Arc Gun	5	Near	Electro, Blast, Cumbersome
Machine Gun	5	Far	Rapid Fire, Spread, Cumbersome
Rocket Launcher	4	Far	Blast, Cumbersome
Sonic Wave Gun	4	Near	Blast, Cumbersome, Unreliable. Targets also suffer from the Deafened Condition
Teleforce Projector	7	Distant	Powerful, Anti-materiel, Rare, Mounted

Heavy Weapon Upgrades: *Accurate, Blast (Huge)* and *Powerful* are +2 Cost each. *Anti-material, Blast, Deadly, Electro, Rapid Fire, Spray* and *Spread* are +1 Cost each. *Fractal* is +1 Cost and must also take the *Rare* Tag for an additional +1 Cost. Each negative Tag reduces the cost of a heavy weapon by ½ a Cred point (round fractions down).

AMMO

There is no need to track ammo in *Tomorrow City*, as you are assumed to carry enough for the duration of your Job. Sometimes, as the consequence of an action, you might have to reload a weapon. In rare cases (such as after rolling a Botch), you might entirely run out of ammo for a particular weapon. In this case, you will have to find or make more ammo. Purchasing ammo from a store costs 1 Cred and refills all ammo for all characters present.

Explosives

Grenades, bombs, bundles of dynamite, and mines are dangerous explosives that can cause a great deal of damage to a large area.

All explosives deal 4 Damage instead of the normal 2 and have the *One Use* Tag unless noted otherwise. Explosives that must be set up in advance have a range of "placed".

When attacking with thrown explosives, such as grenades or dynamite, partial success or failure indicates the weapon ended up somewhere you did not want it to. Perhaps it fell short or went well past the target, landed near something else explosive, or rolled under an ally's car!

A character can attempt to defuse bombs, mines, and other explosives with a Check. In general, explosives have a Danger Rating equal to their Cost.

EXPLOSIVES	COST*	RANGE	TAGS/RULES
Anti-Personnel Mine	2	Placed	Blast, Tripped, One Use
Anti-Robot Mine	3	Placed	Blast, Electro, Tripped, One Use
Anti-Vehicle Mine	2	Placed	Anti-materiel, Tripped, One Use
Demolitions Charge	2	Placed	Spray, Detonator, One use
Dynamite, Bundle	2	Near	Blast (Huge), Fuse, One Use
Dynamite, Stick	1	Near	Blast, Fuse, One Use
Grenade, Explosive	1	Near	Blast, One Use
Grenade, Flash	1	Near	Blast, Stun, Non-Lethal, One Use
Grenade, Gas	1	Near	Blast, One Use, Non-lethal. Inflicts the Poisoned Condition on targets. Cloud persists for D3 Turns
Grenade, Sleep	1	Near	Blast, One Use, Non-lethal. Inflicts the Tired Condition on targets. Cloud persists for D3 Turns

Grenade, Spark	1	Near	Blast, Electro, One Use. Does half Damage to living targets
Molotov Cocktail	1	Near	Spread, Fire, Dangerous, One Use
Satchel Charge	2	Close	Anti-materiel, One Use, Dangerous
Serum Bomb	1	Near	Blast, One Use, Non-lethal. Inflicts one dose of a chosen serum (declared when purchased) on everyone in the blast radius. Halve the duration of the effect and side effect (if applicable)
Smoke Bomb	1	Near	Blast, Non-lethal. Creates an area of thick smoke that obscures vision
Time Bomb	3	Placed	Blast (Huge), Timer, One Use

Explosives Upgrades: *Anti-materiel, Blast, Deadly, Detonator, Electro, Fire, Spray, Stun, Timer,* and *Tripped* are +1 Cost each. *Huge Blast* and *Radio Detonator* are +2 Cost each. An explosive can have the *Fuse* Tag for free. Each negative Tag reduces the cost of an explosive by ½ a Cred point (round fractions down).

*Grenade Bandoliers: Explosives are purchased in bandoliers, boxes, or small crates. When you spend 1 Cred you can choose up to Cost 3 worth of explosives – so you could take three Cost 1 grenades, a Cost 1 grenade and Cost 2 bundle of dynamite, a single Cost 3 time bomb, or any other combination. Spending 2 Cred allows you to select up to 7 Cred worth of explosives.

PERSONAL ARMOUR

Personal armour is gear that a character can don for protection from attacks or other Harm. Armour has Hits equal to its Armour X Tag (so a bullet proof vest has 2 Hits). When a character suffers Damage, they can allocate it to their armour. When all of the armour's Hits have been removed, it offers no more protection until repaired or replaced.

Shields usually improve a character's dice pool, rather than add armour. They require one hand to use and are not common in the city, so may draw attention.

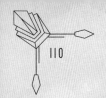

Stacking Armour

A character can wear multiple pieces of armour that are described as covering different parts of the body. For example, they might have a leather jacket, a steel breastplate, and a helmet. When marking Damage against armour you can choose which piece of gear is affected unless the narrative indicates a logical hit location.

PERSONAL ARMOUR		COST	TAGS/RULES
WORN ARMOUR	Airship Gunner's Vest	3	Armour 3, Parachute, Cumbersome
	Bullet Proof Vest	2	Armour 1, Concealed
	Combat Vest	2	Armour 2
	Heat Suit	1	Resistant (Fire)
	Helmet	1	Armour 1
	Ironside Armour	5	Armour 4, Deflect, Intimidating, Cumbersome, Noisy. Has 2 hardpoints (p.121)
	Leather Jacket	1	Armour 1
	Steel Breastplate	2	Armour 3, Obvious
	Trench Armour	2	Armour 2, Immune (Gas), Obvious. Includes coat, helmet, and gasmask
SHIELDS	Arc-shield	2	Deflect, Resistant (Electro), Cumbersome
	Buckler	1	Parry
	Faraday Webbing	1	Resistant (Electro)
	Pattern Collar	2	Resistant (Pattern Energy), Rare
	Riot Shield	1	Deflect

Personal Armour Upgrades: You can add the *+1 Armour* Tag for +1 Cost. *Deflect, Immune (Gas), Intimidating, Resistant (X)*, and *Strong* are also +1 Cost. Any armour may take the *Parachute* Tag for +1 Cost, but also gains the *Cumbersome* Tag, which off-sets the cost. Easily manipulated items, such as small shields and gauntlets, can gain the *Parry* Tag for +1 Cost. *Concealed* is +1 Cost and may only be added to items with *Armour 2* or less. Negative Tags reduce the cost of a piece of armour by 1 Cred each.

TOOLS

Any object that a character might use to help with a task is a tool. A character can have any mundane tool that makes sense for their character concept. If the tool has a Tag or grants a clear advantage in a specific situation, then it will have a Cost of at least 1.

TOOLS	COST*	TAGS/RULES
Acid	1	*Two Uses.* Will eat through a hand-sized area in D3 Turns. May be used like a ranged weapon; *Near Range, Spread, Dangerous*
Adrenalin Injector	1	*One Use.* Automatically stabilise a dying character. If conscious, a character can use this on themselves
Armour Patch Kit	1	*One Use.* Automatically repairs D3 points of Damage on a piece of armour, a robot or vehicle
Autokey	1	+1 Action Die when attempting to open conventional locks
Binoculars	0	Allows you to see great distances
Camera	1	Comes with a large flash bulb and one of the following lenses: *Detect (Thermal), Detect (Pattern),* or *Night Vision.* Additional lenses can be purchased for +1 Cost each, or all lenses can be taken as a go bag. It takes one hour to develop a roll of film
Chloroform	1	*Three Uses.* Inflicts the Tired condition on a victim. Living enemies with a Danger Rating of 1 or less will immediately fall unconscious
Climbing Kit	1	+1 Action Die when attempting to climb surfaces
Disguise Kit	1	+1 Action Die when attempting to change your appearance. Takes D6 x 10 minutes to prepare effectively
Expedition Gear	1	Environment-specific clothing and equipment. +1 Action Die when attempting to survive in a specified hostile environment, e.g. Arctic clothing
Fake Documents	1	*One Use.* Counterfeit papers, ID, or invitation. Good enough to pass a cursory examination. Better documents may be Cost 2 or 3
Fire extinguisher	1	Immediately extinguishes fire in a 10' area
First Aid Kit	1	+1 Action Die when attempting to heal someone

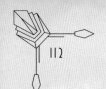

Flashlight	0	Illuminates up to Near
Gas Mask	1	*Immune (Gas)*
Grapple Gun	1	Requires a Check to hook on. Ascend D3+1 stories per turn as a Free Action (or descend twice as fast). Can work as a swing line
Gunsmith Kit	1	+1 Action Die when attempting to repair weapons
Handcuffs	0	Made of steel. Simple to lockpick
Night Vision Goggles	1	Allows you to see in very low light. Everything is in shades of grey and green
Painkillers	1	One Use. Ignore the effects of one Injury for one Scene
Parachute	0	*Cumbersome.* A simple safety device for aircraft crew. More advanced parachutes, including those used for paragliding, are +1 Cost
Poison (Ingested)	1	*Three Uses.* When ingested, apply the Poisoned Condition
Poison (Contact)	1	*Two Uses.* Use an action to apply to a weapon, giving it the *Deadly* Tag for one Scene
Punch Key	1	*One Use.* Automatically unlock one punch-card door
Radio	0	*Unreliable.* These bulky appliances have a range of Distant, but the many strange devices of the city constantly interfere with them
Rebreather	1	Up to 10 minutes of oxygen. Allows you to breathe underwater. A user gains *Immune (Gas)* while using the rebreather
Rocket Pack	2	*Fly, Noisy.* A powerful engine designed to propel a user through the air. This is a much simpler version of the devices used by the Sky Rangers
Spotlight	1	Illuminates up to Far
Tech Kit	1	+1 Action Die when attempting to repair electrical items, robots, and automatons
Tool belt	1	+1 Action Die when attempting to repair vehicles and machines

*Go Bags: Characters may purchase tools in pre-organised kits called "go bags". A go bag costs 1 Cred and contains up to 3 Cost worth of tools. The gear in go bags tends to be poorer quality, or designed for emergencies, and therefore all tools in a go bag gain the One Use tag, if they did not already have it. Example go bags might include:

- Break & Enter Kit: Autokey, Grapple Gun, and Punch Key
- Doctor's Bag: Adrenalin Injector, First Aid Kit, Painkillers
- Expedition Bag: Climbing kit, Expedition Gear, First Aid Kit
- Spy's Kit: Chloroform, Disguise Kit, Fake Documents

SERUMS

A serum is an alchemical drug that provides the user with a temporary enhancement. In most cases, this enhancement adds one or more Tags to the character for a short period of time.

Serums are administered in doses, which provide a specific effect and side effect. The effects of a serum begin immediately after being administered and last for the duration indicated. The Turn after a serum's effects finish, the user suffers the stated side effect. Most side effects have a specific duration; those without a duration listed (usually Conditions) last until removed through the passage of time or by taking an appropriate action.

You take two doses of the Hawk Eye serum: It will last 2D6 minutes in total (one D6 minutes per dose). The turn after the effects end, you suffer the side effect of Blurry Vision.

If a serum has the *Immediate* Tag, gain both the effect and side effect as soon as you administer the dose(s).

SERUM DURATION

When a serum effect and side effect have a random duration, use the same die roll for both. For example, if you use Oxygel and roll a 4, your character does not need to breathe for four Turns but will then suffer *Violent Coughing Fits* for four minutes. You can place two dice on your character sheet to track each effect.

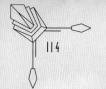

Spikers

Serums are typically administered with specialised auto-injectors called spikers. These syringe-like devices have a rotating cylinder into which single-dose vials of serum are loaded; rotating the cylinder allows you to select which serum and how many doses to administer. When you use a spiker to administer a serum, you can take one or more doses of a single chosen serum as a Quick Action.

You have a spiker loaded with three doses of Hawk Eye and three doses of Amped. You could administer one, two, or three doses of Hawk Eye as a Quick Action. However, you could not administer one dose of Hawk Eye and one dose of Amped as a single action.

Multiple Doses

A character can be affected by a maximum number of doses (from a single serum, or multiple different ones) equal to their Grit value. If you have already taken your maximum number of doses, any further serums only apply the side effects.

You have Grit 3. You have taken 2 doses of Amped and one dose of Celerity. You cannot gain any benefit from further doses until the effects of at least one serum have worn off.

SERUMS	COST*	TAGS/RULES
Amped	1	**Effect:** Your unarmed close combat attacks count as having the *Electro* Tag for D6 Turns per dose used **Side Effect:** You suffer +1 Damage from *Electro* attacks for the same duration
Brutal	1	**Effect:** Your unarmed close combat attacks deal +1 Damage per dose used. The effects last for D6 Turns, no matter how many doses are taken **Side Effect:** Suffer one level of the *Tired* Condition per dose used
Celerity	1	**Effect:** Gain *Quick Reflexes* for D6 minutes per dose used **Side Effect:** Suffer the *Clumsy* Condition for the same duration
Hawk Eye	1	**Effect:** Gain *Excellent Vision* for D6 minutes per dose used **Side Effect:** Suffer *Blurry Vision* for D6 hours per dose used
Heal	2	*Immediate* **Effect:** Heal D3 damage per dose used **Side Effect:** Suffer one level of the *Tired* Condition per dose used
Hercules	1	**Effect:** Gain *Strong* for D6 Turns per dose used **Side Effect:** Suffer one level of the *Weakened* Condition, per dose used
Focus	1	**Effect:** Gain *Accurate* for D6 Turns per dose used **Side Effect:** Suffer one level of the *Dazed* Condition per dose used
Grounded	1	**Effect:** Gain *Immunity (Electro)* for D6 Turns per dose used **Side Effect:** Suffer from the *Weakened* Condition for the same duration
Mellow	1	*Immediate* **Effect:** remove one level of both the *Angry* and *Shaken* Conditions per dose used **Side Effect:** Suffer one level of *Intoxicated* for D6 minutes per dose used
Mr Hyde	2	**Effect:** Gain *Fury, Huge,* and *Strong* for D6 Turns, per dose used. **Side Effect:** Suffer D3 levels of the *Angry* Condition
Nerve Block	3	**Effect:** Ignore the effects and penalties of all Injuries for D3+3 minutes. May only administer one dose at a time **Side Effect:** Suffer D3 Damage. This cannot be absorbed by armour or other gear
Night Eyes	1	**Effect:** Gain *Night Vision* for D6 minutes per dose used **Side Effect:** Suffer from *Blurry Vision* for the same duration

Olympian	2	**Effect:** Gain *Athletic* and *Strong* for D6 Turns per dose used **Side Effect:** Suffer one level of the *Weakened* Condition
Oxygel	1	**Effect:** You do not need to breathe for D6 Turns per dose used **Side Effect:** Suffer *Violent Coughing Fits* for D6 minutes per dose used
Pheromone	1	**Effect:** Gain *Attractive* for D6 minutes per dose used **Side Effect:** Suffer from *Terrible Body Odour* for D6 hours per dose used
Primer	3	**Effect:** Clear the *Tired* Condition. Gain *Alert* for D6 minutes. May only administer one dose at a time **Side Effect:** Suffer from *Shaking Hands* for D6 minutes
Spring	1	**Effect:** Your legs grow huge and muscular. Gain *Mighty Leaps* for D6 Turns per dose used **Side Effect:** Suffer from *Unsteady Legs* for D6 minutes per dose used
Terminus	2	**Effect:** Appear to be dead for 2D6 minutes per dose used **Side Effect:** Suffer one level of *Shaken* per dose used
Vigour	2	*Immediate* **Effect:** Remove one level of both the *Tired* and *Weakened* Conditions per dose used **Side Effect:** Suffer from *Involuntary Muscle Spasms* for D6 minutes per dose used

*Spikers: Serums are usually purchased in pre-loaded spikers. Each spiker costs 1 Cred and contains up to 6 Cost worth of serums (six 1 Cost serum doses, two 3 Cost serum doses, etc.). Each serum loaded into the spiker is a single dose – more expensive serums tend to be thicker or have a higher volume, which is why they take up more of the spiker's capacity. You may fill the auto-injector with any combination of serums you desire. An empty spiker can be refilled with serums that are found, created, or purchased during a Job.

You purchase a spiker for 1 Cred. It can be filled with up to 6 Cost worth of serums. You decide to fill it with one dose of Primer (Cost 3), one dose of Heal (Cost 2) and one dose of Hercules (Cost 1). That is all that can fit into the device. If you use the Primer during a Job, the spiker will have room to refill with other serums – perhaps another dose of Primer, or maybe three doses of Amped.

ROBOTS

Robots are very simple automata that can perform basic tasks. They have limited intelligence and come in all shapes and sizes, depending upon their function, who built them, and where they are operating. They are defined by their size and intellect.

Size

A robot's size determines how big it is and its Grit. A robot is broken or destroyed when it has suffered damage equal to its Grit value, in the same way that Threats are taken out.

SIZE	COST	GRIT	DESCRIPTION
Tiny	1	1	Between 6 and 12 inches on their longest side. *Tiny* robots can move up to a maximum of 10' per Turn. These robots are most often encountered as toys or used in workshops or labs to perform very specific tasks.
Small	2	3	Less than three feet high/long. *Small* robots are commonly used as messengers and for security. Badges and news reporters are sometimes accompanied by small cam-bots that record events.
Large	3	5	About the same size as an average person. Mostly used to automate jobs in the service industry, such as bartenders, doormen, maids, and lift attendants. They are particularly common in the wealthy Inner City where a machine is preferable to an untrustworthy member of the proletariat.
Huge	4	8	Seven or more feet high. Tall, broad, and imposing, *Huge* robots are expensive to build and maintain. They are sometimes used in industry for tasks that are too dangerous for humans, or as security for the very wealthy. It is extremely rare to see a *Huge* robot with more than typical intellect.

Intellect

Robots are incapable of detailed analysis or deep thinking, and they lack any ability to understand human emotions. They do not predict or use their own initiative – they are only capable of responding to events based on the instructions they have been programmed with.

A robot's intellect determines the complexity of commands it can understand. The more intelligent it is, the more detailed the instructions it can receive and follow. Most robots can be given verbal commands, though some varieties require instructions to be encoded on punch cards that are fed into their mechanical brains. A robot's intelligence also grants it one or more free Tags that help to define its role, programming, or purpose.

INTELLECT	COST	TAGS	DESCRIPTION
Simple	+0	1	*Simple* robots have animal-like intelligence. They can understand and act upon a single short command, such as "guard the door", "fetch my gun", "stop anyone from entering", or "record everything I do". *Simple* robots have a very limited vocabulary related to the specific purpose they were built for. Some do not speak at all or can only say a few words that they tend to repeat over and over.
Typical	+1	2	These robots can understand commands that can be expressed as two short sentences or directives. They can parse instructions such as "Only let people with invitations in and protect them from harm" or "Watch the Ministry of Science and come tell me if Gladstone Crowe leaves". They can communicate with rudimentary gestures, such as head nods or hand waves, and have a limited vocabulary that allows them to speak simple sentences. Many people liken talking with them to speaking with a child.
Smart	+2*	2	*Smart* robots can be given instructions with up to three separate clauses or commands. They are particularly favoured in scientific settings where they can perform a logical sequence of steps to speed up tasks. *Smart* robots can speak complex sentences on a specific topic related to their programming and can provide accurate, factual recounts or descriptions. They make for a competent but single-minded assistant.

*Huge robots have an additional +2 cost to give this Intellect rating.

ROBOTS	COST	GRIT	TAGS/RULES
Cam-bot	3	3	*Small, Typical robot. Record Things, Project Things.*
Chauffer-Chauffer	3	3	*Large, Simple robot. Drive.*
Desk Jockey	5	5	*Large, Smart robot. Bureaucracy, Meet & Greet.*
Digger Pete	4	8	*Huge, Simple robot. Construction.*
Guard-O-Matic	4	8	*Huge, Simple robot. Defend.*
Lab Helper	2	1	*Tiny, Typical robot. Grabbing Claw, Bunsen Burner.*
Mr Fixit	3	3	*Small, Typical robot. Repair, Diagnose Machine.*
Robo Jeeves	4	5	*Large, Typical robot. Cook & Clean, Protect the Boss.*
Spider Bot	2	3	*Small, Simple robot. Climb.*
Wind-up Bomb	2	1	*Tiny, Simple robot. Can be set to explode in 1–6 turns (treat as a Grenade).*

Robot Upgrades: Each additional Tag adds +1 Cost.

ROBOTS VS. AUTOMATONS

Robots are the very poor cousin of automatons. They are used for relatively basic tasks and require human input to define the parameters of their actions. By contrast, automatons draw on the thinking brain of Mother and are capable of complex, independent thought. They are, as their name suggests, autonomous beings. Despite their differences, there are still many similarities between the machines. Both are inhuman, metal constructs that feel no pain and will devote themselves completely to a given task. Neither can understand human emotion and, therefore, can be cold and callous in their dealings with the living.

VEHICLES

Getting around the world of Tomorrow City is as simple as finding the right vehicle and taking to the streets or skies. Vehicles are defined by a short profile that describes their key features:

- **Grit.** How much damage the vehicle can suffer before being immobilised or destroyed. Vehicles can also suffer suitable Conditions, such as Blown Tyre, Damaged Ailerons, or Leaking Fuel Tank.
- **Crew.** The first number listed indicates minimum number of people required to operate the vehicle effectively. Operating a vehicle with less than the required crew may incur penalties or be impossible. The second number is the maximum number of passengers the vehicle can transport, in addition to the crew.
- **Hardpoints.** You can attach one weapon to each hardpoint a vehicle has. Heavy weapons take up two hardpoint slots and weapons with the Mounted Tag take up three hardpoints. The driver/pilot can operate one weapon and crew/passengers can operate the others. Most vehicle-mounted weapons fire forward, but the GM can declare which direction each hardpoint is facing at the time a vehicle is acquired. Weapons may be turreted at the GM's discretion.
- Weapons with a Cost equal to or less than a vehicle's Cost are included in the vehicle's Cost. Weapons with a Cost greater than the vehicle's Cost must be purchased separately.

A Cost 4 truck with two hardpoints could have two light machine guns (Cost 3) mounted on it for free. If you instead wanted to mount a flamethrower (a Cost 5 heavy weapon), you would have to acquire it as a separate item, using your Cred.

A Cost 8 tank with four hardpoints mounts a forward-facing light machine gun (Cost 3) and a cannon (Cost 6, Heavy, Mounted) for free. The GM agrees the cannon can be on a turret.

Linked Weapons

If a vehicle has multiple of the same type of weapon, you can declare that they are linked at the time of purchase. A driver/pilot/gunner can operate all linked weapons with one action, as if they were a single weapon. On a successful attack, the linked weapons deal +1 Damage for each weapon after the first.

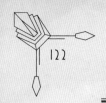

Your Sky Monster aircraft has three linked machine guns. You make a single attack with them, as if they were one weapon, and a success will deal +2 Damage to the target.

Surface Vehicles

Anything that travels along the ground, or perhaps over water, is a surface vehicle. This includes cars, motorcycles, trucks, and watercraft. They tend to be faster on well-maintained roads and hard surfaces.

BASIC SURFACE VEHICLES	COST	GRIT	CREW	HARD	TAGS/RULES
Motorcycle	1	3	1/+1	0	Agile
Car	2	8	1/+5	2	
Truck	3	16	1/+2	2	Cargo (Light), Slow or Sluggish
Armoured Vehicle	6	24	3/+1	4	Thick Armour

Surface Vehicle Upgrades: *Agile, Cargo (Light), Deflect, Fast, Flashy, Off-road,* and *Resistant (X)* are +1 Cost each. *Thick Armour* is +2 Cost. Each level of *Cargo (X)* above Light is an additional +1 Cost. You can also add +2 hardpoints for +1 Cost. Negative Tags reduce the cost of a surface vehicle by 1 Cred each.

EXAMPLE SURFACE VEHICLES		COST	GRIT	CREW	HARD	TAGS/RULES
BIKES	Bicycle	0	1	1/+1	0	Slow
	Heavy Motorcycle	2	4	1/-	2	Agile
	Monowheel	2	2	1/-	0	Agile, Fast
	Motorcycle & Sidecar	2	4	1/+2	2	
	Reconnaissance Bike	2	3	1/+1	1	Agile, Off-road

CARS	Armoured Limousine	4	8	1/+6	3	Flashy, Thick Armour, Sluggish
	Jeep	3	8	1/+4	2	Off Road
	Roadster	3	8	1/+1	2	Fast
	Small Car	2	6	1/+3	1	Agile
TRUCKS	2 ½ Ton Truck	4	16	1/+2	2	Cargo (Medium), Sluggish
	Bus	3	16	1/+24	0	Slow
	Delivery Van	3	14	1/+2	1	Cargo (Light), Slow
	Fuel tanker	3	14	1/+2	0	Cargo (Medium), Slow, Explodes
ARMOURED	Blade APC	5	12	1/+10	2	Thick Armour, Off road
	Dagger Light Tank	6	18	3/+1	4	Thick Armour, Off-road
	Sabre Battle Tank	8	24	3/+1	6	Thick Armour, Deflect, Off-road, Sluggish
	Small Landship	11	36	6/-	8	Thick Armour, Deflect, Off-road, Slow
WATER	Amphibious Truck	4	16	1/+3	2	Cargo (Light), Amphibious
	Kayak	0	1	1/-	0	Slow
	Pleasure Craft	2	8	1/+6	2	
	Speed Boat	3	6	1/+4	2	Fast

Dirigibles

Lighter-than-air vehicles are interchangeably referred to as dirigibles or airships. Most are rigid-framed zeppelins, though hot-air balloons and blimps are also used as pleasure craft and observation platforms.

Dirigibles are slow but surprisingly manoeuvrable; they can hover in place, and can take off and land without the need for a runway. In Tomorrow City, airships frequently dock with platforms at the top of skyscrapers.

While modern airships are filled with non-flammable helium, some unscrupulous captains and transport companies continue to use hydrogen to cut costs. The vehicles described below are assumed to be filled with helium, but you can reduce a dirigible's Cost by 1 to fill it with hydrogen instead. Hydrogen-filled dirigibles gain both the *Flammable* and *Explodes* Tags.

Massive: The high Grit value of dirigibles represents not just their massive size, but also the fact that a few bullet holes or other punctures will not cause the gas to violently escape. An airship strafed with bullet holes could take hours, or even days, to descend. When a dirigible suffers damage equal to half its Grit, it will begin to slowly float to the ground.

BASIC DIRIGIBLES	COST	GRIT	CREW	HARD	TAGS/RULES
Small (100 feet)	2	10	1/+1	0	Light
Medium (200 feet)	4	30	2/+8	2	Light
Large (400 feet)	6	50	2/+12	4	Light
Huge (800 feet)	8	70	4/+25	4	
Massive (1600 feet)	10	100	8/+50	6	Sluggish

Dirigible Upgrades: *Cargo (Light), Deflect, Fast, Flashy,* and *Resistant (X)* are +1 Cost each. *Thick Armour* is +4 Cost. Each level of *Cargo (X)* above Light is an additional +1 Cost. You can also add +2 hardpoints for +1 Cost. Negative Tags reduce the cost of a dirigible by 1 Cred each.

EXAMPLE DIRIGIBLES		COST	GRIT	CREW	HARD	TAGS/RULES
SMALL	Barrage Balloon	1	8	-/-	0	Light, Tethered
	Hot Air Balloon	2	10	1/+6	0	Light, Slow
	Observation Blimp	3	15	1/+1	1	Light, Powerful Searchlight
MEDIUM	Delivery Dirigible	5	30	1/+3	2	Light, Cargo (Light)
	Private Cruiser	5	30	2/+8	2	Light, Flashy
	Sky Cab	3	25	1/+4	0	Light
	Military Recon Ship	5	30	2/+8	4	Light
LARGE	Cargo Dirigible	7	55	2/+3	2	Light, Cargo (Medium), Slow
	Prison Transport	6	45	4/+12	4	Light
	Sky Raider	8	50	2/+12	6	Light, Fast
HUGE	Cargo Hauler	8	70	8/+4	2	Cargo (Heavy), Sluggish, Slow
	Navy Battle Cruiser	14	75	4/+25	6	Thick Armour, Fast
	Sun Seeker Yacht	8	65	4/+25	2	Flashy
MASSIVE	Aircraft Carrier	14	100	8/+50	10	Sluggish, Deflect, Runway
	Container Airship	11	90	8/+6	2	Sluggish, Slow, Cargo (Massive)
	Flying Fortress	17	110	12/+50	12	Sluggish, Thick Armour

Aircraft

From old military planes to personal transports, gliders, and light passenger craft, the skies above Tomorrow City are filled with aircraft of various shapes and sizes. Most are single or twin-propellered vehicles, though a few larger planes have four, six, or even eight!

Many large warehouses in Rimside have rooftop runways, and shorter launch platforms adorn the tops of high-rise structures closer to The Spindle. Gliders must be launched by other aircraft, with vehicle winches, or dropped from dirigibles. Vertical take-off aircraft are virtually unknown due to the prevalence of dirigibles.

BASIC AIRCRAFT	COST	GRIT	CREW	HARD	TAGS/RULES
Small (40' wingspan)	2	8	1/-	0	Light
Medium (80' wingspan)	4	16	1/+8	2	Light
Large (120' wingspan)	6	24	1/+24	4	Slow or Sluggish
Huge (240' wingspan)	8	32	4/+50	6	Sluggish

Aircraft Upgrades: *Agile, Cargo (Light), Deflect, Fast, Flashy,* and *Resistant (X)* are +1 Cost each. *Thick Armour* is +2 Cost. Each level of *Cargo (X)* above Light is an additional +1 Cost. You can also add +2 hardpoints for +1 Cost. Negative Tags reduce the cost of a vehicle by 1 Cred each.

EXAMPLE AIRCRAFT		COST	GRIT	CREW	HARD	TAGS/RULES
SMALL	Antique Biplane	2	8	1/+1	2	Light, Slow
	Personal Glider	2	8	1/+1	0	Light, Silent
	Stormwind Fighter	3	10	1/-	2	Light
	Tornado Stunt plane	3	8	1/-	0	Light, Agile
MEDIUM	Buzzsaw Heavy Fighter	5	16	1/+1	4	Light
	Sky Serpent Bomber	6	16	3/+6	6	Light
	Starfield Gunrunner	4	12	1/+6	2	Light
	Sunbright 8	3	14	1/+8	0	Light
LARGE	Oden Recon Aircraft	6	20	2/+12	4	Sluggish, Detect (Aircraft)
	Loki Heavy Bomber	7	24	3/+6	8	Sluggish, Thick Armour
	"Turkey" Glider	5	20	1/+12	2	Slow, Silent, Cargo (Light)
HUGE	Mercury Sky Cruiser	7	26	4/+50	2	Sluggish, Flashy
	Sky Monster	11	32	3/+50	8	Sluggish, Thick Armour
	Sunbright "Yak"	10	32	2/+50	4	Sluggish, Cargo (Heavy)

INTO DANGER

Revs take on dangerous jobs and deal with dangerous people in return for a little cash, respect, or for reasons known only to them. They prepare as well as they can but, when things start to get messy, there is nothing left to do but throw themselves into danger, roll with the punches, and hope their skills, experience, and sheer grit will get them through. This chapter describes how to apply the rules in a variety of common dramatic situations that the characters might find themselves in.

STORY STRUCTURE

Your characters are going to take on Jobs, sometimes for a client or employer and sometimes to pursue their own Drives. Your games will play out at a pace that makes sense to the plot of your story, which is usually much quicker than real-time. Stories can be divided into the following Increments:

- **Campaign.** A series of Jobs linked by a common setting, group of characters, or overarching plot.
- **Job.** A complete mission with a beginning, middle, and end.
- **Session.** A single period of gameplay, where you might play out several Scenes or an entire Job.
- **Scene.** An encounter during a Job, usually taking place in a single location.
- **Turn.** A moment in a Scene long enough for each character to do something (p.64).
- **Action.** When a single character does something.

The Job

Characters take on high-risk Jobs in the pursuit of their next paycheque or, perhaps, for more noble reasons. Each such mission unfolds with a specific sequence, from the inciting incident to the climactic conclusion.

- **The Hook.** The Revs are employed or coerced to take on the Job.
- **Gear Up.** The characters acquire their gear and plan for the coming Job.
- **Into Danger.** The Job begins in earnest and the characters move through a series of Scenes until it is completed or abandoned.
- **Downtime.** When the action is over the characters have an opportunity to rest and recover. This is also when they advance or improve.

ACTIONS HAVE CONSEQUENCES

The following explanations and examples are accompanied by short tables with example consequences to inspire your own descriptions. A quick way to use them is to look at the highest or lowest remaining Danger Die after a Check and use the corresponding table entry as inspiration for what happens next.

ARGUMENTS & PERSUASION

An argument occurs when someone attempts to persuade another individual or a group of an idea or point of view. Most of the time, persuading someone can be resolved with a single Check, but when you want to play out an intense debate, furious argument, rousing speech, or a dramatic war of words, you can use an Extended Check. In these instances, each success or failure represents one side or the other making an effective point, revealing an important fact, losing interest, or becoming flustered, upset, or engaged. Achieving three successes means your argument has won out and you have convinced your audience. If you suffer three strikes, your argument is unsuccessful, and your character may even have been persuaded to change their own mind or give up entirely!

When creating dice pools for arguments and persuasion, factor in the acting character's most appropriate Trademark and associated Edges. Trademarks like Charming are always going to be useful in such situations, but sometimes a Trademark related to a specific background, occupation, or audience could be helpful. If the audience is friendly, open to suggestions, or likely to be swayed, you might add an extra Action Dice. If the person or group being convinced is disinterested, has a strong opinion of their own, or is hostile, add in one or more Danger Dice.

EXAMPLE ARGUMENT CONSEQUENCES	
1	Become tongue-tied, flustered, or momentarily lost for words
2	Upset or anger someone; Put someone in danger; or Risk an important relationship
3	Tell an obvious lie; Have your bluff called; or Reveal a weakness
4	Become Angry, Dazed, Shaken, or Embarrassed
5	Escalate the situation; Draw unwanted attention; or Put yourself in a tough spot
6	Expose yourself or an ally to Harm; Have your Cred reduced; or Change your mind

Alexi is trying to convince a crowd of drones to make a stand against their factory boss and start a riot. As this is a dramatic moment and could have far-reaching consequences, the GM decides to play it as an Extended Check. The player describes Alexi calling the crowd to him and listing all the injustices they have suffered. He is using his own Drone Trademark to help connect with the audience.

The Check is a partial success, so the GM describes a small group stopping work to listen, but just as many looking angry at this outsider trying to stir up trouble. A Danger Die is added for the changed circumstances. His next Check is a failure – the onlookers are getting hostile, some picking up large tools or shouting him down. That's a strike, and Alexi also suffers the Shaken Condition as his confidence falters. The next Check is another partial success – Alexi is finally gaining some traction and beginning to sway the crowd, though he notices some men at the back sneaking away, perhaps to inform on him. The player prepares the dice pool for the next Check…

CHASES & RACES

Whether on foot or in vehicles, dramatic chase scenes are a staple of pulp adventures and action stories. Participating in a chase or race requires a character's full attention and therefore counts as a Focused Action. If a character wants to do something else while involved in a chase, such as take in the details of their pursuer or shoot while driving at speed, both actions incur a penalty of one or more Danger Dice. During a vehicle chase, passengers can take their own Action or assist by giving directions or pointing out hazards.

Chases and races can be resolved quickly with a single Check or turned into an exciting Scene using the Extended Check rules. Achieving three successes in an extended chase means you have caught up with the target, whereas suffering three strikes indicates that they have gotten away. Conversely, if fleeing from a pursuer, you will need three successes to escape.

Make the chase dramatic by describing the result of each Check with cool moments and interesting events. Does rolling a success mean that you gained on the target, or that they faltered? Did you slip down a convenient alleyway, slide across the hood of a vehicle, or make a dramatic leap? Each Check indicates what happened, but your description tells everyone how it all went down.

Relative Speed

Tomorrow City doesn't worry too much about the exact speeds of people or vehicles – you just want to know whether something is faster or slower than whatever it is competing with. When building dice pools for chases and races, you will want to factor in the relative speed of each participant. As a rule, surface vehicles are faster than anyone on foot, dirigibles are faster than surface vehicles, and aircraft are faster than other vehicle types. In a race between someone on foot and someone in a car, the driver will be at a distinct speed advantage, unless the environment or terrain stops them from using the extra horsepower. Anyone using a similar mode of transport is assumed to be roughly equal in speed, unless they have a Trademark, Edge, Harm, or Tag that suggests they are slower or faster.

A car with the Fast Tag will be at an advantage over the average jalopy. An aircraft with the Engine Trouble Condition might be on an even footing with a dirigible with the Fast Tag.

EXAMPLE CHASE CONSEQUENCES

1	Trip, stumble, skid, or slide; Get caught in a crowd or behind something slow
2	Break something; Cause collateral damage; or Use up an item of gear
3	Draw unwanted attention; Give an enemy an opportunity; Upset someone
4	Become Angry Shaken, Tired, or Weakened
5	Take a wrong turn; Become lost; or Put yourself in a tough situation
6	A character, vehicle, or ally suffers Harm

Emile, driving a roadster (Fast), is in pursuit of a gang of goons in a stolen truck. The player describes Emile swerving through traffic in Rimside. He gets a bonus Action Die because his car is faster than the truck. The Check is a success, and he closes the distance. On his next Check, he only scores a partial success. That counts as another success, but the GM describes his car swiping a fire hydrant – it now has a damaged fender that is scraping the road and slowing him down. A Danger Die is added to the pool. The player makes a third roll, but this time Botches it! The GM applies two strikes against Emile, describing how the truck makes a sudden turn down a narrow side street and increases its lead. That's two successes and two strikes. The next Check is going to determine if Emile catches up, or if the truck escapes into the warren of Rimside alleyways...

COMBAT

In Tomorrow City, violence is common. Everyone has grown up in the shadow of war and, for all too many, their conflicts have been resolved with a gun in the face or a knife in the back. The city authorities use a heavy hand to control the populace, and the gangsters and thugs that rule the streets are quick to deliver a beatdown to those who step out of line. Despite the war having ended, life is still cheap. When words fail and tempers flare, weapons are drawn.

Organising Combats

Combat almost always occurs in Turns, with players making an Initiative roll (p.64) at the start of the combat to determine whether they act before or after any enemies. At the start of each new Turn, the GM should describe the enemy's Actions, or what they are attempting to do, and the players can respond with the Actions of their own characters.

Most of the time, events can be kept straight in everyone's heads, but sometimes a map drawn on scrap paper or a whiteboard can help players visualise the action. A few marks on a page, along with some strategically placed sticky notes or dice, will easily let everyone know where characters are in relation to each other.

Combat Turns & Actions

During a Turn, each character can take one Free Action and either a Quick Action or Focused Action. If taking a Quick Action, you can also move up to Near. When performing a Focused Action, you can do nothing else in the Turn.

Free Actions.

- Draw or ready a weapon
- Shout a warning
- Take a few steps
- Pull an item from a pocket or belt

Quick Actions.

- Make an attack
- Administer first aid
- Take one or more doses of a single serum
- Toss an object to an ally
- Put on a gasmask
- Reload a weapon or clear a jam
- Intimidate someone
- Operate a simple device

Focused Actions.

- Move up to Far
- Aim before shooting (gain +1 Action Die)
- Examine something closely
- Deliver a rousing speech
- Defuse an explosive
- Operate a complex device

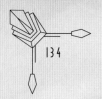

Attacking

When a character attempts to cause Harm to someone or something else, they are making an attack. This requires a Check. Factor in all the things that make the attack easier as Action Dice and all the things that make it more difficult as Danger Dice. An opponent's Tags and Actions are the most likely modifiers, but things like cover or the environment should also be considered. If the intent of an attack is to knock down, stun, restrain, or inflict some other Condition on a target, describe how you do it and make the Check.

A success or partial success will cause damage to the target, and Boons can be used to apply +1 Damage. Partial successes, failures, and Botches should have consequences for the attacker. The default Damage for attacks is 2, though some weapons cause more.

EXAMPLE ATTACK CONSEQUENCES	
1	Out of ammo; Weapon jammed; Weapon malfunction; or Weapon stuck in something
2	Drop, lose, break, or use up a weapon or other item of gear
3	Break something; Cause collateral damage; Injure a bystander; or Alert an enemy
4	Only inflict half Damage on the target; or Action has limited effect or duration
5	Put yourself or an ally in a bad spot; Expose yourself to danger; or Give up an advantageous position
6	Suffer damage; Become Angry, Dazed, Shaken, or Tired; or Suffer other Harm

ATTACK CONSEQUENCES TABLE

When making ranged attacks, lean towards lower-numbered consequences, such as breaking things or weapon jams. Close combat consequences tend to be the things listed as higher results, like an unfavourable position or taking Harm.

Defending

When targeted by an attack, describe how your character is avoiding or resisting it and make a Check. Different Trademarks, Edges, and Tags will be relevant depending on the approach you choose. When dodging, ducking, or weaving to make yourself harder to hit, Tags that increase your mobility are going to be useful. If attempting to resist, endure, block, or deflect an attack, Tags related to strength, toughness, and durability are going to come into play. Remember to factor in an opponent's Danger Rating, along with any Tags or Conditions they might have.

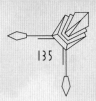

You avoid Harm on a success, while a partial success might mean you only suffer a portion of the Harm or some other consequence. A failed Check means the character suffers the full extent of the Harm and Botches make things much worse, such as double Damage, multiple levels of a Condition, or other serious consequences.

A character usually suffers 2 Damage from attacks, though an enemy equipped with specialised weapons might cause more or different Harm.

EXAMPLE DEFENCE CONSEQUENCES	
1	Alert an enemy; Draw unwanted attention; Expose yourself to future danger
2	Upset or injure an ally or bystander; Damage your reputation; Make a new enemy
3	Put in a bad situation; Knocked back or down; Separated, pinned or restrained
4	Cause collateral damage; Break, drop, lose or use up an item of gear
5	Become Angry, Dazed, Shaken, Tired or Weakened
6	Only avoid half the damage or a portion of the Harm

Emile is in a shoot-out with a hired Hitman who takes several shots at him. Emile's player decides he will avoid the danger by diving behind a nearby car. The GM agrees that both his Veteran and Quick Trademarks are relevant, so he can pick which to use. He decides on Quick, adding one Action Die for the Trademark, and another for his Duck & Weave Edge. Unfortunately, he must add two Danger Dice for the Hitman's Danger Rating, another two for their Shoot and Cold-Blooded Killer Tags, and a fifth because the gunman has a better position! That means Emile will be rolling three Action Dice versus 5 Danger Dice. He fails the roll, indicating he doesn't move quite fast enough, and suffers Damage. The Hitman is equipped with a standard pistol, so inflicts 2 Damage.

JUST TAKE THE HITS

If a character is distracted, busy doing something, incapacitated, or unaware of an attack, they have no choice but to suffer the damage – there is no Check to avoid the Harm. They may be able to use armour to reduce the total damage suffered, at the GM's discretion.

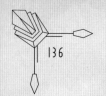

Example Combat

Alexi, Emile, and Carol have ventured down to Underside where a gang of four Hood Scum have taken offence at some smart comments Alexi made.

Kirsty (GM): *The Hood Scum with the facial scars pats the pistol tucked into the front of his trousers and says to Alexi, "You're gonna pay for that, you dumb drone." His three pals chuckle and draw their weapons. Everyone should roll Initiative.*

Charli (playing Emile): *I got four, so will go before the thugs.*

Xander (playing Carol): *Me too.*

Ava (playing Alexi): *Oops, I guess I was laughing at the thug too much to notice the danger. I only got two, so will act after the hoods.*

Kirsty (GM): *Okay, the narrow alley has corrugated iron walls but is cluttered with rubbish and debris, so there are plenty of places to take cover. Two of the Hood Scum remain perched on a rusting girder about six feet above you. They both have pistols and are going to shoot at Emile, as he looks most dangerous with his combat vest and submachine gun. The one with facial scars is shooting at Alexi. The last guy has a broad blade, like an oversized Bowie knife and is advancing on Carol. He grins, exposing rotted teeth. What is everyone doing?*

Charli (Emile): *Well, I'm going to step behind some wooden boxes for cover, then shoot one of the guys aiming at me. [They make a Check, getting a 4.] That's a partial success, so one of the Hood Scum takes two Damage.*

Kirsty (GM): *[Noting the Damage] Sure, but spraying all those bullets around punches holes in the thin metal walls. You hear yelling and a commotion from somewhere beyond. That's probably going to be a problem later. What's Carol doing?*

Xander (Carol): *Umm, I power up my pneumatic gloves and step towards the guy with the knife. [Xander makes his Check, getting a 5.] Yes, I get a solid hit. Two Damage and a level of Dazed.*

Kirsty (GM): *Sure, but it's only a partial success, so there's a consequence. What's the highest remaining danger die? Let's say the guy with the knife manages to get a hit on you too, so take two Damage.*

Xander (Carol): *Ouch!*

Kirsty (GM): *It's the Hood Scum's turn now. Scarface points a rusty pistol with an exaggeratedly long barrel at Alexi. How do you respond?*

Ava (Alexi): *I'm going to dive for cover behind some of the rubbish. [She makes a Check, getting a 5.] A partial success. Can I avoid getting hit, but now be in amongst this pile of filthy garbage? Kind of in an awkward position?*

Kirsty (GM): *Sure. You sprawl face-first into a pile of mildewy cardboard that collapses on top of you. You're kind of flat on your stomach and it will take a Quick Action to get up. The two Hood Scum on the balcony both shoot at Emile. You're tucked behind some debris, Charli, so make a Check to see if you can duck into cover. Add an extra Danger Die for being outnumbered.*

Charli (Emile): *[They roll the dice, getting a 4.] Hmm... Partial success. I'm not sure what might happen. I'm already wedged behind the cover so don't think I can get into a worse position.*

Kirsty (GM): *I think since it's a hail of bullets from two guys, it's very hard to avoid all the Damage. You try to duck behind the cover but get grazed by a bullet or splintering wood. You take half Damage, so one point.*

Charlie (Emile): *I'll mark one point of armour to soak that.*

Kirsty (GM): *[Looking at Xander] The Hood Scum fighting Carol dodges under another swing of your pneumatic fist and attempts to stick you with their blade. How do you respond?*

Xander (Carol): *I leap back a bit and try to use my Scrapper Trademark and Dodge a Blow Edge to avoid the knife. [He makes a Check, getting two 6's.] A success and a Boon! Alright! I guess I avoid Harm. Can I have him backed into a corner?*

Kirsty (GM): *Absolutely. You use the Boon to put him in a bad position, which will give you a bonus Action Die when you act against him. It's now Alexi's turn to act. You're face down in a pile of garbage, with Scarface pointing a gun at you. What are you going to do?*

Ava (Alexi): *Can I get up and charge at him?*

Kirsty (GM): *You're face down in an awkward position, remember? It will take an Action to get up, so you won't be able to attack him in close combat this turn.*

Ava (Alexi): *In that case, I'll draw my hand cannon and shoot him from where I'm lying, if that's okay.*

Kirsty (GM): *Sure, but add an extra Danger Die for the awkward position.*

Ava (Alexi): *[She makes the Check, getting a 6.] A full success! That's two Damage, plus one for the Deadly Tag. Actually, I'll also spend a Moxie to change that Action Die with a five into a six, too. That gives me a Boon, which I'll use to inflict one extra Damage. Four total.*

Kirsty (GM): *[Whistling] Wow. There's a smoking hole right through his head. He stands looking down at you for a moment, wobbles, then falls. That's the end of the Turn, so it's back to the top. The Hood Scum with the knife is going to continue fighting Carol, and the two on the balcony are going to keep shooting, one each at Emile and Alexi. What is everyone going to do?*

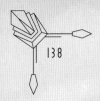

Take-Downs

When you attack an unaware opponent with the intent of disabling them, you are performing a take-down. Knocking someone unconscious from behind is a classic example of this. Make a Check, factoring in Action and Danger Dice for things like the better position, the target's toughness or alertness, and their Danger Rating. Success or partial success disables the target, perhaps knocking them unconscious, or killing them outright. A failure or Botch means the target was not taken out, though they may have suffered Damage or a Condition at the GM's discretion.

EXAMPLE TAKE-DOWN CONSEQUENCES	
1	Alert an enemy; Draw unwanted attention; Expose yourself to future danger
2	Drop, lose, break, or use up a weapon or other item of gear
3	Cause more Harm than intended; Cause collateral damage
4	The target is only subdued for a short time
5	Become Angry, Dazed, Dishevelled, Shaken, or Tired
6	Suffer Damage or other Harm; Put yourself in a bad spot

Emile Franks is infiltrating a philomath's hideout and spots a sentry. He wants to sneak up, put him in a chokehold, and render him unconscious. He builds his dice pool, adding Action Dice for his Veteran Trademark, Brawl Edge, and a better position (the sentry is unaware). The sentry has a Danger Rating of 2, so the player must add two Danger Dice, plus another for the thug's Alert Tag. The roll is made, and Emile gets a partial success; the sentry is subdued, but at a cost. The GM decides that the guard puts up more of a fight than expected and Emile is hurt in the struggle.

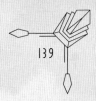

DOGFIGHTS

A dogfight is a combat between flying vehicles at very close range. In a dogfight, each pilot tries to outmanoeuvre their opponent and line up a good shot. It is a cross between a chase and a combat, and you can use either system to resolve a dogfight. If one side is simply trying to escape the other, use the chase rules. If the aircraft involved are seeking to shoot each other down, then it is a true dogfight. Dogfights flow much like a standard combat; however, they do not use the standard Initiative rules. Instead, at the start of each Turn, each Rev piloting a flying vehicle makes a manoeuvre Check.

Manoeuvre Check

A manoeuvre Check represents the pilots jostling for position and determines who attacks first each Turn. Modify the Check with an appropriate Trademark (such as Aviator or Windborn), applicable Edges, the highest Danger Rating on an enemy pilot and any relevant Tags. A success or partial success means the Rev's vehicle can attack before the enemy. Boons can be spent by the pilot and/or gunners to add Action Dice to their attack Checks this Turn. A partial success means the Rev can attack first, but it puts pressure on their aircraft or crew that may result in a Danger Dice to an attack, Damage to the plane, or some other consequence. If the manoeuvre Check is failed, the enemy attacks first and, if it is Botched, the character's aircraft or dirigible does not get to attack at all!

Emile engages in a dogfight with two light fighters. He starts the combat Turn with a manoeuvre Check, gathering his dice pool. He adds an Action Die for his Windborn Trademark and another for his Pilot Edge, then adds two Danger Dice for the enemy's Danger Rating and a third because they have the Dogfighting Tag. He rolls a partial success, so gets to act before the enemy but there is a consequence. The GM suggests that his manoeuvre has left the aircraft in a tough spot, meaning that he suffers an extra Danger Dice on his attack this Turn.

Air-to-Air Combat

Once manoeuvre Checks are completed, combatants act. All characters in the same vehicle act at the same time, in an order that makes sense to what they are doing. Players should describe how their aircraft, dirigible, or rocket-pack-equipped Rev are flying and perform an Action. Usually this will be blazing away with any weapons mounted on hardpoints, but it could be any number of other things, such as landing

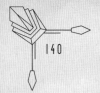

on a passing zeppelin, spotting, repairing something, or leaping from a burning aircraft (hopefully with a parachute!). Resolve attacks as you would in any combat.

The key to describing a good dogfight is to remember that the events take place in three dimensions, so the vehicles can dive, swoop, climb, and twist in ways that someone on foot or in a car cannot. The terrain and environment will also be quite different – instead of rubble, pedestrians, cars, and streetlamps to watch out for, a pilot might use cloud cover, the sun, and other flying vehicles for cover or advantage. If flying over and through the city itself, then the aircraft might weave between high-rises, duck under bridges, and twist about the spires, masts, and radio towers that adorn many buildings.

EXAMPLE DOGFIGHT CONSEQUENCES	
1	Out of ammo; Weapon jammed; or Weapon malfunction
2	Cause collateral damage; Injure a crewmate; or Put an ally in a bad spot
3	Momentarily blinded by the sun; Lose sight of the target; or Expose yourself to danger
4	Only inflict half Damage on the target; or Suffer additional Damage
5	Become Angry, Dazed, Shaken, or Tired
6	Put stress on your vehicle; Pilot or vehicle suffers Damage; or Trail smoke

Air-to-air combat typically happens at a different scale to standard combat; Close and Near ranges could be dozens or hundreds of yards, and movement speeds are measured in miles per hour. Ground combatants don't make manoeuvre Checks and always act after flyers that do. Attacking flyers from the ground (or even from atop zeppelins or high buildings) will incur at least one Danger Dice penalty.

INTERROGATIONS & QUESTIONING

When you want answers from someone and they resist your efforts, make a Check. Whether you're interrogating a witness, coaxing information from a victim, or threatening a goon, it all plays out the same way. Often, a single check will get you the answer you need. Use an Extended Check to play out an interrogation where both sides could potentially suffer emotional harm or give away more than they bargained for. Achieving three successes during an interrogation means you learn what you need, or at least gain some useful information. If the interrogator suffers three strikes, their line of questioning was not effective, or the target resisted their efforts.

EXAMPLE INTERROGATION CONSEQUENCES	
1	Hurt someone; Take things too far; or Accidentally break something
2	Upset someone; Draw unwanted attention; or Make an enemy of someone
3	Reveal a secret; or Give away more than you intended
4	Become Angry, Dazed, or Shaken
5	Give an enemy power; Make a bad deal; or Put yourself in a tough situation
6	Expose yourself or an ally to harm; or Use up your Cred

Carol Grimes is questioning a Foreman of Moloch about some recent disappearances and the GM decides this should be an Extended Check. The player makes a Check and gets a partial success. They mark one success, but the situation is complicated by the arrival of some of the Foreman's followers. This could mean trouble if Carol doesn't get answers quickly. The player rolls a second time but fails. That's a strike and a consequence. The followers surround Carol in an intimidating semi-circle, inflicting the Shaken Condition on her. Her third roll is a success, and the player explains how Carol's quick wit and fast thinking confuses the Foreman a little, keeping the gang of workers at bay a moment longer. The next roll is another partial success. That's three in total, so the Foreman reveals an important clue related to the disappearances. Unfortunately, there is also a consequence; angry that he has been manipulated, the Foreman tells his followers to throw Carol out of the factory, which they do – roughly. She suffers a point of Damage as a result.

Bribery

Offering money, services, or favours is a common way to coerce someone into cooperating with you. Characters can make whatever bribes they wish, and the GM might give them a bonus Action Die if the target is open to it. Characters offering cash or other valuable items can also spend 1 Cred to roll with Mastery when attempting to bribe someone. This represents them offering a significant reward in return for cooperation.

INVESTIGATIONS

An investigation is any search for information, clues, or evidence that will assist the player characters in overcoming a problem or solving a mystery. It might involve searching a room, questioning a witness, or combing through racks of journals at the University of Science & Technology. Given enough time and attention, most clues will be found, and it often won't even require a Check, just asking the right questions or looking in the right place should do the trick.

However, when the evidence you seek is buried a little deeper or is harder to obtain, a Check may be called for. In these situations, it is not so much about whether you find a helpful detail, but how. When you make an investigation Check, don't think about it as asking, "Do I find the clue?" Instead, it is more like asking "Do I find the clue quickly? Or without too much effort? Or without costing me anything?"

Any success will find what you are looking for, though a partial success means that there was some consequence or drawback – perhaps it took a while, or you had to pay a bribe or offer a favour. Failure could mean no clue was found, or the clue was discovered but with some hard consequence or serious cost.

EXAMPLE INVESTIGATION CONSEQUENCES	
1	Break something; Give something up; or Use up an item of gear
2	Alert an enemy; Make a new enemy; Upset someone; or Burn Bridges
3	Waste Time; or Waste money
4	Become Angry, Shaken, Tired, or Weakened
5	Make a bad deal; Put yourself in a tough situation; or Undermine an ally
6	Suffer damage or a social or emotional injury

Alexi arrives at a missing friend's apartment, finding it torn apart as if someone was furiously searching for something. He wants to see if there are any clues as to the identity of whoever ransacked the place, so proceeds to look around. The GM knows the person responsible is a Broken Doughboy, and the long slashes in the sofa and walls indicate strong mechanical arms with sharp claws. He could just tell the player that the damage was done by someone with a pair of mechanical arms but instead calls for a Check. Alexi's player rolls the dice and scores a partial success. Alexi makes the appropriate deduction, but it takes quite a bit of time.

PATTERN POWERS

Characters with Pattern Weaver Trademarks can sense and manipulate the otherworldly energy of the Pattern. While each Pattern Weaver Trademark has one or more Advantages that describe unique things they can do, that is not the limit of what is possible when manipulating the strange metaphysical force. Using the Pattern is meant to be quite freeform, letting the players and GM decide the extent of the effects. Here are a few things any Pattern Weaver might attempt:

- **Detect the Pattern.** Detect the presence of reality tears, aberrations, or other Pattern weavers. Follow the invisible trail left by aberrations, or sense where or when Pattern energy was used. The smaller or further away the energy is, the harder it is to detect.
- **Manifest the Pattern.** Reach through the thin barrier between realities to draw out and manipulate Pattern energy. Use it to create swirling shapes that distract, dazzle, or delight a target. Perhaps create a tiny (or large) reality tear, or pulse of Pattern energy that frightens or Harms a target.
- **Summon an Aberration.** Rip an aberration into our reality. This is never a good idea, and difficult to do (add D3 +1 Danger Dice). Perhaps the Pattern Weaver is skilled enough to determine the type of aberration ahead of time. Perhaps.
- **Warp Reality.** Manifest the Pattern to form abstract objects or obstacles out of nothing or to render cosmetic changes to man-made structures such as lamp posts, vehicles, signs, or parts of buildings. Alternatively, you might attempt to undo the reality-warping effects of aberrations, returning the world to the way it should be.

When interacting with the Pattern or using Pattern Advantages, players should clearly describe their action, the desired outcome, and point out anything that is working in their favour. The GM will use this description and the scene details to decide if the effect is possible, and whether a Check is needed.

Pattern Power Checks

Factor in the standard modifiers, paying particular attention to the scale of the desired effect. For example, a Metaphysical Geometrist using the Destination Anywhere Advantage will find it much easier to open a door to somewhere nearby, than halfway across the city. Use the following modifiers as a guide:

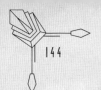

ADD AN ACTION DIE FOR...	ADD A DANGER DIE FOR...
Trademark: A single relevant Pattern Trademark related to the desired effect	**Aberrations:** Targets already infused with pattern energy may be harder to affect
Edges: Each Edge that enhances the character's chance of success	**Finesse:** The effect requires an unusual amount of precision or accuracy
No Pressure: There is plenty of time, a willing target, and/or no distractions	**Scope & Scale:** The power affects a large area or multiple targets
Strange Geometry: Performing the action in a site strong with Pattern Energy	**Barrens:** Areas strangely devoid of Pattern energy are known as barrens. It is harder to use the Pattern in such places
Force of Will: A Pattern user can infuse their own life force into the effect. Add an Action Die for each point of Damage they choose to suffer	**Exception:** The effect is an unusual use of the Advantage or other Pattern power

Pattern-related Checks are resolved like any other, with a success indicating a character achieves the desired effect and a partial successes coming at a cost. A failure usually means that the power does not work or does not work the way it was intended, which will probably lead to new problems!

EXAMPLE PATTERN POWER CONSEQUENCES	
1	Something comes through a reality tear; or Something is lost through it
2	Temporary cosmetic change, such as skin colour or tessellated skin patterns
3	Put someone in a bad spot; Expose yourself to danger; Cause collateral damage
4	Only inflict half Damage on the target; or Power has limited effect or duration
5	Become Dazed, Shaken, Tired, or Weakened
6	Suffer damage; or Suffer other Harm

Bystander Reactions

While everyone knows about the devastation of the Pattern bombs used in the war and have heard rumours of the aberrations that can claw their way into our reality, relatively few citizens have come face-to-face with such horrors. When they do witness the Pattern, they may react with shock, fear, or anger. The GM is encouraged to do what is dramatically appropriate in the situation. Use the following table as inspiration.

2D6	BYSTANDER REACTION
2	Faint in shock
3-4	Cower and hide
5-7	Flee, screaming in terror
8-9	Paralysed with fear
10-11	Run, seeking help from the authorities
12	Attack the apparent cause of the horror

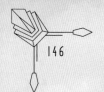

RESISTING HARM

Resisting Harm is done in much the same way as defending against an attack in combat; declare what you are doing to dodge, avoid, endure, or soak the Damage, gather a pool of Action and Danger Dice, and make a Check. On a success, you get away relatively unscathed. Partial successes might mean that you only take a small amount of Harm or some other consequence. Failures and Botches result in your character taking the full Damage, and maybe something extra.

The car the characters are riding in skids off the road and down a steep embankment. The GM tells the players to each make a Check to see how badly their character is injured. Carol has the Scrapper Trademark and argues she is used to getting roughed up. The GM agrees and she gets to add an Action Die to her pool. The GM also agrees that Alexi's Drone Trademark and Tough Edge both benefit him. The GM then tells each player to add two Danger Dice as the drop was significant and the car had been travelling at high speed. Carol fails the roll and suffers 2 Damage, while Alexi achieves a partial success; it is decided that he doesn't suffer any damage but takes the Dazed Condition instead.

RESISTING HORROR

Revs are often confronted by terrifying aberrations, overwhelming force, gruesome crime scenes, and horrors beyond their understanding. When situations or enemies are shocking, frightening, or unexpected, the GM may call for a Check. Add Action Dice for Trademarks and Edges that suggest the character has experience dealing with shocking scenes or that reflect strong willpower. They might also gain bonus Action Dice if the character was expecting something like what they have encountered and have braced themselves for it. Apply an additional Danger Dice if the cause of the horror is particularly bizarre, unnatural, or gruesome, and another one if the situation involves someone the character knows. Always add the Danger Rating of Pattern aberrations if they are encountered, or if the Threat is purposely trying to frighten or intimidate a character.

Success means the character keeps their cool and continues acting as normal. A partial success might indicate they suffer the Shaken Condition, are frozen, cry out in fear or some other consequence. If the Check is failed, then the character always suffers at least one level of Shaken and might have other consequences.

EXAMPLE RESISTING HORROR CONSEQUENCES	
1	Freeze in fear; Drop whatever you are holding; or Forget what you are doing
2	Scream, squeal, or shout in surprise or shock; or Stumble back, making a noise
3	Hide behind an ally; or Put them in a bad spot
4	Become Dazed, Shaken, Tired, or Weakened
5	Lash out at the nearest person or thing in shock or fear
6	Flee; Put yourself in a bad spot; or Faint

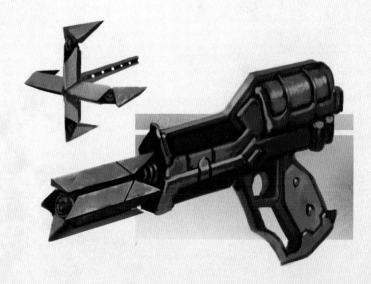

DOWNTIME

When a Job is over, characters get to rest and recuperate in a period of Downtime, during which they recover from their Injuries, reflect on their experiences, and improve their skills. Sometimes Downtime represents several weeks, or even months, between big jobs, while at other times it could be only a matter of hours or days. It is up to the GM to decide how long each Downtime period is based on the needs of the stories and the interests of the players.

REST & RECOVERY

Characters automatically refresh their Moxie and Cred during Downtime. They also clear their Conditions and heal all lost Hits. At the GM's discretion, any or all Injuries can be healed, if the Downtime is long enough. Otherwise, they might remove one or two points of Damage from each Injury.

If a character is suffering from a Trauma, discuss what is required to heal it. Do they just need time to rest, or are professional help, medical attention, or even robotic parts required? Will the Downtime be enough for the character to heal, or will the Trauma persist for another Job? Can the character afford surgery, or are they going to be in serious debt? Does any of that have further ramifications for the character?

GROWING FROM EXPERIENCE

As characters overcome obstacles, push through tough situations, chase their goals, and get back up after being knocked down, they come to better understand themselves and their capabilities. This is reflected through the accumulation of Experience Points (XP). Experiences can be positive or negative, but all ultimately provide opportunities for a character to grow.

At the end of a Job, talk through the events with the GM and other players and use the following list as a guideline to award characters with XP. For events that were mostly positive for your character, mark an XP box with a tick. For negative experiences or setbacks, mark an XP box with a cross.

Mark XP for each of the following that applies, in order:

- **On the Job.** Characters earn one experience point for participating in a Job, no matter the outcome. If the Job was successful, tick an XP box, otherwise, put a cross in it. Success or failure should be determined by the objectives of the characters, client, victim, or employer.
- **Knowledge.** Did your character learn something new about the city, its inhabitants, or the world at large? Perhaps they found answers to a problem, discovered an enemy's weakness, or learned of some tragedy. Tick an XP box if this new knowledge is positive, helpful, or will make your character's life better. Put a cross in an XP box if you discovered a new threat or danger, or if your eyes have been opened to some terrible feature of life in the city.
- **Drive.** If you made some gains towards your Drive or took some significant action inspired by it, tick an XP box. If you suffered a setback, acted against your own best interests, or found yourself further from a goal than ever, cross an XP box.
- **Ties.** Did you engage with other characters in an interesting or meaningful way? Did you authentically interact with one or more of your ties in a way that revealed new details about your relationship? If this was a positive interaction, tick an XP, if it was negative put a cross in it.
- **Harm.** Did your character become incapacitated by a Condition, suffer a serious Injury or Trauma, or come close to death? If so, cross one XP box.

Whether you tick or cross an XP box will often depend on the character, their personality, and the specifics of a Job. It is entirely possible that some characters tick a box while others put a cross in one in response to the same situation.

At the end of a Job, Charli and the other players determine what XP their characters earn. This Job was successful, and Emile Franks learned some important information about a long-term enemy, so Charli ticks two XP. Emile made no real progress towards his Drive, but didn't suffer a setback either, so doesn't mark any XP for that. He did have some positive interactions with Alexi, so that's a third tick. Emile was also knocked unconscious from the Dazed condition during the Job, so crosses an XP box.

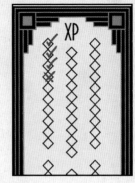

ADVANCES

When you have marked 10 XP, you can take an Advance for your character. An Advance allows you to do one of the following during Downtime:

- **Choose a New Edge.** This new Edge can be for any Trademark. Be inspired by the Trait lists or add something related to the stories your character has been involved in.
- **Choose a New Advantage.** This new Advantage can be from any Trademark your character currently has. At the GM's discretion, you might be able to pick an Advantage from a totally different Trademark, based on the experiences your character has had over the course of their Jobs.
- **Improve your Moxie, Cred, or Grit.** Increase any one of these values by 1, to a maximum of 6.
- **Write a New Trademark.** Every fifth advance can be a new Trademark. This new trademark should relate to the stories that you have told and represent new skills or interests, the accumulation of resources, or a changing reputation. A character can never have more than five Trademarks.

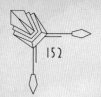
School of Hard Knocks

When you take an Advance, put a line through ten XP boxes and note how many boxes were ticks and how many were crosses.

- **Six or More Ticks.** You've had some wins and are currently feeling pretty good about life. No further effect.
- **Five Ticks & Five Crosses.** You've had ups and downs that have left you feeling drained. You begin the next Job with 1 less Moxie than usual. However, it can be refreshed as normal.
- **Six or More Crosses.** Life has been tough, and you've learned some lessons the hard way. You have had sleepless nights, hit the bottle hard, or indulged in a vice. You begin the next Job with D3 Conditions. These can be marked as levels in a single Condition or spread across multiple. You cannot begin a Job with three levels in a single Condition.

Carol Grimes has completed a few Jobs and accrued twelve XP. The player puts a line through ten boxes and gives Carol an Advance. Counting the ticks and crosses, they find that she has six crosses struck out, meaning she will start the next Job with one or more Conditions. The player rolls a D3, scoring 2 and decides to put both points into the Tired condition. They explain that Carol has been burning the midnight oil in her spare time, looking for her sister's killer.

CHANGES

During any Downtime, you can also change details about your character, should you feel it merited. You might rewrite an Edge to better reflect the character's skills or abilities as you learn about them through play. You can also change or replace a Flaw if an existing one has been resolved or overcome in some way, or if you feel a different problem will be more interesting to play. Likewise, you can rewrite Drives or Ties, representing changed goals or relationships. Any such changes should be discussed and agreed with the GM first.

Sometimes, a player may wish to change one of their Trademarks as it no longer fits the story. Perhaps there is no need for an Aviator, or maybe a Trauma has left the character so crippled that the Quick Trademark just doesn't make sense. In these situations, player and GM should discuss the issues and work to re-write the existing Trademark. It might be as simple as changing a name or tweaking the list of Traits. If it really is impossible to adjust the current Trademark, a GM can allow a player to switch it (and any attached Edges or related Advantages) for something new. The player should describe how they have used their Downtime to learn new skills or switch careers.

RETIREMENT

Eventually you may decide that it is time for your character to hang up their hat and retire. This might be at the end of a campaign, or just because a particular Rev's story has come to a logical conclusion. When considering the final chapter of your character's story, have a conversation with the GM and other players and discuss what might be an interesting and fitting ending for them. Do you want them to go out in a blaze of glory, or in a dramatic moment during a Job? Or will they quietly disappear into the night now or in a future Downtime? Planning in this way gives all the players and their characters an opportunity to contribute to a memorable finale for the Rev.

NEW REVS

When a character retires or dies you can introduce a new one. Create them in the same manner as your previous Rev. They also get a number of Advances equal to the previous character, but with their experience track unmarked.

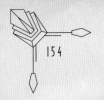

ON THE JOB

Revs do a wide variety of work – they undertake missions for desperate citizens and shadowy Ministry Agents; they pursue their own agendas; and they help radical groups grow in power and sow discontent. Sometimes they must carefully investigate strange mysteries or terrible crimes, while at other times they just set out to make some money, create havoc, or cause as much damage as possible! Each distinct scenario is called a Job and, while the details of each may be very different, they all share a similar structure that helps the Game Master organise the information and events, as well as ensure that the players have an entertaining time while uncovering secrets, rescuing victims, exploring the ruined wastelands, and bringing down dangerous organisations. Jobs generally fall into two broad types – missions and mysteries.

MISSIONS

A mission is any job where the characters are provided with a clear objective and then left to decide how to accomplish it. These are often the most straightforward of Jobs, though they can quickly become complicated due to wrong turns, poor choices, or the consequences of Checks. Preparing an interesting and entertaining mission is a simple process that can be done with just a little planning. You just need to keep in mind the "Rule of C.O.O.L."

- **Concept.** Start with a cool idea. What is the fun thing that will make players excited about this Job? This could be an interesting location, unique problem, nefarious villain, or fun piece of technology or gear. Beg, borrow, or steal from films, books, and TV shows for inspiration.

- **Objective.** Decide what goal the Revs must achieve. What person, piece of information, or thing do they need to find, protect, kill, or steal? How will they know when the Job is complete? Often laying out a simple but difficult goal will be enough for an entire evening's entertainment.
- **Obstacles.** Make a list of interesting problems or enemies that the Revs might face over the course of their mission. What stands in their way? What obstacle, foe, or tech is going to stop the characters from achieving their objective? It might be easiest to work backwards, starting with what "big" Threat must be overcome at the climax of the Job, and then noting three or four other interesting Scenes or encounters the characters might have along the way.
- **Link.** Consider how this Job ties in with the details already established about the characters and the setting. Can you link it to a character's past, an old friend, a Drive, or a Flaw? Or perhaps you can introduce a sneaky twist that will throw the characters into hot water and spark opportunities for new Jobs in the future. Find ways to weave this story into the broader lives of the characters.

Missions don't need to be complicated affairs with twists, turns, and convoluted subplots. In fact, you're better off keeping your plans relatively straightforward, as the nature of Checks will throw up all kinds of complications as you play. Keep things simple – an objective, an obstacle, and some motivated characters will see you through most of the time!

Planning for the next Job, you have an idea that a struggling actress asks the player characters to retrieve some expensive personal items from an ex-lover who lives in a penthouse in the Inner City. She cannot return to the apartment as the doorman and staff know her, and her former beau has threatened to have her taken away by the Ministry of Peace if she ever shows her face there again. This Job is going to be a heist! That's the cool concept and the objective sorted.

You make a list of interesting problems for the characters to overcome, including a very protective doorman, an elevator that requires a punch card (or a way around it), a robotic guard dog, and maybe an unexpected party of wealthy revellers. Thinking about it, a stealthy getaway, chase, or even a fight in the middle of a party in a luxury suite complete with jazz band, flappers, and bodyguards would make a fun climax. You jot these notes down.

Finally, for the link to the Revs, you remember one of the characters has the Drive "Bring down the Anti-Robot League". You decide the jilted actress is actually working for the League, and whatever the characters steal will go to fund their propaganda efforts. If the characters discover this information, they may have a tough choice to make.

MYSTERIES

Many Jobs may involve the investigation of a mystery or crime, such as uncovering the identity of the mad scientist terrorising the neighbourhood, finding the location of a lost piece of technology, or bringing a murderer to justice. Sometimes, an investigation will be a small part of a bigger Job, whereas, other times, it will be the central focus. In these cases, the GM should spend some time planning out the details, considering the character's Trademarks, Edges, and other abilities in order to present a satisfying mystery to be solved. Start by thinking about the following elements:

- **The Low-down.** This is the truth of the mystery – the facts as known only by the victim or the perpetrator. Begin by working out what the mystery is and who is behind it (and why). This information is usually for the GM's eyes only, at least until the players have unravelled the plot.
- **Web of Clues.** A series of clues, suspects, and Scenes that will lead characters from the inciting event of the Job to the dramatic solution of the mystery. Each person or place of interest should reveal new evidence that will ultimately lead the player characters to the showdown. A variety of clues that require a range of different skills and approaches to uncover is always the best option to get all the player characters involved in the action.
- **Showdown.** The climax of the mystery is a moment of exciting drama, where all the clues fall into place, the bad guy is stopped, the victim is rescued, and/or the mystery is solved. It might involve a fight, a chase, or a dramatic revelation before a group of assembled suspects.
- **Fallout.** The Job is over, but things may have changed – for the characters, their neighbourhood, or the city itself. Who benefitted from the Rev's actions, and who lost out? What are they going to do now? How will this lead to future Jobs?

Web of Clues

Once you know what has happened, who is responsible, and how the mystery might end, you need to create a web of clues for the player characters to discover and interpret. You do this by leaving a trail of breadcrumbs for the Revs to follow. Work backwards from the showdown, asking yourself at each step *"What do the characters need to know to get to this point?"* Whatever your answer is should become a clue attached to a person, place, or point of interest. Try and have two or more clues that lead to each important piece of information that the characters need so that, even if they miss the first one, they still have a chance to discover the facts from the second. Require different skills, abilities, or approaches to find the clues, so that everyone has an opportunity to contribute to solving the mystery. The clues can be as subtle or obvious as you like, and a combination of both is generally advisable. For each clue you create, ask yourself again how the characters will find this person, place, or piece of information, and continue working backwards until you get to the starting point of your story.

When you are done, you should have a list or flowchart detailing the web of clues and overarching plot of your mystery.

When your web of clues is complete, fill in the details. Give all the non-player characters names, make notes about the locations that might be visited, and prepare a list of Threats for the Revs to encounter. With this information complete, your Job is ready.

You have an idea for a mystery where an agent of the Ministry of Truth is killing witnesses to a crime. You decide a City Councilman murdered his lover, and the Ministry is helping to cover it up. The player characters are hired to find out who is killing locals in a Midtown neighbourhood. That's the crime, the culprit, and the motive sorted. For the showdown, you like the idea of a fight with the ministry agent, maybe on a rooftop, or in a power station. You now have all your key pieces and need to weave a web of clues that will get the Revs from their initial meeting with their client, a neighbourhood leader, to the fight with the agent. Working backwards, the final piece of information the characters need is the agent's identity and location, so you start by planting a few clues that will reveal this.

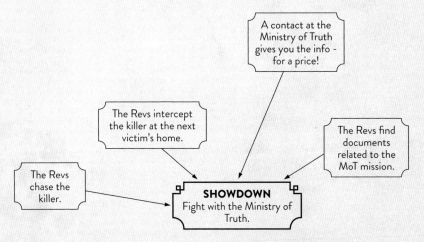

Next, create several clues that point to each of these clues. For instance, how do the character's find out that the Ministry of Truth is involved? What could lead them here? Or how are they able to intercept the killer at the next victim's home? Go through the same process for each clue you invent, until you have a list, mind map, or flowchart of people and places of interest that will lead from the hook to the showdown. The web of clues for this mystery might look like the one below.

Notice how most clues have multiple arrows pointing to them – this gives you lots of flexibility for how the Revs unravel the mystery.

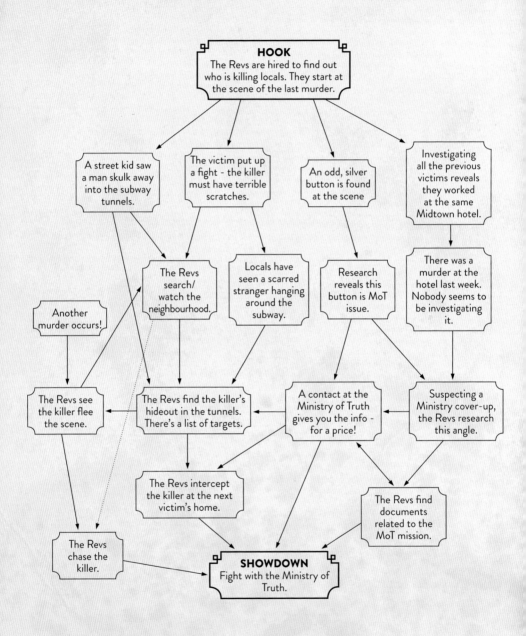

HOOK
The Revs are hired to find out who is killing locals. They start at the scene of the last murder.

A street kid saw a man skulk away into the subway tunnels.

The victim put up a fight - the killer must have terrible scratches.

An odd, silver button is found at the scene

Investigating all the previous victims reveals they worked at the same Midtown hotel.

The Revs search/ watch the neighbourhood.

Locals have seen a scarred stranger hanging around the subway.

Research reveals this button is MoT issue.

There was a murder at the hotel last week. Nobody seems to be investigating it.

Another murder occurs!

The Revs see the killer flee the scene.

The Revs find the killer's hideout in the tunnels. There's a list of targets.

A contact at the Ministry of Truth gives you the info - for a price!

Suspecting a Ministry cover-up, the Revs research this angle.

The Revs intercept the killer at the next victim's home.

The Revs find documents related to the MoT mission.

The Revs chase the killer.

SHOWDOWN
Fight with the Ministry of Truth.

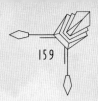

STRUCTURING JOBS

As explained in the Into Danger chapter (p.127), each Job follows a simple structure with a Hook, Gearing Up, Into Danger, and Downtime. It doesn't matter whether you are planning a mission or a mystery, each job should have the following elements:

- **Hook.** Take your cool ideas and devise a way to throw the characters right into the action. Perhaps they are approached by someone with a job, hear an interesting rumour, or are made an offer they cannot refuse? Think of it as the opening to a movie – you want to grab everyone's attention immediately and immerse them in the story. It's totally okay, advisable even, to begin with the Job already underway and the characters in the thick of the action. What cool moment might the characters be involved in as the curtain rises? A strong hook should get the players and their characters excited about the Job.
- **Gearing Up.** Either before the hook or shortly after it, the player characters should have an opportunity to grab some gear and make plans. Players should have a clear idea of what they have been engaged to do before acquiring their equipment. If the players always choose the same gear for their characters, it might already be recorded on their character sheet. In this case, you can skip the gearing up step.
- **Into Danger.** This is the sequence of Scenes from the inciting event to the exciting climax. The easiest way to prep a Job is to break it into a collection of rooms, locations, people, and situations that might be interacted with. Incorporate a variety of Scenes that require different skills and abilities and see if you can work in social encounters, moments of action, puzzles, and combat. Think about what the characters are good at and give them each a chance to shine.
- **Downtime.** Eventually the Job will end and the player characters will get to lick their wounds and reflect on the events they have been through. This usually happens when the goal of a given Job is achieved, though a period of Downtime might also occur if there is an extended lull in the action where everything seems to settle down and life seems a little bit normal for a while. During Downtime, the players go through the XP checklist and determine whether or not their characters grow and change because of what they have seen and done.

If you're stuck for ideas, use the Random Job Generator (p.215) to generate ideas for your own Jobs. Play around with the prompts you generate and think about how they might be combined to create something interesting and fun for your players.

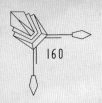

GAME MASTER ADVICE

As the GM, you will help to bring the world to life and throw the player characters into the turmoil of the dangerous future city, with its swarming masses, diabolical scientists, and unknowable automaton caretakers. You will present problems and puzzles to be solved, enemies to confront, and monstrous products of science to overcome. You will devise exciting Jobs for the characters to take on and challenge them in interesting and exciting ways. While it may sound daunting, it is not a difficult task if you fall back on the rules, your imagination, and common sense. This chapter provides some advice to help you run games that are fun for everyone at the table, yourself included.

CHARACTER CREATION

Before players create their characters, talk about the sorts of stories everyone is interested in telling. Discuss the kind of game everyone would like to play, the general tone of your story, and what features of the dieselpunk genre players are most interested in exploring. The Characters chapter (p.66) has several suggestions to get you started. As players make their characters, ask them questions about their Trademarks and Edges, and work together to discover their history, motivations, and place in the world. Help the players develop their characters' Flaws, Drives, and Ties, fleshing out the details so that they are more than just a generic statement. The more information that everyone has about each of the characters, the more real they will feel and the easier they will be to roleplay. Make a note of all the interesting stuff that the players come up with so that you can draw on it in play, weaving details of the characters' lives into the Jobs they pursue.

Also ensure that you take the time to establish some safety tools and set boundaries. *Tomorrow City* delves into elements of horror, science-gone-mad, and the darker side of human nature, and it is important to address this upfront. What are people okay with, what is going to be relegated to the background, and what is totally off-limits?

RUNNING THE GAME

While a great deal of responsibility falls on the shoulders of the GM, the following ideas will help to keep the game flowing and the players engaged.

Bring the World to Life

Create a world that feels alive. Fill it with characters that belong, have their own agendas, and will get on with their lives in response to, or in spite of, the actions of the player characters. Give the NPCs names and evocative descriptions – and note them down so you don't forget later! Villains should have goals and plans to achieve them.

Places should be just as evocative, helping to establish the setting and tone of your game. Make them interesting, challenging, and fun. Use the descriptions in the The City of Tomorrow chapter (p.16) to add cool details. When describing scenes, do what the great pulp writers did and layer description on top of description, using figurative language and drawing on all the senses; don't just describe the colours of the Cable Market, but also the sounds and smells and what it's like to taste the strange gruel the cook in the Great Factory serves you. Use all the tools of novels and film to draw the players into the unfolding story.

Be a Fan

Be a fan of both the players and their characters. They are the cool protagonists of your story, so set them up to show off what they can do. A character's Trademarks, Edges, Flaws, Drives, and Ties are flags that tell you what each player is interested in, so use this information to guide the Scenes you create.

Give the players a sense of agency and let them make choices that feel meaningful to the plot. Listen to what they say, to you and to each other, and incorporate it into the story in interesting or unexpected ways. Always remember that the players are just as responsible for the story as the GM.

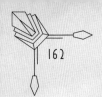
Ask Questions

Ask players questions so that you understand their actions, motivations, and goals, then use this information to create more cool moments for them. When a new Scene begins, ask players where their characters are, or where they want to be. When players make statements about their characters, dig further. What is their home neighbourhood like? Why do they hate the Peace Officers so much? What is it about the robot bartender that makes them uneasy?

Ask either open-ended questions or leading questions and then use the answers to add details to a Scene or bring information into the story at a later stage. Every answer adds to the world and presents another opportunity for the players to engage with the story.

Do What the Fiction Demands

Part of the GM's role is to apply the rules through the lens of the story. Pay attention to the details that have been established and always follow the fiction. React to the player characters' actions with logic and imagination, presenting consequences that make sense in the context of the story.

Put pressure on the characters when appropriate, hit them hard when they mess up, and reward them when they come through a tough situation. Following the fiction creates a consistency that makes the world more believable and gives players confidence to continue to throw their characters into the action.

GETTING THE MOST OUT OF SCENES

Jobs play out in a sequence Scenes, one after the other, until the characters achieve their goal, reach their destination, or defeat the villain. Then you get to do it all over again! There are no hard and fast rules about how many Scenes you should have in a Session or Job, or what should happen in each, but here are a few pieces of advice that will keep your Scenes focused, moving forwards, and entertaining.

Enter Late, Exit Early

An old film-making adage is to "enter late, exit early", meaning that you should focus your Scenes on the cool and exciting parts. Begin Scenes where the interesting stuff is about to happen and keep the pace going from there. How far into the Scene can you start and still have things make sense? Start there! The characters are pinned down, the deal has gone sideways, the Hood Scum have just arrived. It's totally okay to set the Scene up with a little exposition and throw the characters straight into the action.

Likewise, when the bad guys or obstacles have been overcome, the clues found, or the objective achieved, end the Scene. Move the characters on to the next important moment of the story. There is no need for a long, detailed wrap-up – the characters defeat the guy, get the thing, and escape in the nick of time. Scene done, on to the next.

Give Players Something to Do

Don't just tell players that they are in a room or situation and leave them to guess what they should be doing. Every Scene should have an objective, a danger to avoid, a character to talk to, or something to investigate. Don't leave the players trying to work out what they need to do in the Scene, doing so can drag the story out and frustrate the players.

Think Cinematically

Describe Scenes and action like it's a movie or novel. Use the language of film – pan, zoom, and cut – describe an establishing shot, or give the players a close-up of the monstrous aberration's face and their jagged kaleidoscope eye. Use descriptions like *"As the camera pans across the room you see..."* or *"We see a low shot of the building you are about to enter, its art deco ornaments glinting in the sun..."*. Describe impactful actions in detail, imagining them as slow-motion shots. Don't be afraid to cut away to give the narrative structure, show what the villain is doing, or tell the story out of chronological order.

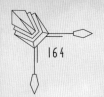

If a Scene begins to falter or the characters seem lost for what to do next, reveal something dramatic or interesting. It could be anything that spurs the characters into action, be that giving them a new clue to follow or a new danger to respond to. Perhaps a character they were going to meet later arrives now, somebody suddenly drops dead, or a convenient phone call unlocks a helpful clue.

MASTERING CHECKS

Every time you call for a Check, it should mean something interesting is going to happen, no matter the result. Nothing will slow a game down faster than rolling for every little thing that isn't going to have any real impact on the story.

Establish the intent of an action before a Check. If the character is attempting something dangerous, ensure that the player understands what is at risk should they fail. Be clear about the consequences of actions up front and be consistent with their application. When an action is resolved, do what seems most interesting and appropriate. Feel free to ask for input from the players and collaborate on the outcomes.

Check Difficulty

Use the Scene details and common sense to determine how hard an action is. Reading down the list of modifiers is a good start and paying particular attention to positioning, Scene Tags, and scale will give you clues as to whether the characters are going to have it easy or are in a whole mess of trouble.

If players are succeeding too easily, ramp up the pressure. Don't be afraid to pile on the Danger Dice; player characters are both capable and durable. Look at how you are applying modifiers and ensure that you are as particular and careful with how you use Threats as the players are with their characters. Apply Danger Dice for a Threat's advantages, put the characters under time or resource pressure, and remember that Conditions and Injuries can make Checks tougher. It is always okay to add an extra Danger Die or two to an action simply because it is hard!

If players are failing a lot of Checks and finding things too hard, help them to identify the advantages they have in any given situation. Encourage them to assess and prepare before diving in, and don't forget that Conditions and Tags applied to Threats might add Action Dice to a pool. Working together and playing smart should instantly give the player characters a boost.

PRESSURE

Pressure is a tool for creating tension and providing unexpected moments of danger. Make sure you track it somewhere that enables the players to watch it with growing dread! When the Pressure reaches a total of 6, something bad happens. This could be anything related to the story or the current situation the characters find themselves in. Some examples might include the following:

- The character's current situation gets much worse (there are more enemies than expected, a specific item is required, someone raises an alarm)
- The Danger Rating of a Threat increases, or it reveals a new ability, skill, or advantage
- Time passes (now the players have to fight the villain only minutes before their death machine activates!)
- The villain or adversary strikes again (the characters are attacked, another victim is found, or an explosion rocks Midtown…)
- The villain's plans progress (either behind the scenes, or in an obvious manner)
- A new, unrelated Threat is introduced to the story (an old enemy turns up, the Badges get involved, a rival group of Revs arrive)

For maximum effect, the new danger should be obvious and occur soon after the Pressure reaches 6. Perhaps the characters hear sirens, or an approaching enemy, or screams in a nearby building. Perhaps they realise that someone has gone missing, they don't have the right equipment, or their attacks are not as effective as they should be. If the repercussions of the Pressure are happening off-screen, consider using a cut-away shot to show what is happening elsewhere, or worry the players with the menacing phrase *"I'll let you know what that means in one moment…"*.

Reset the Clock

Reset the Pressure to 0 after you reveal the new trouble. You can do this immediately to keep the squeeze on the characters, which is particularly good in high-tension situations, such as combat or other altercations. Alternatively, you can wait to reset the Pressure at the start of the next Scene, or even after a rest. You might do this if the characters have already gone through a number of intense Scenes or are purposely taking their time to do things carefully.

MASTERING MYSTERIES

Many *Tomorrow City* Jobs will involve characters investigating disappearances, strange devices, or other weird happenings. As the player characters investigate a mystery, they should have the opportunity to uncover whatever clues are there. You never want to be in a situation where the investigators do not find an essential clue, as this could result in dead ends and frustration for both you and the players. Let's look at some ways to get clues into the character's hands.

- **Natural Talent.** Speaking to the right people, asking appropriate questions, or looking in the right direction might let characters automatically find a clue. In such situations, you can simply tell the players what information is found. This could be particularly applicable if a character has a Trademark that suggests an affinity with the person, place, or object of interest. This approach ensures that nothing is missed but can sometimes feel a little anticlimactic. The key to making it work is through interesting description and entertaining roleplay.
- **Investigating.** Another approach is to assume that the characters will find the clue, but they must make a Check to see how effectively, thoroughly, or quickly they do so. The type of Check will depend on the investigator's actions and what they are trying to uncover. In these situations, even a failure might turn up a useful piece of information, but at a significant cost, such as time, a Condition, or some other trouble. This is not to say that every clue must be found – sometimes a failure is just that and the clue remains undiscovered. In these situations, characters will have to try a new approach or investigate a different lead to get where they need to be.
- **Dumb Luck.** A final option, if used sparingly and subtly, is to just have a clue fall into the character's laps. For example, someone might give them a hot tip, the criminal just happens to show up at an opportune moment, or a helpful contact interprets a clue. Such a device might be useful to patch some unforeseen plot hole, or to help the characters out when they seem hopelessly lost or confused. However, don't be too obvious about it, and don't do it too often, as it can take away the players' sense of agency and make them feel like their characters' actions don't really matter.

Help the players find clues by giving clear descriptions and pointing out interesting details. Some things to keep in mind include:

- When characters succeed at Checks, give them the information they need to progress
- Don't be obtuse – what seems obvious to you isn't always clear to the players
- If in doubt, have NPCs speak plainly and overshare
- Have clues be actionable – a name to research, a place to visit, or a revelation that connects two previously unrelated clues

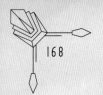

Sometimes an investigation will flounder despite your best efforts. When players seem unsure how to progress, suggest courses of action or remind them of what they already know. Say things like *"You have a list of witnesses to question"*, or *"Nobody has actually searched the room yet"*, or *"There's a pipe runner at the back of the break room trying hard to avoid eye contact"*. If the players end up way off track, drop a clue in their laps; perhaps a piece of evidence that was meant to be found elsewhere is in their current location, or someone can provide the same information that a missed witness was going to share. If they misinterpreted a clue, have someone or something add extra information to clarify. Introduce new clues based on the actions of the characters to guide them back on track.

MASTERING COMBATS

The key to running exciting combats is to be heavy on the description. Begin with a clear explanation of the environment, enemies, and situation. Point out the important features, paying particular attention to the dangers and opportunities – *"There's a big guy with a pattern gun standing by the door and sharp pieces of machinery are scattered across the floor"*. Once the combat has begun, continue to use clear and evocative description. Nobody ever just stands still and punches; they sidestep and swing, reel from a blow, duck behind cover, or clench their fists in rage before charging. Most combats won't last very long, so make them memorable.

How Many Threats?

Threats, such as hoods, robots, and Ministry agents, are described in the next chapter (p.170). Generally, a single alert enemy or group of two to three mooks is a reasonable challenge for one player character. Most Threats require two or three successes to overcome, which means two or three opportunities for the situation to get worse! The more enemies that are in a Scene, the more complicated things will get, so use the Tough Guy and Mook rules to keep the number of Threats manageable. If the Revs find themselves seriously outnumbered, ensure that there are plenty of environmental features for them to take advantage of and a way of escaping should things go south. Fleeing a dangerous or terrifying enemy is always a valid option!

FLAWS & MOXIE

While a character's Flaws are important features of their personality and backstory, they are also an integral element of the game's core mechanics. They need to come into play for a character to refresh their used Moxie points. As using Moxie is both fun and an easy way to improve a character's chances of success, players will soon find the resource depleted and look for ways to introduce their Flaws – you want to be ready for this.

During character creation, encourage players to write two Flaws that can be used in clearly different situations. It is also a good practice to note down each character's Flaws so you can plan for complications that let players hook into their troubles. If a character has difficulty keeping their emotions in check, throw them into a tough social situation. If they have an old injury or physical drawback, present them with challenges that will be much harder if the player wants to highlight their Flaw.

Don't be shy in pointing out when a character's Flaw might be appropriate to draw on or asking a player if one of their Flaws might be triggered as the consequence of a Check. Working together like this will avoid the dreaded situation where a player realises that they need a top-up of Moxie only after it's too late.

REWARDS

Reward players and characters for the things they achieve, such as when a player does something cool, or a character achieves something significant related to the Job or their Drive. Rewards do not have to be huge advantages – even a small bonus can make a player feel like the efforts they have made and the troubles their character has suffered have been worthwhile. You might give a reward when:

- A player roleplays in a way that improves everyone's enjoyment
- A character discovers an important detail related to their Drive
- Characters explore their Ties in an engaging and/or entertaining way
- A character does something cool or dramatic that causes everyone to stop, cheer, or cry

Any story element can be a reward, such as introducing a situation or character a player wants to engage with or hooking a dramatic moment into a character's backstory. More tangible rewards include:

- Gaining a piece of gear or changing one or more Tags on an item. A single use item (or one dose of a serum) can be a handy bonus during a Job
- Refreshing a single Moxie point or Cred point (A character can never have more than their maximum value)
- A free Boon that can be used on a future successful Check in the current scene. A GM may stipulate a specific use or type of Check
- The temporary use of an Advantage the character does not have
- Turning one or more crosses on the XP track into ticks, representing a reversal in fortunes
- Ticking an extra box on the XP track

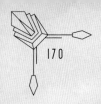

THREATS

A Threat is an enemy, obstacle, or other problem that the Revs must overcome during the course of their Job. They can be anything from a hood with a gun, to a blazing inferno, an arrogant clerk, or sinking boat. Whatever gets in the way of the player characters achieving their goals is a Threat. Each Threat is defined by a short profile, including its Name, Drive, Tags, and Actions.

| THREAT NAME | DANGER RATING | X |
	GRIT	X
A description of the Threat.		
Drive	What the Threat wants. This is usually an immediate desire or goal.	
Tags	The Threat's strengths, weaknesses, skills, equipment, and flaws. These Tags might add Action or Danger Dice to Checks, depending on how the characters interact with the Threat.	
Actions	What the Threat does, or what they might do. These are both a guide to roleplaying the Threat and a list of potential consequences that it might inflict on the player characters during a Scene. Use a Threat's Actions as a hint to how it behaves around or responds to the characters.	

Danger Rating: A Threat's Danger Rating is an indicator of how competent and/or dangerous they are. When making a Check to interact with or overcome a Threat, add Danger Dice equal to its Danger Rating. Additional Danger Dice or Action Dice can then be added based on the situation and the Threat's Tags.

Grit: How much Damage a Threat can suffer before it is taken out or overcome.

ATTITUDES & REACTIONS

How a Threat reacts to the characters will always depend on the fiction. However, when encountering strangers with no prior knowledge of or relationship to the player characters, or with no specific agenda, you can roll 2D6 to determine their attitude.

2D6	ATTITUDES & REACTIONS
2-3	Hostile. The Threat is antagonistic or aggressive
4-5	Dislike. The Threat demonstrates obvious scorn, distaste, or aversion
6-8	Indifferent. The Threat shows no obvious curiosity, care, or dislike
9-10	Approachable. The Threat has a friendly disposition
11-12	Helpful. The Threat is eager to assist in a manner proportionate to their skills or position

HARM

Threats suffer Harm just like the player characters do and can receive a number of points of Damage equal to their Grit value. If a Threat's Grit is reduced to 0, it is taken out in whatever manner is most appropriate. Threats can also suffer Conditions in the same way the player characters do. Use your common sense as to whether a specific Condition can affect a Threat, based on its description and purpose.

Mooks

Any Threat can be designated as a Mook. Mooks are very weak opponents with a single point of Grit. However, they keep their full Danger Rating and Tags. The GM can choose to form Mooks into squads of two or more, which then act as if they were a single character, meaning the squad only gets one action per Turn. As the squad takes Damage, remove Mooks from it – one for each point of Damage suffered. When a player character acts against a Mook squad, they suffer an additional Danger Dice for being outnumbered.

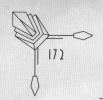

Emile shoots at a squad of four Hood Scum who have been designated as Mooks. He builds his dice pool, making sure to add a Danger Die for being outnumbered and another for the Hood Scum's Danger Rating. His Check result is a success and one Boon, for a total of 3 Damage. The player describes Emile pulling the trigger of his revolver several times and three of the thugs falling under the hail of bullets. There is a single Hood Scum remaining in the squad, which means that Emile is no longer outnumbered.

Tough Guys

Particularly resilient enemies or major antagonists can be designated as a Tough Guy. Tough Guys have additional Grit points equal to twice the number of player characters facing them.

Emile, Carol, and Alexi are fighting a RoboGuard that the GM has designated as a Tough Guy. Normally, a RoboGuard would have 6 Grit, but this one has 12 – an extra 6 from facing three player characters.

Villains

Major antagonists and important NPCs can be designated as Villains. Create Villains using the full rules for creating a player character. Consider their function in the story, choose Trademarks, Edges, and Flaws as appropriate and treat them like any Threat's Tags. Villains suffer Harm like Revs.

Non-Player Characters

An NPC is a character in the story that is neither a Threat, nor a player character. They are often allies, extras, or bit-players. Some Trademarks also grant characters subordinate NPCs, such as lackeys or animal companions. NPCs suffer Damage and Conditions in the same way that Threats do. In combat, they will act when the GM decides it is appropriate – allies and companions will usually act with the player character(s) they are helping.

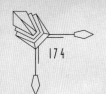

THREATS & GEAR

Threats don't interact with gear in the same way Revs do. They are assumed to have the equipment or items that make sense for whatever they are. If an item is particularly important to the Threat, it might be listed as a Tag. In these cases, apply Action or Danger Dice to Checks as the circumstances require.

Well-armoured or particularly tough Threats will have a higher Grit value. If they have a Tag such as *Armour, Made of Metal*, or *Iron Hide*, simply add a Danger Die to Checks whenever a character attempts to injure them.

Threats may be equipped with weapons, serums, tools, or vehicles as the GM deems fit, but most of the time it will not be necessary to track the specific details.

MINISTRY AGENTS

The Ministries oversee almost every aspect of life in the city, from law enforcement and sanitation to traffic signals and taxation. They are enormous bureaucracies with both literal and figurative armies keeping them running.

BADGES	DANGER RATING	1
	GRIT	5

	Named for the large silver shield they wear on their black uniform; Badges are police officers in the employ of the Ministry of Peace. They ensure crimes, public disturbances, and troublemakers are dealt with swiftly, if not always justly.
Drive	Keep the streets peaceful
Tags	Bully, Restrain, Brawl, Authority, Law, Stun Baton
Actions	Stare you down, Move you along, Give you a beating, Call for backup, Arrest you

- **Detective.** These hard-nosed investigators make it their business to know yours. They gain the *Investigate* Tag.
- **Patrol Team.** Pairs of Badges in a patrol car, or occasionally on heavy motorcycles. They gain the *Drive* Tag and are equipped with radios to call for backup or an observation blimp.
- **Riot Bull.** Highly trained Badges, they are often well armed and armoured. Their black metal riot shields are sometimes called "Coffin Lids". They gain +2 Grit and the *Deflect* Tag.

| BUREAUCRAT | DANGER RATING | 0 |
| | GRIT | 2 |

Focused, pedantic, and officious, bureaucrats fill every level of office in the Ministries. They are the primary workforce, acting as clerks, managers, registrars, record keepers, and attendants.

Drive	Do my job to the highest standard
Tags	Bureaucracy, Research
Actions	Demand paperwork, Make you wait, Alert a manager, Lose your paperwork, Cut through red tape, Tip someone off, Reveal a secret

- **Management.** Be they a department head, executive, station chief, or deputy liaison to a senior clerk, bureaucrats in management roles hold on to their meagre authority any way they can. They gain the *Bully* and *Cunning* Tags.

| MINISTRY OPERATIVE | DANGER RATING | 2 |
| | GRIT | 6 |

Elite, loyal agents in the employ of various Ministries, these operatives are secretly dispatched to undertake business that cannot be entrusted to anyone else.

Drive	Protect the Ministry's interests
Tags	Break & Enter, Stealth, Shoot, Intimidate
Actions	Steal something, Hurt you or an ally, Erase information, Threaten you or the ones you love, Put you in a compromising positions

- **Zero.** Cold-blooded killers and assassins, Zeroes are dangerous operatives and experts in wet-work of all kinds. They gain the *Professional Killer* and *Duck & Weave* Tags.
- **Honey Trap.** These seductive operatives manipulate targets and lure them into compromising situations. They gain the *Attractive* and *Charming* Tags.
- **Peace Officer.** The Ministry of Peace's sinister secret police, they often arrive in the middle of the night to take targets away. They gain the *Restrain* and *Brawl* Tags.

PROPAGANDIST	DANGER RATING	1
	GRIT	4

Smartly dressed, charming, and clever, every Ministry employs a cadre of public relations specialists to deliver information and keep the masses happy.

Drive	Deliver the Ministry's truth
Tags	Charming, Spin Doctor, Cool Under Pressure
Actions	Deceive you, Stall for time, Twist your words, Turn the public against you, Have you detained

- **Ink Finger.** Experts in counterfeiting and doctoring official records, these propagandists often work behind the scenes to re-write the truth. They lose *Charming* but gain the *Counterfeit* and *Research* Tags.
- **Smooth Badge.** Working for the police, these spin doctors dress in immaculate uniforms adorned with badges and medals. They gain the *Intimidate* Tag.

SPINDLE GUARD	DANGER RATING	2
	GRIT	4

The City Council's personal protection detail, the Spindle Guard are recognisable by their chrome cuirass and mirrored faceplates. Indoctrinated through a demanding regime of psychometric conditioning and specialised serums, they act without question to protect The Spindle and the Council.

Drive	Protect the City Council at any cost
Tags	Veteran Soldiers, Deadly Weapons, Fiercely Loyal, Threaten
Actions	Stop you, Demand to see your papers, Arrest you, Intimidate you

- **Ironside Trooper.** Piloting the heavy diesel-powered Ironside armour, these troopers are called in when the threat of force alone is not enough. They are equipped with light machine guns or heavy weapons and gain +6 Grit and the *Deflect* and *Strong* Tags.

CITIZENS

Encounters with the people of the city are common, from questioning local bartenders and cab drivers to interacting with store owners and domestic staff. The citizens of Tomorrow City represent all the various walks of life you would expect to see in a thriving metropolis.

DOMESTIC STAFF	DANGER RATING	0
	GRIT	3

	The hardworking staff of a wealthy household, hotel, apartment building, or other service provider. Some are terrible gossips, some are lazy slouches, and others jealously protect jobs that offer security, prestige, or good tips.
Drive	Keep my job
Tags	Stamina, Notice, Blend In, Gossip
Actions	Keep a secret, Ignore you, Spread a rumour, Spill a secret, Take a bribe

- **Driver.** Private chauffeurs, cab drivers, and personal pilots ferry the wealthy about the city in a relative comfort. They gain the *Drive* or *Pilot* Tag and the *Know a Shortcut* Tag.
- **Doorman.** Well-dressed and formal, doormen, butlers, desk clerks, and concierges all have a certain air of authority. They gain the *Strong-Willed* Tag, and some may also have the *Intimidate* Tag.
- **Robotic.** Any simple domestic task can be done by a robot. They lose *Gossip* but gain +2 Grit and the *Made of Metal* Tag.

MECHANIC	DANGER RATING	0
	GRIT	4

	Experts at maintaining machines and vehicles, repairing things when they break down, and scrounging just the right part for a client, mechanics are often covered in grease and grime, and deal with machines better than people.
Drive	Keep things running
Tags	Repair, Vehicles, Analyse a Machine
Actions	Fix something, Keep a vehicle running just a little longer, Overcharge for parts, Sabotage a machine, Make things messy or dirty

- **Pipe Runner.** They climb across the city, laying new cables and ducting, or pulling it up as the districts turn about The Spindle. They operate in teams, with rival companies often sabotaging each other's work. They gain the *Parkour*, *Navigate*, and *Sabotage* Tags.

PHYSICIAN	DANGER RATING	0
	GRIT	3

Steady hands, an expensive qualification, or access to large amounts of serums makes a physician a welcome addition to any neighbourhood.	
Drive	Heal the sick or injured
Tags	First aid, Medicine, Serum Expert, Educated, Arrogant
Actions	Patch you up, Administer a shot, Write a prescription, Drug you, Convince you there's nothing wrong

- **Combat Medic.** With skills honed on distant battlefields, these medics' methods are not always orthodox, but are effective. They lose *Educated* and *Arrogant* but gain +1 Danger Rating and the *Veteran* Tag.
- **Cutter.** Part drug dealer, part street surgeon, many of the poorer neighbourhoods have no one else to turn to when they get sick. They gain +1 Danger Rating and the *Poison Expert* and *Knives* Tags.

REPORTER	DANGER RATING	0
	GRIT	4

Muckrakers, gossip columnists, paparazzi, and tabloid reporters have a nose for a good story and a bad habit of sticking it where they're not wanted. They stalk celebrities and city officials and flock to public disturbances like scavengers on roadkill.	
Drive	Get the scoop
Tags	Nose for a Story, Eye for details, Embellish a Story, Interrogate, Gossip
Actions	Get you to open up, Catch you in a lie, Publish rumours or lies, Expose you to danger

- **Paparazzi.** Professional photographers and serial pests, they often have high quality cameras, film cameras, or even a cam-bot. They lose *Interrogate* and *Embellish a Story* but gain the *Photography* and *Stealth* Tags.
- **Blackmailer.** Sometimes reporters just seize an opportunity, while at other times unscrupulous souls make it their business to blackmail in return for money or power. Blackmailers lose *Interrogate* but gain the *Intimidate* Tag.

SCIENTIST	DANGER RATING	0
	GRIT	3

Seekers of knowledge and champions of reason, scientists infest the city, congregating in schools, private clubs, and secret laboratories. Some conduct legitimate research, but just as many delve into esoteric topics and use questionable practices.

Drive	Unravel how the world works
Tags	Science, Research, Investigate
Actions	Barrage you with facts, Ask way too many questions, Become distracted, Steal an interesting device, Leave you with more questions than answers

- **Philomaths.** Obsessive and dangerous, these scientists pursue knowledge with little regard for the consequences of their research. They gain the *Serum Expert* and *A Little Unhinged* Tags.

SOCIALITE	DANGER RATING	1
	GRIT	3

Wealthy skyrisers, trust fund brats, politicians, and celebrities make it their business to be seen at all the most glamorous parties and fashionable nightspots. They are often famous for little more than their name.

Drive	Be the talk of the City
Tags	Charm, Money, Arrogant, Inner City Contacts
Actions	Draw all the attention, Ridicule you, Seduce you, Invite you, Point out your flaws, Pay for someone or something to go away

- **Playboy.** With plenty of money and time on their hands, the young and rich often indulge in parties that go on for days. They make a game of seduction and don't care who they hurt along the way. They gain the *Seduction* Tag.
- **Performer.** Actors, musicians, lounge singers, and film makers often make a living on the party circuit. Sometimes they are genuine celebrities, while other times they are just the latest muse or plaything of the rich and powerful. Performers lose Arrogant but gain the *Perform* and *Make a Scene* Tags.

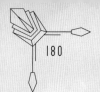

AUTOMATONS & ROBOTS

Automatons and robots are machines imbued with limited intelligence that makes them capable of performing a variety of tasks. Automatons are advanced artificial beings that draw upon the power and intellect of Mother to operate independently and engage in complex activities. Some are at least as intelligent as the average citizen. Robots, on the other hand, require programming or clear instructions to perform simple, repetitive tasks.

While most automatons and robots have a humanoid form, they lack any capacity to understand or evoke human emotion. Many automatons (and some smarter robots) have self-preservation sub-routines that will cause them to act in their own self-interest at times.

All automatons and robots suffer +1 Damage from weapons with the *Electro* tag, as it interferes with their machine-brains. They are immune to the *Shaken, Poisoned*, and *Tired* Conditions.

| ANGEL | DANGER RATING | 3 |
	GRIT	13
Perched upon The Spindle like gold or chrome-clad gargoyles, angels are sophisticated automatons that Mother uses to guide the citizens of Tomorrow City. Each is a unique construct, ten feet tall and fashioned like a beautiful man or woman with glorious chrome wings and a telescreen in place of their heads. They soar across the city skyline, accumulating data, assessing situations, and delivering messages directly from Mother.		
Drive	Be the messenger of Mother	
Tags	Unknowably Inhuman, Awe-inspiring, Steel Sinews, Huge, Graceful Flight, Razor Sharp Sword	
Actions	Fill you with awe, Frighten you, Deliver a message, Warn you	

- **Hermes.** The most famous of the Angels, Hermes is also known as Mother's Voice. In place of a telescreen, its head is an array of loudspeakers and instead of a sword, it carries a burning torch. Hermes appears when Mother wishes to make an important proclamation. It gains the *Intimidating* and *Must be Heard* Tags.

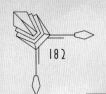

BROKEN DOUGHBOY	DANGER RATING	1
	GRIT	8

A relic of The Long War, it is unclear whether broken doughboys are entirely robots, or if they were once human. Their metal bodies are designed to look like uniformed soldiers, complete with helmet, though most are rusting, dented, and very worn. They are commonly found employed as security bots or bodyguards.

Drive	To serve, fight, and die
Tags	Shoot, Fight, Trench Warfare, Old & Rusting
Actions	Hit you hard, Take cover, Impale you on a bayonet, Prepare defensive position, Charge an enemy

CHERUB	DANGER RATING	1
	GRIT	6

Copper-skinned automatons fashioned in the image of a Renaissance cherub, they have saucer-like eyes and speak in an echoing voice like that of a child down a well. They creep across rooftops and beneath sewer grates, watching the city's inhabitants and reporting back to Mother.

Drive	Watch and report
Tags	Awareness, Night Vision, Climb, Quiet
Actions	Observe you, Report on you, Narrate your actions, Whisper warnings

ORPHAN	DANGER RATING	2
	GRIT	6

An automaton that has lost its connection with Mother. Often damaged, rusting or falling apart, they wander the city, behaving erratically until some sight, sound or interaction sparks a memory of its former purpose. Many attempt to dress in human clothes, which only adds to their disturbing appearance.

Drive	Find a purpose
Tags	Disturbing Appearance, Confused Programming, Steel Body
Actions	Question you, Offer to help, Suddenly turn on you, Speak cryptically, Malfunction

- **Orphaned Watcher.** The most dangerous of orphans, these broken automatons use their bladed hand to rend flesh and sow fear in the neighbourhoods they wander into. They gain the *Long Sharp Blades* and *Bloodthirsty* Tags.

| **ROBOGUARD** | **DANGER RATING** | 1 |
| | **GRIT** | 6 |

Purpose-built to work as bodyguards and sentries, the RoboGuard has become a staple in warehouses on Rimside, where cynical factory owners don't trust humans to keep their stock or machines safe. Most RoboGuards are seven feet tall with huge fists.

Drive	Guard this place
Tags	Alert, Fight, Iron Plating, Grappling Hands, Slow
Actions	Spot you, Alert the authorities, Detain you, Hit you hard

- **BoxerBot.** Modified to compete in illegal robot fighting competitions, a BoxerBot's grappling hands are replaced with large steel boxing gloves. They lose *Grappling Hands* and *Slow* and gain +2 Grit and the *Heavy Fists* Tag (4 Damage).

| **ROBOTIC HOUND** | **DANGER RATING** | 1 |
| | **GRIT** | 4 |

A robotic hound used for security everywhere from glamorous penthouses to warehouses and factories. Most have the proportions of a large dog, though they can come in all shapes and sizes.

Drive	Protect my master
Tags	Alert, Leap, Razor Teeth, Run
Actions	Run you down, Bark loudly, Alert the master, Bite

- **Exotic Forms.** It is fashionable amongst skyrisers to commission robotic pets in the form of exotic animals, styled with intricate designs and inlaid with precious metals. They gain the *Flashy* Tag and any others appropriate to the chosen animal form.

WATCHER	DANGER RATING	3
	GRIT	8

Sinister, dark copper automatons with long bladed claws on their left hand, watchers often appear where there is unrest in the city – though it is unclear if they arrive before or after the trouble begins. They warn citizens to keep out of city business, intervene to protect important infrastructure, or occasionally punish those who have transgressed against Mother's plans.

Drive	Be the hands of Mother
Tags	Intimidating Presence, Steel Sinews, Fight, Long Sharp Blades
Actions	Threaten you, Hold you back, Watch your suffering, Slice you open

- **Deadly Blades.** A Watcher's close combat attacks always count as *Deadly*, dealing 3 Damage to Revs.

EXPERIMENTS GONE WRONG

Whether intentionally built to meet some need of an ambitious but misguided creator, or a horrifying accident, the following Threats represent some of the misbegotten and pitiable creatures that might be found in the dark recesses of the city.

BODY HORROR

When describing failed experiments, lean into the grotesque. Open wounds, stitches and staples, mutations and disease, things that pulse and throb, obvious medical procedures, and zombification are all common tropes. When introducing these elements, do keep in mind the safety tools and decisions made at the start of play to ensure everyone continues to enjoy the story.

| BRAIN IN A JAR | DANGER RATING | 1 |
| | GRIT | 3 |

Literally a brain in a jar, this intelligence is kept alive with complicated machinery and electronics, interacting with the world via telescreens and speakers. Extremely rare, they were intended to preserve the consciousness and knowledge of great thinkers and scientists, but the state of disembodiment has driven them quite mad.

Drive	Escape this jar
Tags	Genius, History, Cunning, Persuasive Liar, Network of Spies, Quite Mad
Actions	Tell you a dangerous truth, Conceal their motives, Hire you for an important job, Trick you into helping them, Convince you to swap places

- **Ambulatory Brain.** These brains have escaped the confines of the vast machinery that contains them and now control or ride a robotic body. They gain +1 Danger Rating, +3 Grit and the *Robotic Body* Tag. Add other Tags, such as *Spider Legs*, *Razor Claws* or *Strong*, as you see fit.

| LIVING CADAVER | DANGER RATING | 1 |
| | GRIT | 4 |

A corpse, reanimated with robot machinery or stolen automaton parts. Metal rods, cables, and cogs project from their rotting flesh, tearing bloodless wounds as they move. Intended as a cheap, tireless workforce, they know nothing but their resentment and hatred for the living.

Drive	Punish the living
Tags	Not Alive (Neither the Deadly nor Electro Tags affect this creature)
Actions	Chase you, Hunt you, Bite & claw you, Overwhelm you with their numbers, Cry out in rage, Call to others

- **Reanimator.** These hate-filled corpses retain memories of their past life as inventors, mechanics, or scientists. They use this knowledge to build more living cadavers from their victims. They gain the *Corpse Builder* and *Cunning* Tags.

SERUM BRUTE	**DANGER RATING**	**2**
	GRIT	**10**

Monstrously large men and women, their muscle tissue and bone structure increased beyond what should be possible through a regime of drugs, serums, and radium exposure. Their backs and shoulders are covered with auto-injectors that allow them to instantly dose themselves with serums.

Drive	Flex my muscles and demonstrate my power
Tags	Huge, Strong, Brawl, Cocktail of Serums, Lumbering
Actions	Break or crush something, Use a serum, Intimidate you, Hit you hard, Take damage and laugh

- **Auto-Injectors.** A serum brute can use any one serum as a Free Action each turn. Effects and side effects apply as normal.
- **Rage Brute.** Subjected to enormous pain during experimentation, these brutes have become little more than feral animals filled with rage. They gain the *Mighty Rage* Tag and are immune to the *Dazed, Shaken* and *Tired* Conditions, even if they are serum side effects.

TAINTED BLOATER	**DANGER RATING**	**1**
	GRIT	**5**

The failed product of a chemical warfare programme, the tainted bloater constantly generates toxins within their body that must be expelled in noxious clouds. Even after death, their corpses build up poisonous gases until they explode!

Drive	Rid myself of these poisonous gases
Tags	Fast, Poisonous, Immune to Poisons and Serums
Actions	Belch a cloud of poisonous gas, Skulk in the shadows, Beg for their life, Explode in a cloud of poisonous gas

- **Belch.** A tainted bloater can belch once every D3 Turns, inflicting the *Poisoned* Condition on everyone within Close range. If killed, they will release one final poison cloud D3 Turns later.

| TWO-HEADED NIGHTMARE | DANGER RATING | 2 |
| | GRIT | 6 |

The fusion of two or more people or animals, stitched together for some horrifying purpose. These miserable wretches come in many forms, and are often used by their twisted masters as lab assistants, guards, or simply amusements.

Drive	Do Master's bidding
Tags	Eyes in the Back of their Head, Extra Limbs, Cunning, Horrifying Appearance
Actions	Disgust you, Menace you, Fawn over you, Beg you for mercy, Run and hide, Betray you to Master, Stab you in the back

- **Manticore.** These nightmares are the amalgamation of several large animals, such as tigers, wolves, gorillas, horses, bison, or even elephants! They gain +1 Danger Rating and +4 Grit but lose the *Extra Limbs* and *Cunning* Tags. They might have other Tags, such as *Sharp Teeth, Horns, Claws*, or *Huge*, depending on the combination of beasts.

TROUBLEMAKERS

The city is full of troublemakers, from no-good street thugs to criminal organisations, violent cults, and ne'er-do-wells out to make a buck or have some fun.

| ABERRATIONIST | DANGER RATING | 2 |
| | GRIT | 6 |

Able to manipulate the Pattern, these misguided fools summon aberrations to do their bidding. The creatures they summon only obey them for a limited time, and all too often the city is subjected to the ravages of these uncontrolled terrors.

Drive	Command aberrations to do my bidding
Tags	Pattern-attuned, Summon Aberrations, Manipulate the Pattern, Run
Actions	Convince you they can help, Summon something dangerous, Lose control of their creation, Open a tear in the Pattern

CROOKS	DANGER RATING	1
	GRIT	4

Thieves, burglars, and no-good swindlers, criminal types have made the city their playground. They use stealth and deception to do whatever they think they can get away with but usually flee at the first sign of trouble.

Drive	Make some easy money
Tags	Stealth, Climb, Break & Enter, Run, Weak-willed
Actions	Trick you, Rob you, Make a fool out of you, Disable your security, Tie you up, Flee into the night

- **Grifter.** Silver-tongued swindlers who use their wits and charm to trick people out of their valuables. They lose *Climb* but gain the *Charming* and *Expert Liar* Tags.
- **Vultures.** These burglars specialise in high-rise heists, using rocket packs, climbing gear, and other gadgets to reach their targets. They gain the *Rocket Pack* and *Brave* Tags.

FANCIER OF THE COURT OF PIGEONS	DANGER RATING	1
	GRIT	4

The Feathered King runs an extensive network of messengers and information brokers throughout the city. Each Fancier in the Court protects their position through deals, blackmail, and bribery.

Drive	Control information
Tags	Cunning, Pigeons, Gossip, Information-brokering, Network of Spies
Actions	Hire you, Blackmail you, Reveal your secrets, Tell you an unwelcome truth, Set their goons on you

| **FOLLOWER OF MOLOCH** | DANGER RATING | 1 |
| | GRIT | 5 |

Devotees to the blood-thirsty Machine God, Moloch, these cultists are recognisable by their shaved heads and the ritual scarring across their bare arms and backs. They control parts of Rimside and the Great Factory with violence and intimidation, and drag the unwary to sacrifice to their hungry deity.

Drive	Appease Moloch
Tags	Strong, The Great Factory, Fight, Restrain, Intimidate, Resist Pain
Actions	Demand your supplication, Tithe you in blood, Threaten you, Attack you, Drag you to their temple

- **Foreman of Moloch.** Leaders of the Cult of Moloch, foremen are priests, mechanics, and rabble rousers. They gain +3 Grit and the *Command* and *Repair* Tags.

| GANGSTER | DANGER RATING | 3 |
| | GRIT | 4 |

Cunning men and women in charge of criminal syndicates, organised crime families, and illegal businesses, such as smuggling rackets, counterfeit operations, and illegal casinos. They have money, influence, and a network of goons, crooks, and other underlings to do their bidding.

Drive	Control this town
Tags	Cunning, Wealthy, Tough, Shoot, Friends in High Places, Henchmen
Actions	Threaten you, Set you up, Hire you, Blackmail you, Have you roughed up, Make you disappear

| GOON | DANGER RATING | 1 |
| | GRIT | 6 |

Thugs, enforcers, and standover men, goons use force and the threat of violence to get what they want. Many are little more than common crooks, though some make legitimate money as bouncers and bodyguards.

Drive	Make you pay
Tags	Big, Tough as Nails, Brawling, Intimidate, Not Too Bright
Actions	Threaten you with violence, Break something, Demand your cash, Hit you hard

- **Hitman.** Professional killers rarely dabble in petty crimes – they make their money from assassination. They gain +1 Danger Rating and the *Cold-Blooded Killer* and *Shoot* Tags.

| HOOD SCUM | DANGER RATING | 1 |
| | GRIT | 4 |

Gangs of youths roam the streets of every district, looking to stir up trouble and have some fun. They are fiercely loyal to their comrades, and it takes little provocation to start a fight.

Drive	Stir up some trouble
Tags	Brawling, Reckless, Brave in Numbers
Actions	Terrorise a neighbourhood, Protect their turf, Challenge you, Hit you when you're down

There are many gangs of hood scum in the city. Some of the better-known ones include:

- **The Weenies.** Natives of Rimside, these youths wear disturbing oversized Halloween masks and carry rusty blades. They gain the *Unsettling Appearance* and *Knife Fighting* Tags.
- **Townies.** Self-styled protectors of various Midtown neighbourhoods, these violent youths like to play target practice with the property of anyone who is late on their insurance payments. They gain the *Intimidate* and *Shoot* Tags.
- **The Hellions.** This predominantly female gang specialises in stealing cars, planes, and dirigibles and terrorising neighbourhoods as they race each other and other gangs. They gain the *Drive* and *Hotwire* Tags.

REVOLUTIONIST	DANGER RATING	1
	GRIT	4

	Anarchists, rabble-rousers, terrorists, or freedom fighters – they seek to overthrow the City Council and bring about a regime change. They operate in loosely affiliated cells, each of which seems to have its own agenda and way of doing things.
Drive	Bring down the Council
Tags	Stealth, Lie, Strong-willed, Hide, Explosives, Network of Allies
Actions	Preach at you, Convince you, Lie to you, Trick you into helping them

- **Vox Populi.** Experts at swaying an audience and stirring up a crowd, they are often the voice and face of a revolutionist cell. They gain the *Passionate* and *Sway a Crowd* Tags.

SKY RAIDER	DANGER RATING	2
	GRIT	4

	Merciless pirates who periodically swoop upon wasteland settlements, or even Tomorrow City if they are feeling particularly bold. They usually travel in well-armed fleets of aircraft and dirigibles, bristling with a motley array of weapons.
Drive	Blitzkrieg!
Tags	Pilot, Gunnery, Fight, Intimidate
Actions	Attack from the sun, Take out the defences, Pick off the weak one, Gang up on you, Demand your surrender

- **Breacher.** Experts at boarding dirigibles and other large aircraft, or fast-roping to ground targets, breachers are formidable close combat fighters. They gain the *Tough, Skydive* and *Boarding Action* Tags.

PATTERN ABBERATIONS

The Pattern seeps into our world through tears in reality, and transforms whatever it touches as it does so. Aberrations are creatures that either originate from somewhere beyond these dimensional rifts or have been corrupted by the power of the Pattern. Either way, they are otherworldly and horrifying to behold.

Pattern aberrations always halve the Damage they take from attacks (rounding down), unless the weapon/attack has the *Fractal* Tag.

BLINKER	DANGER RATING	1
	GRIT	4

Attuned to the Pattern, these creatures can "blink" out of our reality and instantly reappear somewhere else. While technically human, constant travel through alternate realities has twisted and transformed them into an aberration. Some use their ability to steal and rob, while others are little more than crazed killers.

Drive	Shock, rob, and hurt
Tags	Fast, Blink, Surprise Attack, Sleight of Hand, Long Blades
Actions	Surprise you, Dodge and disappear, Attack you from behind, Cut you deep

CUBIST RAVAGER	DANGER RATING	2
	GRIT	8

These pitiable creatures appear to have been cut up and reassembled in a jumble of pieces like cubist art come to life. Once human, exposure to the Pattern has transformed them into mockeries of their former selves, their minds as fractured as their bodies. No longer able to make sense of the world, they are driven to tear things apart and put them back together in a manner more pleasing to their own sense of reality.

Drive	Reassemble the world in their own image
Tags	Inhuman Anatomy, Immensely Strong, Anger and Fear in Equal Measure
Actions	Pull things apart, Rampage through the city, Stack objects in strange formations, Lash out at you, Try to rearrange your features

FRACTAL WELL	DANGER RATING	2
	GRIT	6*

A floating, multi-coloured ball of barely contained Pattern energy, it draws things to it like a miniature black hole. The closer a living creature gets to a Fractal Well, the harder it is to escape its pull and, should you touch it, you are absorbed. Fractal Wells tend to appear when large tears in reality occur, such as after the use of a powerful fractal weapon or the appearance of a great number of Pattern aberrations. They do not move, but grow in size and power as they absorb people and objects.

Drive	Absorb everything
Tags	Bright, Intense Heat, Suck You In
Actions	Float menacingly in the air, Mesmerise you with its changing colours, Draw you to it

- **Absorb.** Anything that touches the Fractal Well suffers D6 damage and, if they die, are absorbed. The Fractal Well increases its Grit value by +2 each time it absorbs a living creature or a large object, such as a car. A Fractal Well cannot be killed, even if its Grit is reduced to 0 by attacks, but will disappear when its Grit reaches a total value of D6x10.

PAIN PANE	DANGER RATING	2
	GRIT	8

This impossibly thin aberration looks like a stained-glass image of a man, often imitating the shape of a knight or biblical figure. It hides as windows on buildings, ready to pounce on prey. Being no thicker than a pane of glass, it almost disappears when it turns on its side. When light passes through this aberration, it sprays a kaleidoscope of colour in front of it, and anyone caught in the pattern is stained with colour and wracked with pain.

Drive	Transform the bleak world into one of colour
Tags	Thin as Glass, Razor-sharp, Colour Spray
Actions	Sneak up on you, Cut you open, Drop from above, Transform things into glass, Turn you into glass, Explode in a shower of glass

- **Kaleidoscope.** Anyone who spends a Turn in a Pain Pane's "shadow" immediately suffers 1 Damage that cannot be soaked by armour. If a Rev suffers an Injury from this Damage, it must be a new one that represents their flesh slowly being transformed into glass. If it becomes a three-point Injury the damage is permanent – note it as a Trauma!

REALITY GREMLIN	DANGER RATING	1
	GRIT	4

These small creatures look like a tangle of geometric metal shapes. They are particularly attracted to machinery, which they pull apart and rebuild into strange devices that often intensify Pattern energy and act as a beacon to other aberrations.

Drive	Build strange fractal machines
Tags	Small, Quick, Sharp Edges, Engineers
Actions	Leap and dodge in excitement, Chatter in metallic banter, Scratch or bite you, Steal your gear, Tear apart machines, Build a strange device

- **Robo-Gremlin.** One or more gremlins have infested and taken over a robot, or even an automaton. These crazed machines often manifest strange inbuilt weapons. They Lose *Quick* and *Small*, but gain the *Made of Metal* and *Shoot* Tags. If the gremlins infest larger or stronger robots, they might also increase their Grit.

TESSELLATED STALKER	DANGER RATING	2
	GRIT	12

A large humanoid figure seemingly made of millions of polygonal shapes that clink and rattle as it moves. Impenetrable darkness oozes from the spaces between the flesh-tiles, while its body shifts in colour to match its surroundings. When the faceless creature attacks, its torso tiles swirl into a jagged maw, and it feeds its victims into the darkness within.

Drive	Devour the world
Tags	Large, Camouflage, Tough Like Stone, Move & Swirl, Great Stone Fists
Actions	Hide in plain sight, Surprise attack, Menace you from the shadows, Strike you hard, Hold you tight and swallow you whole

- **Living Mosaic.** These two-dimensional tessellated stalkers move across the ground or walls, attempting to devour living things they come into contact with. Once devoured, the victim becomes part of the mosaic. They lose *Great Stone Fists* and gain the *Stealthy* Tag.

BIZARRE HORROR

Aberrations are manifestations of incomprehensible realities. Make them creepy, unnatural, and weird. Describe them in terms of feelings, shapes, patterns, sounds, or smells that don't seem to go together, and highlight how confusing and unnatural they are. It's hard to tell where their head is, or if you are looking at an aberration's front or back. Emphasise that these are things that do not belong in our world.

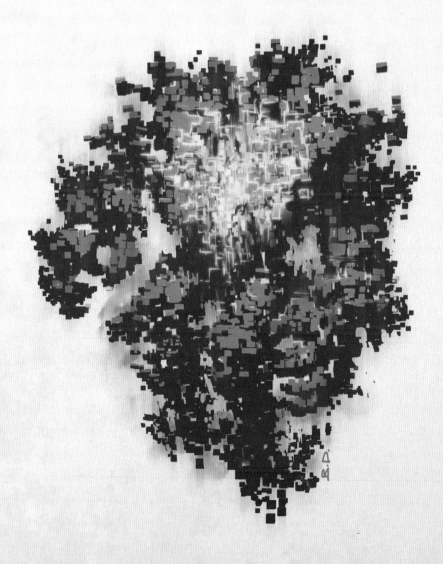

ENVIRONMENTS

Threats can also represent environmental hazards, nefarious traps, and other troubles. Such Threats cannot be fought in the normal sense but might be overcome by other means. Usually, environmental Threats must be navigated around or endured.

BLAZING INFERNO	DANGER RATING	2
	GRIT	3

Whether a small warehouse, crowded tenement, or a luxurious penthouse, buildings can become death traps when fire is involved.	
Drive	Spread and burn
Tags	Searing Flames, Thick Smoke, Loud Crackling, Unseen Obstacles
Actions	Burn you, Choke you, Intensify, Spread

DARKENED BUILDING	DANGER RATING	1
	GRIT	3

Unlit warehouses and apartments, abandoned buildings, darkened factory corridors, and wasteland ruins can all be treacherous places to visit without a good torch.	
Drive	Keep its secrets
Tags	Moving Shadows, Echoing Footsteps, Scattered Boxes or Rubble, Oil Spills, Hidden Steps or Drops
Actions	Disorient you, Frighten you, Trip you

DRAINS & TUNNELS	DANGER RATING	1
	GRIT	3

The city is woven with a complex of sewers, access tunnels, and hidden passages that are used to run cables or deliver infrastructure.	
Drive	Make you uncomfortable
Tags	Impenetrable Darkness, Tight Spaces, Grime & Oil, Strange Ticking & Clicking, Rats the Size of Cats
Actions	Make you filthy, Confuse you, Frighten you, Tangle you in cables, Waste your time, Cause you to become you lost

| **FACTORY MACHINE ROOM** | **DANGER RATING** | 1 |
| | **GRIT** | 4 |

Great pistons, relentless conveyor belts, and thumping machinery fill this space, ready to crush, burn, and catch the unwary in their steel limbs.

Drive	Just keep working
Tags	Deafening Machinery, Chains & Hooks, Conveyor Belts, Smoke & Steam, Exhausting Heat, Great Wheels & Pistons
Actions	Get in your way, Obscure your view, Drag you, Crush you

| **MAZE-LIKE CITY** | **DANGER RATING** | 1 |
| | **GRIT** | 3 |

The crowded city is constantly in motion, the landscape changing as you sleep. Getting anywhere quickly can be a challenge, even on the best days.

Drive	Get you lost
Tags	Crowded streets, Freshly-laid Cables, A Missing Tramline, Winding Alleys
Actions	Waste your time, Lose your bearings, Cost you resources, Make you Angry or Tired, Cause an Injury, Cause you to become lost

| **SWAMP CANALS** | **DANGER RATING** | 2 |
| | **GRIT** | 4 |

The foetid swamps and muddy canals of Old Cali sprawl in the shadow of the city. Here, mud and water are the least of your worries.

Drive	Suck you into their depths
Tags	Thick Mud, Swarms of Mosquitos, Putrid Pools, Sloshing Mulch, Overwhelming Stench, Leeches
Actions	Cover you in filth, Cause a rash, Trap you in mud, Drown you, Poison you, Cause you to become Tired or Weakened

UNDERSIDE GANTRIES	DANGER RATING	1
	GRIT	3

Rusting girders and narrow catwalks run between tin shanties, all hung fifty stories above the ruins of Old Cali. Here, you never know quite where you're going and a slip could be your end.

Drive	Strand you
Tags	Narrow Girders, Unstable Catwalks, Strong Winds, Large Holes, Rusting Chains, Warren of Alleys
Actions	Confuse you, Cause you to slip, Frighten you, Separate you, Give you vertigo

ZEPPELIN TOP	DANGER RATING	2
	GRIT	3

Moving across the top of a dirigible or other precarious surface can quickly lead to injury or death if you are not careful.

Drive	Rock and roll
Tags	Buffeting Winds, Unsteady Footing, Drone of Engines, Cables & Ropes
Actions	Knock you off your feet, Make you hold on tight, Cause you to drop something, Frighten you, Expose you to an enemy, Give you vertigo

ORGANISATIONS

Cults and leagues, organised crime syndicates, gangs, secret societies, the Ministries, and other groups can be represented as Threats. These might be long-term enemies or enterprises that the Revs must work to overcome. In this case, Grit represents the strength of the organisation. When the Revs successfully take action to erode the power of the organisation, reduce its Grit.

THE COLLECTOR

DANGER RATING	1
GRIT	4

An underground art smuggling ring that primarily deals in strange Pattern objects, dangerous artifacts from The Long War, and stolen goods. Run by the mysterious Collector, it is said that they can procure anything you want – for a price.

Drive	Obtain precious artefacts
Tags	Money, Fleet of Smuggling Dirigibles, Loyal Goons, Well-informed, Secret Auction Rooms
Actions	Steal from the rich, Send out an expedition, Rob an expedition, Bribe you, Threaten you, Dispose of the evidence

THE CULT OF MOLOCH

DANGER RATING	2
GRIT	6

The followers of Moloch wish to appease their hungry Machine God with blood, and ultimately to see Him usurp Mother's place as the most important machine in the city.

Drive	Feed Moloch
Tags	Legions of Workers, Secret Boltholes, Eyes in the Great Factory, Well-equipped, Intimidation & Fear
Actions	Threaten you, Block access to the Great Factory, Cause a riot, Stop your supply of gear, Kidnap you, Give you a savage beatdown, Feed you to Moloch

THE MINISTRY OF TRUTH

DANGER RATING	4
GRIT	10

The Ministry of Truth controls information throughout the city and has a vast supply of resources to draw upon. They can make anyone look like anything they want, and often do.

Drive	Control the narrative
Tags	Expert Spin-doctors, Tomorrow's News Today, Control the Telescreens, Propaganda Experts, Spies Everywhere
Actions	Spread mistruths, Revoke your paperwork, Steal your identity, Frame you, Make you look foolish, Turn the city against you

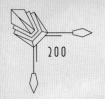

JOB: ESCAPE PLAN

The following information has been
classified by the Ministry of Truth as:

FOR GAME MASTER'S EYES ONLY

Douglas Baker, a low-level clerk and one-time thief has found himself in the custody of the Badges. The Revs are hired to break him out of a detention facility. However, the clock is ticking, as he is due to appear before the Municipal Court tomorrow afternoon.

This is a simple introductory mission that throws the Revs straight into the action and lets them resolve the Job using whatever skills they may have. They simply need to come up with a plan to rescue a prisoner, with the Job essentially falling into two or three set pieces. Be warned, however, the danger is high if the players do not carefully prepare. The Rev's actions will likely draw the attention of the Ministry of Peace, making this an excellent Job to launch an ongoing campaign with this powerful organisation nipping at their heels.

THE LOW-DOWN

Douglas Baker is a former employee of the Ministry of Agriculture, working in a low-level records position. He was a hardworking employee, but weak-willed with a gambling habit that got him into a great deal of debt. A few months ago, however, someone offered to pay off his bookmaker in return for regularly altering the stock records of one of the Ministry's greenhouses. He did so, and everything worked well for him up until forty-eight hours ago, when an internal audit uncovered his actions, and he was arrested. He is due to appear before the Municipal Court tomorrow.

The group that hired Baker was stealing from the greenhouse and, with his arrest, they risk exposure. Under cross examination, and with the threat of a long prison sentence, he is likely to reveal all kinds of sensitive information. It is better to facilitate his escape than have him tell the Ministry of Truth what he knows about them.

He is currently being held in a small Midtown detention facility and will be transported to the courthouse via dirigible tomorrow afternoon.

THE HOOK

The player characters are likely hired to complete this job by someone involved in the thefts at the greenhouses. The most important detail will be deciding which group originally coerced Baker to adjust the books.

- **The Revolutionists.** A cell of this radical group have been stealing from the Ministry of Agriculture to feed the poor of Rimside. They do it as both an act of charity and a way to disrupt the system. They would call on like-minded individuals who have no love for the city authorities.
- **Gangsters.** The Belafonte family, or a rival syndicate, has been skimming from the factory farm to sell to the markets and delis of Midtown. They will hire troubleshooters, criminals, or people who owe them to get the job done.
- **The Ministry of Science.** A minor division of the Ministry has been conducting secret experiments at the greenhouse, misappropriating stock and other resources at the Ministry of Agriculture's expense. They will hire efficient operators to cover up their involvement.

Consider the character's backstories, Trademarks, and descriptions and use this information to decide who hires them for the Job.

No matter how the Revs get involved, they will be given the following details:

- Douglas Baker is a middle-aged, balding man with a pencil moustache and nervous disposition. He has a scar on the back of his right hand.
- Baker is being held at a small holding facility in Midtown. It has a skeleton staff, with robots operating as guards. They might be able to obtain a map of the facility from the Ministry of Public Works, or someone with good connections.
- Baker will be transported by small dirigible (from a rooftop dock) at 2pm tomorrow afternoon. The airship will travel directly to the courthouse – a journey of about thirty minutes. The route is regular, never changing.
- The courthouse is a veritable fortress – getting Baker out of there is probably impossible.
- Baker needs to be delivered to The Black Gull, a rough drinking establishment in Rimside. The Revs are given a strict warning, however, that they must not be followed.

OBSTACLES

The Revs have some basic details to go on and a strict timeframe in which to complete the mission. They must come up with a plan to help Douglas Baker escape. Below are the primary locations or obstacles they might encounter along the way.

DANGER RATINGS

Throughout this Job, you will see suggested Danger Ratings for actions noted in brackets, such as (DR1). Use these as a base for determining how many Danger Dice you might add to Checks.

Research

The characters might attempt to get a map of the detention facility, a schematic of the transport dirigible, its flight route, or information about the Badges guarding Baker. This can be achieved by calling on contacts, breaking into the City Planner's office (DR2), bribing someone (DR1), or doing some reconnaissance. Ask the players how their characters go about getting the information and play out Scenes or call for Checks where necessary. This research should be relatively straightforward, as the bulk of the adventure should be focused on the rescue attempt itself. The Rev's employer might even be able to provide some of the information they need.

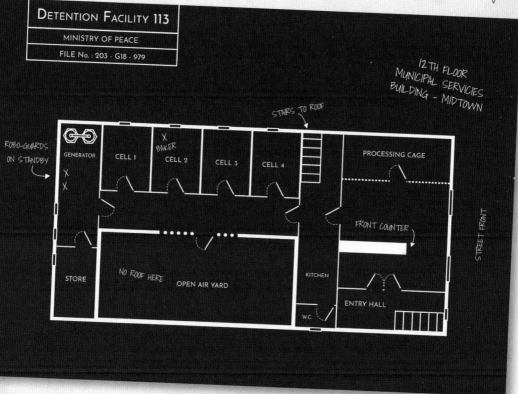

DETENTION FACILITY 113

MINISTRY OF PEACE

FILE No.: 203 - G18 - 979

12TH FLOOR MUNICIPAL SERVICES BUILDING - MIDTOWN

STAIRS TO ROOF

ROBO-GUARDS ON STANDBY

GENERATOR

X BAKER

CELL 1

CELL 2

CELL 3

CELL 4

PROCESSING CAGE

FRONT COUNTER

STREET FRONT

STORE

NO ROOF HERE

OPEN AIR YARD

KITCHEN

ENTRY HALL

W.C.

Detention Facility 113

This secure facility is on the top floor of a twelve story Midtown walk-up. The lower floors are leased to a variety of Ministry departments and government offices, and security is light but efficient. The detention facility is staffed by two **Badges** and four **RoboGuards**. Two of the robots are always active, while the others are on standby near the generator in the back storage room. A staircase leads to the roof where there is an airship dock, used to transport prisoners.

The holding cells are dingy, brick-walled rooms with a single small window high up on the wall. The doors are steel and have complex punch-card locks; the RoboGuards have the access cards.

Baker is being held in Cell Two. Another prisoner, Clive Lowans is in Cell One and will beg to be released. At a glance, Lowans looks similar to Baker, with a pencil moustache and receding hairline. He is a grifter and con-artist who will seek to turn the situation to his advantage, so might help the Revs, flee at the first opportunity, or even turn on them.

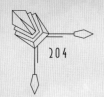

The open-air yard is rarely used, but it is indeed open to the sky above. Thick steel bars form a cage across the top of the yard.

The Revs might attempt one or more of the following to gain access to the facility:

- **Aerial Assault.** The player characters might climb the building's exterior (DR2); swing, jump, or zipline from a nearby building (DR1); or use their own airship to land on the roof. Each comes with its own set of problems and potential dangers! Falls, injuries, losing gear, making a lot of noise, and being seen by passing SkyTrain passengers are the most likely consequences for such actions.
- **Bluffing.** The player characters might obtain counterfeit documents, or attempt to deceive the Badges (DR2) at the front counter. Even if they achieve this, the deception won't last for long. Perhaps the Revs will be caught out while still there, or as they attempt to flee the scene. This approach may result in a **Detective** or **Ministry Operative** being set on their trail.
- **Frontal Assault.** Daring (or reckless) Revs might just attempt to force their way into the building from the front. This will quickly draw a lot of attention and, if the characters don't have a good escape plan, they may find themselves besieged!
- **Break & Enter.** If the Revs do make it inside the facility, they may still have to break Baker out. Stealing access cards or picking locks (DR2) can be straightforward, though the RoboGuard patrols (DR2) will need to be carefully avoided. Consequences might include alarms, being trapped, or suffering Harm.

Transport Dirigible

Instead of breaking into the detention facility, the Revs might choose to free Douglas Baker from the prisoner transport.

This dirigible has a crew of four: the pilot, co-pilot, and two Badges. While it can carry up to a dozen prisoners in a combination of cells and seats, today it has just two – Douglas Baker and Clive Lowans.

The dirigible is armed with a pair of machine guns, one on each side near the doors, which allows it to cover a wide area, should it be assaulted from the air. As well as the two side doors, the airship's rigid envelope has a single hatch on top and an internal hatch in the hallway between the radio room and office. It is conceivable that someone could enter the gondola by moving through the envelope.

The Revs might attempt to get on board the dirigible while it is transporting Baker. This could present several challenges depending on how they go about it. The Badges will defend the airship, opening fire on a hostile or suspicious aircraft (DR2 to avoid Harm, with machine guns dealing 4 Damage each).

- Attempting to land on a dirigible while in flight has a Danger Rating of 2.
- The envelope hatch is easy to open, but the airship's side doors are securely locked (DR1 to breach).
- The gondola is relatively small, making fighting inside difficult. Everything will be at Close or Near range, and there is a risk of harming the pilots or Douglas Baker himself if characters are not careful.
- The transport will call for backup if attacked, and the characters may soon have to face rocket-pack equipped Badges (one per Rev), small fighter planes (one per aircraft the characters have), or other Threats.
- Fast-roping or parachuting from the transport is possible but dangerous, with many rooftop hazards and tall skyscrapers to navigate around (DR2).

The players and their characters may be presented with some tough choices should they damage the dirigible, set it on a collision course with a building, or do anything else that endangers citizens. What can, and will, they do to minimise harm? If they do nothing, what are the repercussions?

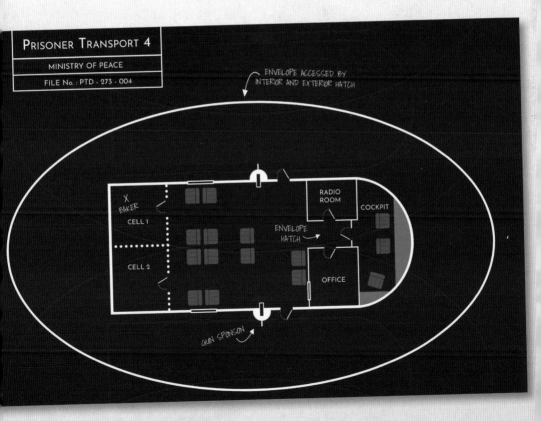

Get to the Black Gull

If the characters are successful in freeing Douglas Baker, they must get him to The Black Gull in Rimside. The authorities will likely be hot on their tail, and this is an opportunity to play out a car chase or dogfight. Remind the players they were warned not to be followed – their employer does not want the meeting location revealed to the authorities. As the GM, you should make it difficult for the characters to escape detection.

- **An Ever-tightening Net.** If the Badges managed to follow them to Rimside, they will send in patrols and slowly sweep through the district. This takes time but, unless the characters have allies or backgrounds connected to Rimside, they will have few places to hide. Make them sneak past a police cordon (DR2), bluff or bribe their way past a lazy Badge (DR3), or attempt to evade capture by taking a route through the sewers under the streets.
- **Opportunists.** The hood scum and other troublemakers of Rimside are always looking to make a quick buck, and nothing makes a buck faster than selling out a stranger. They will happily point the law in the Rev's direction, unless they can be threatened (DR3), persuaded (DR3), or bribed (DR2) to do otherwise. A failed Check might result in a fight or other disturbance that draws the Badges' attention!

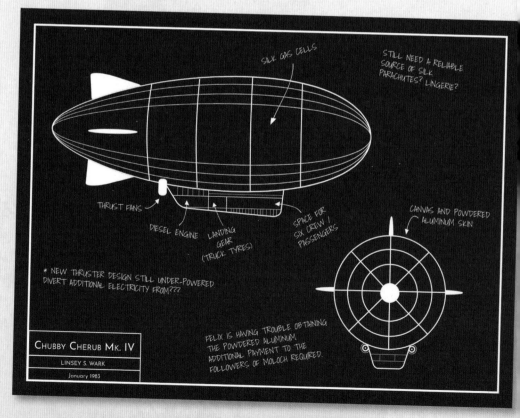

- **Air Support.** If the characters have been particularly careless, messy, or dangerous, the Ministry of Peace may have dirigibles scanning the city for them. If the Scene takes place at night, their spotlights will punch down into the streets, seeking them out. Moving from shadow to shadow is a slow process, giving the Badges on the ground a chance to close their net.

WHAT IF BAKER DIES?

If the Revs go in all guns blazing on this Job, then Baker could end up as collateral damage. This should only be done for dramatic effect, and as the consequence for a major stuff-up on the character's part. His death may be a neat solution, or a dismal failure, depending on the employer's point of view.

The Black Gull

A dingy basement bar in a warehouse neighbourhood of Rimside, The Black Gull is frequented by labourers after their long shifts. It is dark and full of cigarette smoke, making it hard to really make out anyone, and the noisy banter of drunken men and women drowns out conversations. Here, the Revs will meet their contact and deliver Douglas Baker.

If the characters have managed to lose their pursuers, their employer quickly departs with Baker, disappearing into the crowd with him. They could be convinced to smuggle the Revs out of Rimside (DR2, or DR3 if there is a lot of heat). Should the Revs bring the law to the door, however, the contact will set the bar on fire before fleeing with Baker – the characters may be caught between the Badges and a blazing inferno!

LINKS

Eventually, the Revs will either make it to The Black Gull, get caught, or escape into the night. Whatever the resolution, there will likely be fallout! The player characters may have made a powerful new enemy (or two) but could also now have a valuable ally – if they managed to get Baker to safety. Consider how these events tie in with the Rev's Drives, and what might happen next. Are they going to be on the run from the Badges? Have they earned themselves a reputation amongst the citizens of Rimside? Does Douglas Baker owe them one, and will they ever see him again?

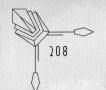

THREATS

DOUGLAS BAKER	**DANGER RATING**	0
	GRIT	2

Baker is a weak-willed and snivelling bureaucrat in the employ of the Ministry of Agriculture. He is middle-aged, balding, and has a pencil moustache. Baker is willing to do anything to avoid prison and may attempt to flee from the characters if given the chance.

Drive	Not get killed or go to prison
Tags	Bureaucracy, Research, Gambling, Duck & Cover
Actions	Run & hide, Tell you what you want to hear, Flee, Cry for help

MINISTRY OF PEACE ROBOGUARD	**DANGER RATING**	1
	GRIT	6

Custom-built to support Badges in the execution of their duties, the so called "Badge Bot" is painted black and typically equipped with a shock baton.

Drive	Not get killed or go to prison
Tags	Enforce the law
Actions	Spot you, Raise the alarm, Detain you, Stun you, Hit you hard

CLIVE LOWANS	**DANGER RATING**	1
	GRIT	3

Middle-aged with a pencil moustache and a sneering smile, Lowans is a grifter and con-artist. He will look for ways to exploit the Revs to his own advantage at every opportunity.

Drive	Make some easy money
Tags	Charm, Lie to Your Face, Cunning, Break & Enter, Run
Actions	Trick you, Rob you, Double-cross you, Help you, Flee into the night

POLICE CORDON	DANGER RATING	2
	GRIT	3

Barricades and flashing lights indicate the Badges have set up a checkpoint; they're checking papers and stopping anyone who looks suspicious.

Drive	Capture the fugitives
Tags	Cops Everywhere, A Spotlight, Wooden Barricade, Nervous Onlookers
Actions	Spot you, Stop you, Question you, Check your papers, Put you into a patrol car, Raise the alarm, Call in air support

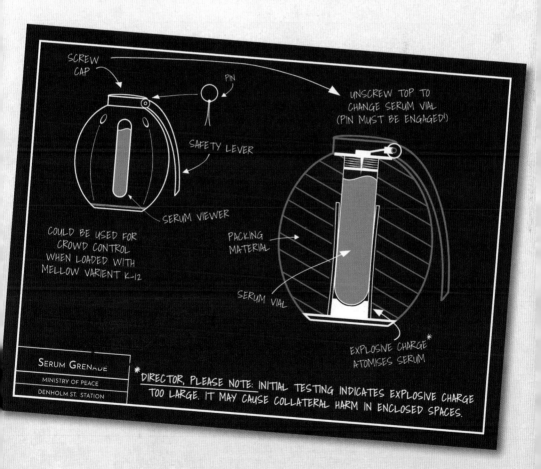

APPENDIX: RANDOM GENERATOR

Use the following tables to quickly generate people and places to populate the city.

PEOPLE

Names

D66	MALE	FEMALE	NEUTRAL	SURNAME	NICKNAMES
11	Carter	Vivian	Quincy	Grimes	Legs
12	Mike	Faye	Carol	Thompson	Smiley
13	Jack	Gigi	Morgan	Masaki	Cogger
14	Sergey	Lauren	Jesse	Cooper	Rat
15	Drake	Vlada	Cam	Banks	Drums
16	Steel	Pepper	Adrian	Grigorenko	Brick
21	Maurice	Gloria	Dana	Torres	Graves
22	Saul	Marta	Charlie	Robinson	Spinner
23	Thomas	Veronica	Jamie	Ricci	Knuckles
24	William	Maria	Aubrey	Green	Knots
25	Humphrey	Katarina	Kit	Spyrou	Blockhead

26	Carlo	Wren	Tracy	Chan	Ticks
31	Trip	Audrey	Alex	Walker	Ruby
32	Jackie	Helen	Georgie	Neumann	Tooth
33	Brutus	Sylvia	Lee	Ryan	Stretch
34	Kai	Lana	Pat	Kohl	Zip
35	Alan	Phoebe	Kim	Colby	Chuckles
36	Duke	Aurora	Viv	Moreau	Ratchet
41	Nicholas	Asari	Zou	Powell	Nox
42	James	Ingrid	Frances	Ivanov	Slice
43	Gunnar	Edda	Peyton	Willis	Scruffy
44	Burt	Mildred	Addison	Delcroix	Measles
45	Emilio	Bette	Kelly	Yurchenko	Meat
46	Archie	Ivanna	Vic	Vargas	Pretzel
51	Spencer	Sybil	Grey	Batty	Cyclops
52	Cary	Lucia	Gene	Steed	Coffin
53	Sham	Carmen	Lane	Scott	Sparks
54	Walter	Olga	Sam	Esposito	Tuesday
55	Bruno	Hazel	Ashley	Flanagan	Beans
56	Anton	Summer	Max	Goldstein	Link
61	Harry	Anika	Blair	Lopez	Droopy
62	Dino	Margaret	Lou	Takuro	Quirk
63	Tony	Beverly	Dallas	Hernandez	Cookie
64	Hector	Diane	Sydney	Kline	Stitches
65	Oscar	Wakata	Casey	Romanovich	Honey
66	Vladimir	Flora	Ainsley	Hudson	Weasel

Distinguishing Traits & Features

D6	PERSONALITY TRAITS			PHYSICAL FEATURES		
1	Arrogant	Distracted	Slow-witted	Shifty eyes	Broken	Very short
2	Overeager	Stand-offish	Blunt	Facial scar	Huge	Tattoos
3	Tired	Cautious	Charming	Very thin	Attractive	Hairy
4	Sleazy	Friendly	Surly	Balding	Dishevelled	Limp
5	Aggressive	Calculating	Unhappy	Well-dressed	Obese	Filthy
6	Talkative	Thoughtful	Formal	Sweating	Tall	Injured

PLACES

Rough Neighbourhoods

D6	ROUGH NEIGHBOURHOOD NAMES				DESCRIPTOR	
1	Cabbage	Rustburn	Baffles	Tinkerer's	Turn	Shambles
2	Soot	Barbed	Dagger	Mastiff	Ditch	Run
3	Red Eye	Grist	Cable	Battery	Lock	Patch
4	Runny	Stackhouse	Thorn	Longdrop	End	Cross
5	Groper	Clergyman's	Radium	Sugar	Fork	Bend
6	Clatter	Sharp	Dangerfield	Broken	Trap	Lane

Rough Neighbourhood Encounters:

1. The traffic lights at an intersection are malfunctioning
2. Delicious smells tempt you into a restaurant
3. A dead pigeon falls from the sky, apparently shot
4. The telescreen on this corner is smashed
5. A pair of street vendors have a loud argument over who gets to work the corner
6. Children splash and play in the spray of a broken fire hydrant
7. A dead body is found floating in the river
8. A gang of hood scum are shaking down a deli owner
9. A large clock chimes loudly from somewhere nearby
10. The stink of a recent fire pervades the area
11. A lost child is crying on a street corner
12. A long queue of drones is lined up outside an automat

Classy Neighbourhoods

D6	CLASSY NEIGHBOURHOOD NAMES				DESCRIPTOR	
1	Silver	Chromium	Crystal	Golden	Skyway	Bridge
2	Spindle View	Darling	Deco	Prosperity	Green	Place
3	Atlas	Sunburst	Lunar	Ruby	Square	Way
4	Zephyr	Tesla	Skylark	Elysium	Steps	Plaza
5	Heart	New	Pacific	Paradise	Atrium	Square
6	Broadway	Phoenix	Enterprise	Horizon	Towers	Heights

Classy Neighbourhood Encounters:

1. There is a great scandal when a moving sidewalk stops operating
2. A huddle of photographers waits outside The Beecroft for some celebrity
3. An Anti-Robot League protest has blocked a busy street
4. A red carpet opening of a new film
5. Someone is roughly tossed out of an apartment building by the doorman
6. An elevator stops working
7. Someone rushes from a jewellery store, pursued by a security robot
8. A swarm of bees has caused part of the park to be closed off
9. A Badge cruiser slowly follows you down the street
10. An obviously working-class family cannot get a cab to stop for them
11. The trees on this skywalk have all died
12. You see a robot struggling to walk a pair of inquisitive dogs

Bars, Clubs & Nightspots

D6	BARS, CLUBS & NIGHTSPOTS				DESCRIPTOR	
1	South Seas	Dalmatian	Grease Trap	Antidote	Tower	Arcade
2	Brown's	Finch	River View	Bushell	Palace	Bar
3	Red Door	Swill	Divine	Wingman	Taverna	Diner
4	Gunmetal	Heaven	Terracotta	Joker	Loft	Palace
5	Salted	Engine Room	Blue	Piston	Club	Grill
6	Turk's	Barracuda	Aviator's	Robotica	Cabaret	Hall

Distinguishing Features:

1. Extremely narrow building
2. There is a secret backroom casino
3. Known for risqué performances
4. There is always a line to get in
5. Frequented by Badges
6. The booze here is watered down
7. There is a strict dress code
8. Stinks of mould and rot
9. Live animals in cages hang from the ceiling
10. All the staff are robots
11. Only serves army rations
12. Dim lighting and sticky floors

Brands, Businesses & Factories

D6	BRANDS, BUSINESSES & FACTORIES				INDUSTRY	
1	Whirlblitzer	Castle	Skyward	Newtopia	& Sons	& Co.
2	Omni	Ardor	Motion	Harmony	Corp.	Bros.
3	Automatica	Flywheel	Vulcan	Teslatronic	Devices	Holdings
4	New City	Central	Alliance	Weaver	Industries	Dynamics
5	Flare	Volt	Stratos	Majestic	Enterprises	Company
6	Lacuna	Resolute	Atlas	Daedalus	Inc.	Union

Brand, Business & Factory Industries:

1. Food services, food preparation, and/or agriculture
2. Electronics, appliances, and/or specialised equipment
3. Fashion design, manufacture, and/or retail
4. Chemical manufacturing and/or supplies
5. Manufacturing, industrial equipment, and/or construction
6. Logistics, freight management, warehousing, and/or transport
7. Finance, banking, and/or insurance
8. Car, dirigible, or aircraft construction and/or maintenance
9. Communications, media, entertainment, and/or public relations
10. Munitions manufacture, supply, training, and/or support
11. Robotics design, maintenance, and/or construction
12. Health, medicine, and/or scientific research

JOBS

Random Job Generator

YOU ARE...	
1	Hired
2	Coerced
3	Blackmailed
4	Paid well
5	Begged
6	Inspired

TO...	
1	Rescue/Recover/Help
2	Extract/Steal/Infiltrate
3	Eliminate/Destroy/Dispose of
4	Protect/Guard/Defend
5	Sabotage/Discredit/Undermine
6	Investigate/Research/Discover

A...	
1	Group. A desperate neighbourhood committee, University students, Anti-Robot League, The Badges, an Archeocult, Society of Philomaths
2	Artifact. Dangerous weapon, Pattern-infused object, Work of art, Vehicle prototype, Automaton, Masterwork prosthetics
3	Pattern. Aberration, Pattern weaver, Fractal weapon, Reality tear, Site of power
4	VIP. City Councillor, Celebrity, Ministry official, Neighbourhood leader, Visiting dignitary, Gangster
5	Information. Code to a safe, Map of a Fragment, Identity of a Ministry informant, Location of a secret laboratory, Blueprint, Counterfeit documents
6	Criminal. Murderer, Hostage, Political agitator, Prisoner, Thief, Escapee

BUT YOU ARE OPPOSED BY...	
1	Aberrations or Failed experiments
2	A Ministry: Badges, Ministry of Truth, Ministry of Science, Ministry of Agriculture
3	Other Revs: Private security, Treasure hunters, Random troublemakers
4	Mother and Her automatons
5	A Cult or League: The Court of Pigeons, The Followers of Moloch, The Revolutionists, Sanitation Union
6	Criminals or Thugs: The Pillbox Mafia, Sky Raiders, Hood Scum, Gangsters, Crooks

AND...	
1	A horde of goons
2	An old enemy
3	Angry locals
4	This time it's personal
5	They're expecting you
6	A dangerous piece of technology

THE TWIST IS...	
1	It's a double cross
2	There's a time pressure
3	You must complete a second Job at the same time
4	Someone else has been hired for the same job
5	Nobody is who they appear to be
6	The Revs are the real victims

Job Hooks

D66	JOB HOOK
11	Stop a runaway airship from crashing into the city
12	Explore the ruins of Old Cali for a powerful lost weapon
13	Rescue a City Councillor who has been kidnapped by gangsters
14	Steal or investigate a Pattern artefact in a museum
15	Find out who is poisoning a Midtown neighbourhood's water supply
16	Fight off an incursion of sky raiders
21	Stop a warehouse of robots that have gone wild
22	Search for a criminal in the Swamplands
23	Get involved in, or foil, an Anti-Robot League plot to bring down Mother
24	Find the killer of a Midtown business owner
25	Search the sewers for a serum brute that escaped a secret facility

26	Escort a dirigible shipment to/from the wastelands
31	Infiltrate a prestigious society ball and steal a valuable artwork
32	Rescue an heiress from Underside kidnappers
33	Break someone out of New Alcatraz
34	Uncover the identity of a factory saboteur
35	Battle sky raiders above the city
36	Investigate a wasteland herd farm that has stopped sending shipments
41	Explore an abandoned munitions factory in the wastelands
42	Bodyguard a movie star
43	Kidnapped by Followers of Moloch!
44	Aunty Maude has gone missing – what has happened to her?
45	Protect/Find a political dissident the Ministry of Truth wants dead
46	A dead body is floating in the Midtown River
51	Discover who is using robots to commit murder
52	Rimside tenements have been blacked out for days – something has to be done
53	Hunt a Pattern aberration in The Great Factory
54	Stop a Ministry of Science clinic experimenting on the local neighbourhood kids
55	Disable the telescreens of Enterprise Plaza, for just a short time
56	Break up a smuggling racket importing dangerous artefacts
61	Search for ingredients and recipes for new serums in the wastelands
62	Broker peace between warring gangs of hood scum
63	Fran Tutti has fallen ill, and rumour has it they were poisoned
64	Spread/Refute Ministry of Truth propaganda
65	Capture mutated animals in the wastelands for a rich scientist to experiment on
66	A zeppelin arrives with no passengers or crew – what happened?

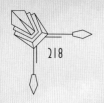
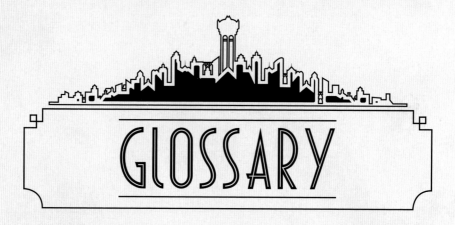

GLOSSARY

Action Die: A die you add to a Check when things are in your favour

Boon: An advantage you get when a Check result has multiple 6's

Botch: A very bad result when making a Check where only 1's or no Action Dice remain

Check: Rolling dice to see what happens next

Condition: A physical, social, or emotional status

Conflict: When two groups act in opposition to each other

Cred: An abstract indicator of a character's wealth, resources, and ability to acquire gear

Danger Die: A die you add to a Check when things are not in your favour

Danger Rating: An indicator of how difficult a Threat is to overcome. Add this many Danger Dice to a Check

Experience points (XP): A reward for playing your character

Extended Check: An action that requires three successes to accomplish

Game Master (GM): The player who facilitates the game

Grit: An indicator of how tough a character or Threat is

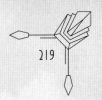
Hits: The amount of Damage a character can suffer before they start taking Injuries

Injury: A serious harm a character is suffering

Mastery: When a character makes a Check "with Mastery", they may re-roll one Action Die

Non-player Character (NPC): A character controlled by the GM

Pattern, The: The powerful extra-dimensional energy that flows into our reality

Player Character (PC): A character controlled by a player

Pressure: An indicator of how badly things are going. When the Pressure reaches 6, things will get worse

Moxie: A resource players spend for a variety of cool effects

Rev: Another name for a character controlled by a player

Scene: A portion of the story that takes place in a single location

Stabilised: When a dying character is attended to by someone

Strike: Three strikes will end an Extended Check

Tag: A word or statement that describes an aspect of the imagined world

Threat: An enemy, obstacle, or challenge that must be overcome in some manner

Tie: An important relationship

Trademark: A notable feature of a character, such as a past, occupation, or special ability

Turn: A period where each character in the scene can perform one Action

TOMORROW CITY

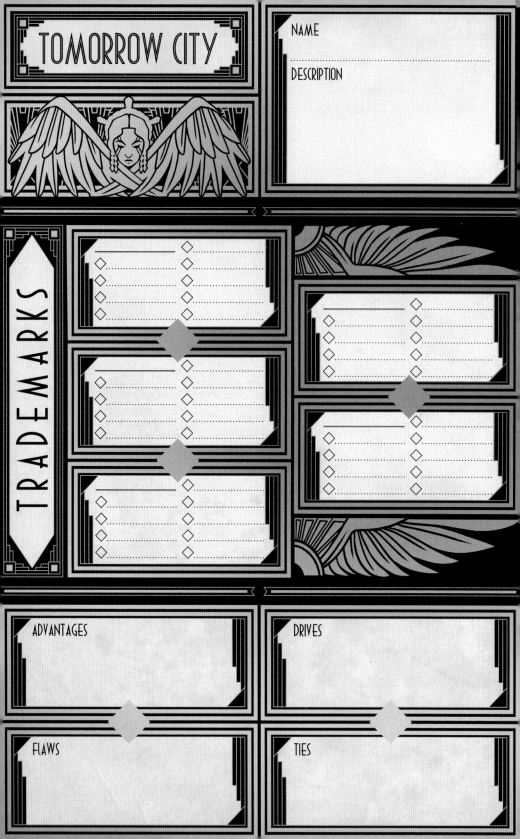

NAME

DESCRIPTION

TRADEMARKS

ADVANTAGES

DRIVES

FLAWS

TIES

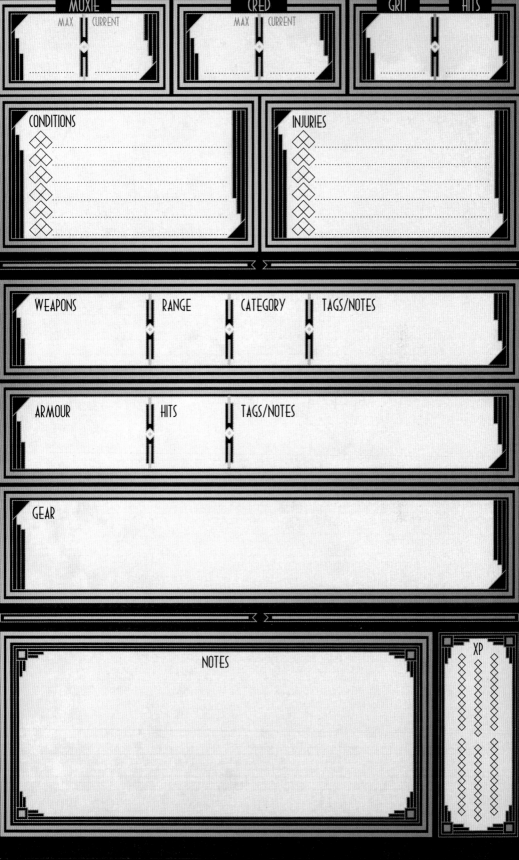

MOXIE

CRED

GRIT HITS

MAX CURRENT

MAX CURRENT

CONDITIONS

INJURIES

WEAPONS RANGE CATEGORY TAGS/NOTES

ARMOUR HITS TAGS/NOTES

GEAR

NOTES

XP

TOMORROW CITY

NAME

....

DESCRIPTION

TRADEMARKS

ADVANTAGES

DRIVES

FLAWS

TIES

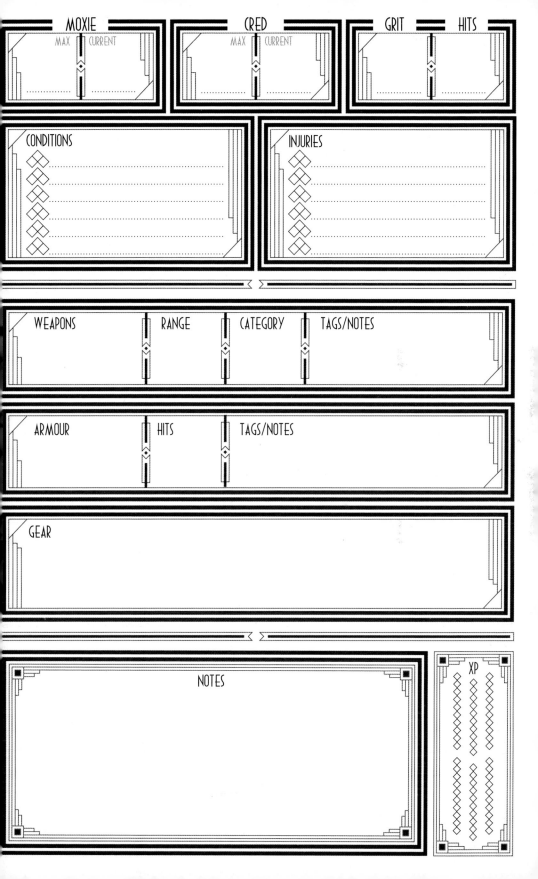

ACKNOWLEDGEMENTS

A huge thank you, once again, to my loving wife and children who put up with so much as I went down the rabbit hole of dystopian futures that might have been. At times, I was probably imagining this all too viscerally and I am ever so glad you put up with me!

I also owe a great debt of gratitude to my band of Revs who were always ready to play another scenario, offer advice, and be a sounding board for my ideas. Cheers to Chris Wark, Rosalind Staines, Mat Robertson, Casey Johnston, Brad Hockey, Jason Drane, Matt Denholm, and Lindsey Deanshaw.

CREDITS

About the Author

Nathan Russell is a teacher, writer, father, and man of imaginary action. He has fought vampires, flown spaceships, plundered dungeons, and rescued Viking princesses. That is what he loves about tabletop adventuring – you can go anywhere and be anything. He has been playing, tweaking, and writing roleplaying games for 30 years and, in 2005, began publishing games for others to enjoy, including the popular Freeform Universal and Neon City Overdrive. Nathan lives in Australia with his far-too-indulgent wife, children, and pugs.

About the Artist

Biagio D'Alessandro is an Italian illustrator. After graduating in fine art, he decided that drawing monsters, demons and aliens would be more fun. In a decade as a professional illustrator, he has collaborated with a wide range of publishers such as Paizo Publishing, Monte Cook Games, and AEG.